He was out somewhere

Who was he and what was he doing right now? Was he asleep? Was he watching late-night TV? Or was he driving around the city? Maybe her house. Thinking about creeping inside.

A shudder convulsed her shoulders, chilling her even though the night was warm.

"Why are you doing this? Why do you hate us?" she whispered.

When she realized she had said "us," that she had grouped herself with Ruby Alder, Diane Gates and Elizabeth St. Marks, another violent shudder tore through her.

Spinning away from the window, Laura hurried back to bed and curled into Max's warmth. He murmured in his sleep and his arm tightened around her, pulling her into the curve of his body. She snuggled close to him, glad they had made love earlier. Laura didn't know how many nights she had left.

ABOUT THE AUTHOR

Margaret St. George has been satisfying a
creative need to write since she was sixteen
years old. She has written more than fifteen
novels, many of which have been historical
romances. A full-time writer, Margaret
enjoys gardening and traveling. She lives
with her husband and family in the
mountains of Colorado.

Books by Margaret St. George

Don't miss any of our special offers. Write to us at the
following address for information on our newest releases.

Harlequin Reader Service
901 Fuhrmann Blvd., P.O. Box 1397, Buffalo, NY 14240
Canadian address: P.O. Box 603,
Fort Erie, Ont. L2A 5X3

Jigsaw
Margaret St. George

Harlequin Books

TORONTO • NEW YORK • LONDON
AMSTERDAM • PARIS • SYDNEY • HAMBURG
STOCKHOLM • ATHENS • TOKYO • MILAN

Harlequin Intrigue edition published March 1990

ISBN 0-373-22133-9

Copyright © 1990 Margaret St. George. All rights reserved.
Except for use in any review, the reproduction or utilization of
this work in whole or in part in any form by any electronic,
mechanical or other means, now known or hereafter invented,
including xerography, photocopying and recording, or in any
information storage or retrieval system, is forbidden without
the permission of the publisher, Harlequin Enterprises Limited,
225 Duncan Mill Road, Don Mills, Ontario, Canada M3B 3K9, or
Harlequin Books, P.O. Box 958, North Sydney, Australia 2060.

All the characters in this book have no existence outside the
imagination of the author and have no relation whatsoever to
anyone bearing the same name or names. They are not even
distantly inspired by any individual known or unknown to the
author, and all incidents are pure invention.

® are Trademarks registered in the United States Patent and
Trademark Office and in other countries.

Printed in U.S.A.

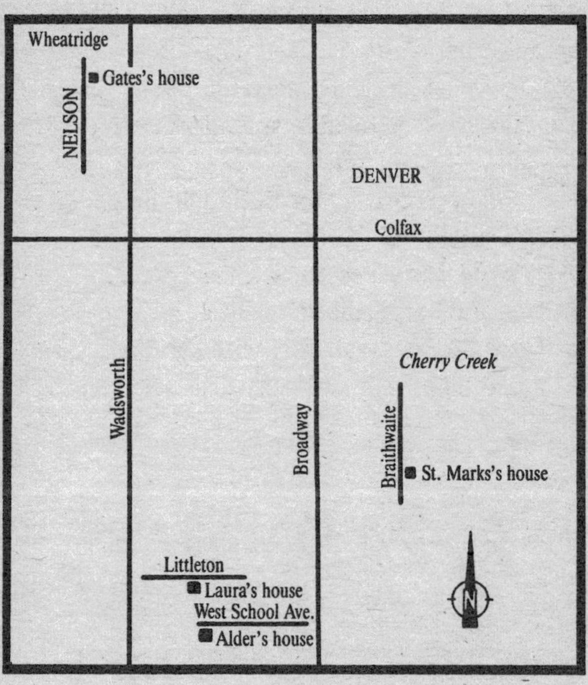
Wheatridge
NELSON
Gates's house
DENVER
Colfax
Wadsworth
Broadway
Cherry Creek
Braithwaite
St. Marks's house
Littleton
Laura's house
West School Ave.
Alder's house
N

CAST OF CHARACTERS

Laura Penn—Could one of her students be pulling deadly pranks?

Max Elliot—He wanted to make an honest woman of her.

Ruby Alder—Her death started it all.

Diane Gates—She lived in splendor, until the day she met her maker.

Elizabeth St. Marks—Her Philadelphia pedigree couldn't shield her from murder.

Dave Penn—He asked for a former wife's loyalty—and jeopardized her life.

Dr. Bruce Latka—A dentist with scratches on his face, did he wield a deadly drill off the job?

Chapter One

Laura Penn parked her Subaru in the lot in front of the Anchor Bay Restaurant and cut the engine. Because it was noon on Saturday, a steady flow of weekend customers moved in and out of the restaurant doors. She gripped the steering wheel, watching and frowning, wondering if Dave was already inside waiting for her.

That wasn't likely, she thought, opening the car door and stepping into the April sunshine. Dave Penn was never on time for anything. He had been fifteen minutes late for their wedding six years ago, and half an hour late for the divorce proceedings two years ago. There was no reason to think anything had changed.

As predicted, Dave was not inside. For an instant, Laura felt a familiar flash of anger, then she reminded herself it didn't matter anymore and shrugged off the irritation. As she had done a hundred times during their marriage, she approached the front desk and asked to be seated immediately rather than wait in the small crowded area beside the door. Once she was seated, Laura ordered coffee and looked at the parking lot through the window, wondering if Dave still drove the Lincoln he had bought shortly before the divorce. He had kept the Lincoln; she had kept the house.

Mostly Laura wondered why she had agreed to meet him for lunch.

Curiosity, of course. Maybe guilt; the divorce had been her idea. And sympathy. She had always been a sucker for someone needing a shoulder to cry on.

"Am I late?"

"You're always late," she said lightly, watching him slide into the booth across from her.

In high school and college she had thought Dave Penn was the handsomest man in the world. Looking at him now, she decided it was true that love was blind. He was nice looking but conventional, certainly not a man most women would describe as drop-dead handsome. His chin was on the weak side, his gaze indirect. And, unless she was mistaken, his sandy-colored hair was beginning to thin.

"You look wonderful, Laura," he said, speaking too fast. He gave her a quick smile over his menu. She didn't remember Dave's being a nervous type, but today he was positively jittery, his movements jerky and uncoordinated. "That's a new hairdo, isn't it? And you've lost weight since I saw you last."

Her dark hair was shorter than it had been six months ago, but she wore it in much the same style. And she hadn't lost weight, although she kept telling herself she was going to lose five pounds. Before she could say so, assuming she would have, he pointed to the menu.

"Let's order and get that out of the way, then we can talk." His fingers drummed on the tabletop and he cursed when the waiter didn't instantly appear.

After giving her order, Laura tasted her coffee and watched him fumble for a cigarette, then a book of matches. When he finally brought the flame to his cigarette, she noticed his hands shook slightly.

"I thought you quit," she commented. His nervousness was making her uneasy, too. Eventually she would have to say something about Ruby Alder. She guessed Ruby's murder was what he wanted to talk about and she dreaded it.

"I started again. A couple of days ago." His eyes grazed hers then slid to one side. "Are you still teaching at Columbine?"

"Yes. Are you still selling real estate?"

"Off and on. The Denver market's been slow."

After that, there didn't seem to be anything to say.

Throughout high school and college she had loved him, blindly, without objectivity, loving him with the intensity of awakening emotions. Whether it was the real thing or not was a question that no longer held any significance. The fact was, they had shared four stormy years together. And now they had nothing to say. There was something sad about that, Laura thought. But then she wondered if they had ever really known each other or had much to talk about.

Because the silence bothered her, she drew a breath and cleared her throat. "I'm sorry about Ruby. Her death must have been terrible for you."

"You don't know the half of it." He sucked on the cigarette, exhaled toward the plants hanging in front of the stained-glass panels.

"Maybe I do. Someone told me you and Ruby had planned to get married."

Whatever he had been about to say, he changed his mind and gave her a curious look instead. "How did you feel about that?"

His expression annoyed her. He looked as if he expected her to object; maybe he thought she would feel jealous.

"The truth? I felt a little sorry for both of you."

For a moment he stared at her, then he stubbed out his cigarette as the waiter placed salads in front of them.

Immediately Laura regretted the unkind words. They made her sound bitter, and she wasn't bitter. Not anymore.

"Look, I'm sorry," she apologized. "I only met Ruby once or twice—I didn't know her well. It's just that she seemed..." Her voice trailed off and she spread her hands.

"Obvious? Honest? Sexy?"

A rush of color flooded her cheeks. Laying aside her napkin, Laura reached for her purse. "I think this was a mistake," she said quietly. "If you'll excuse me..."

"Oh, hell." Reaching across the table, he caught her wrist. "Don't go. I'm sorry, all right?" When she hesitated, he added, "I really need to talk to you."

Suspecting she would regret it, she eased back into her chair and pushed her salad aside. "You'll think this is funny, but a minute ago I was thinking we didn't have anything to say to each other. But that isn't true, is it? It's just that the time for saying everything is past."

"It wasn't all bad, Laura. We had some good times."

The direction of the conversation made her uneasy. "Yes," she admitted slowly. "But the bad times were very bad."

"Remember the year we went to Puerto Vallarta?" His gaze dropped to her mouth. "The private pool behind our rental unit?"

Her cheeks flooded again with color. He was right. They had shared some good times. But she was right, also. There had been some disastrous times, some frightening times.

Tilting her head to one side, she studied him. It was odd how it all came back to her. This expression, that affectation. The silences, the tension in her stomach.

"I know that look, Dave. You want something." She had not intended to speak so bluntly. The words just slipped out.

He waited until the waiter replaced their salads with lemon sole, then he darted a look over his shoulder and leaned forward, speaking in a low voice.

"Laura...the police think I did it."

"What?" Shock smothered her gasp.

"They think I murdered Ruby."

She stared at him, not knowing what to say. When she recovered her voice she, too, leaned over the table and spoke in a whisper. "Dave, that's terrible! But why...why would they think that?"

The lemon sole steamed in front of him and he pushed it away with an impatient motion. "Because they've got their heads up their—"

"Come on, Dave. If you're a suspect, there has to be a reason." She kept staring at him. Dave could be violent, she had reason to know. But murder?

He lit another cigarette. "Ruby and I had a big fight the night before it happened." Turning his head, he looked out the window. "I hit her. I didn't mean to—it just happened."

In the silence, Laura looked down at her sole and blinked against a rush of unwanted memories. "Were you drinking?" she asked finally.

"I'd had a couple of beers. Big deal." He glanced at her, then away. Neither of them spoke as the waiter passed their table. "Ruby wasn't the type to go for a teetotaler. She knew how to have a good time."

Briefly Laura closed her eyes. "You know how you get when you drink."

"Look, Laura. I didn't kill her." A shrug lifted the light sweater he wore. "Okay, I lost control and I hit her. But that was the night before she was murdered. I didn't see her the next day."

It was impossible to eat. Her appetite was gone. Putting her fork down, she asked, "How do the police know about the fight?"

"It was loud. The neighbors told them. Her town house has walls about as thick as card paper. There's more," he said, looking at her, hesitating. "I did something really stupid. I threatened to kill her."

"Oh, God, Dave."

"You know I didn't mean it." His voice was rising and he cast a swift glance at the table behind him. "I was angry. I didn't know what I was saying. People say things they don't mean when they're angry."

How often had he given her that excuse? As though it was all right to say stupid hateful things if you were angry enough or drunk enough. And the person who had to hear them was then expected to forgive and forget and go on as if the accusations or threats had never been spoken.

"What was the fight about?" she asked, because she felt compelled to say something.

"I thought she was seeing someone else."

Laura blinked against a sense of déjà vu. "Was she?"

"I don't know." He raked a hand through his hair. "It doesn't matter now, does it?" When he recognized the shock in her eyes, he clenched his jaw. "Well, it doesn't. What matters is that I'm in a lot of trouble."

"If you didn't do it, you don't have to worry."

"God, Laura. You can be so naive! Think about it. Ruby and I had a big fight about another guy, and I threatened to kill her. Face it, I am the cops numero-uno suspect. They're going to try to hang this on me."

"Just tell them where you were when it happened."

He met her eyes. "That's the problem. I don't have an alibi."

She spread her hands. "You must have been somewhere Wednesday afternoon."

"I was trying to solicit listings. It was a waste of time. Nobody was home. Not one single person. There's no one to verify where I was at four o'clock."

She lifted an eyebrow and gave him an uneasy look. "You spent the afternoon knocking on doors? And not one person was home? What area were you working?"

"Willow Hills, I think. Yes, it was Willow Hills."

"There was no one home in the Willow Hills division?"

"See? Even you don't believe me. What do you think the police would say?"

She stared. Then she leaned forward. "What do you mean, what would they say? Didn't you tell the police where you were?"

"Oh, come on. Do you think I'm crazy? The police would react just like you did. Hell no, I didn't tell them." After drawing a long breath, he reached for her hand. "I told the police I was with you at four o'clock."

The blood rushed from her face and she felt her hand go cold inside his grasp. "Dave! How could you do that?"

"I told them I met you at our house after school. About three-thirty. I told them I stayed until after six, then I left because you had papers to grade."

"Oh, my God!"

He licked his lips and gripped her hand harder. "You have to back me up, Laura. You have to. If I don't have an alibi for that time period, they're going to think I did it. And I didn't. I swear to you, I did not kill Ruby!"

The clink of silver, the tinkle of ice in glasses, and the hum of voices rose in her ears like thunder. "How could you do this? How could you involve me in a murder!"

"Believe me, honey, if there was any other way, don't you think I'd take it? But there isn't."

She noted he called her honey and put it down to habit, to the emotion of the moment. Or maybe he did it on purpose, a ploy calculated to remind her of better times.

"David, what makes you think I'd lie for you?" She couldn't believe what he was asking. She felt sick inside.

"Because once you loved me," he answered simply. "That has to count for something. And because there's no one else. And because if you tell the police that I lied, they'll be certain I'm involved. They'll stop looking for whoever killed Ruby. The real murderer."

Biting her lip, she jerked away from him. It seemed to her the waiter was staring at her. It seemed like everyone in the restaurant was staring at her. She felt certain everyone had overheard the conversation.

"I can't believe you did this," she whispered, turning back to him. On the other hand, she could. Lying wasn't new to Dave Penn. He had perfected the skill by practicing on her. Still, each time was a shock. And this was the worst.

"Laura, please do this for me, this one last thing. Then, I promise you, I'm out of your life forever. If you don't back me up, they'll put me away for this."

"I can't just . . ."

He met her troubled eyes. "Do you think I killed Ruby? Do you think I could kill anyone?"

Obviously her memory was better than his. Suddenly she recalled the night she had finally left him. She didn't remember what they had been arguing about, maybe the Lincoln, but she remembered he had been drinking. And she remembered the crack of his hand across her face. A shudder rippled down her spine. Two days later he had tracked her to her friend's house. And, as always, he claimed to remember none of it. As if not remembering meant it had never happened, meant she had invented it all. He had seemed genuinely stunned when she refused to go back to him, when she told him no man would ever hit her twice.

"Dave, is it possible you . . . you did something . . . and you don't remember it?"

"No!" A look of anger and betrayal clouded his eyes. "That hasn't happened in over a year." His stare made her uncomfortable. "Are you saying you think I did it? That I killed Ruby?"

"Of course not. I just—"

"Because you know I didn't. You and I had fights a lot worse than I had with Ruby. And I didn't hurt you!"

"Yes, you did," she said quietly.

"You're never going to let me forget that one time, are you?"

"When you're sober, Dave, you can be wonderful. But when your're drinking . . ."

"There's no point rehashing the past. I didn't do it. I didn't kill her." After squeezing her fingers, he released her hand and lit another cigarette. "Look, if you don't want to get involved, then don't. Tell the police I wasn't with you." He shrugged.

"Then they'll know you lied." God, she hated this. "That's going to look very bad. Like you have something to hide."

He nodded, frowned out the window. "It wouldn't happen again in twenty years—knocking on doors all afternoon and finding no one home. But that's what happened. Except I can't prove it."

"Maybe someone saw your car," she suggested hopefully.

"Laura, there was no one home in the neighborhood I was working. No one answered their door; no one to see and remember my car. I'm screwed."

He was right. He was also frightened. She saw it behind his eyes, saw it in his unsteady fingers. Hating herself, she bit her lip and started to think it through. Had she seen anyone on Wednesday? Had she gone straight home after school? Could the alibi be disproved?

"God, I hate this!" When he didn't say anything, she drew a breath. "West School Avenue is only a block from my street. Ruby's town house is about three blocks from me. Telling them you were at my house puts you in the area. Have you thought about that?"

He gave her the smile she had once loved. "Not until after I told the police I was with you."

Neither of them spoke. The waiter removed their untouched lemon sole and brought them coffee.

"Does the waiter look familiar to you?" she asked absently, her mind a million miles away.

"Who pays any attention to waiters?"

She shrugged and returned to their discussion.

"Look, Dave, I'll think about it, okay? That's the best I can do right now." And she loathed herself for even that much. She had believed he was out of her life. She had believed she was finished with the messes he continually managed to involve her in. Appointments set with salesmen that he later asked her to cancel. Bill collectors he asked her to deal with. Family squabbles he expected her to solve. The list went on and on, four years' worth.

"If you don't want to do it—" he paused and looked out the window "—I'll understand."

Now he was playing the martyr. She knew him so well. First he reminded her of shared good times, then he told her he had involved her in a lie, then came the pitch about how only she could save the situation. Then he told her in essence that it didn't matter if he went to the electric chair. If she, the only person who could save him, didn't want to lift a finger, that was all right. He would understand. He had managed to trigger all the guilt responses. Guilt because she had ended the marriage, guilt because she hadn't gone back to him and stuck by him when he'd tried to quit drinking, guilt because she was making it on her own and he, apparently, was not.

She looked at him, at the weak chin and the gaze that didn't quite meet hers, and she thanked God she had divorced him. In retrospect, she wondered why she had stayed with him as long as she did. Pride, maybe. She hadn't wanted her family or friends to know she had made a mistake. Hadn't wanted to admit it to herself. And she had told herself he would quit drinking, the violent episodes of smashing dishes and furniture would end, and he would change. Then the threats began. And finally one night he struck her. . . .

The problem had been the good times. Even in bad marriages, there were a few good times. And they had had their share. When he wasn't drinking. The good times were what had kept her on the battlefront, trying when good sense told her trying wasn't going to change anything. She had hung in longer than she should have because she was an optimist. She remembered the good times and told herself there were more good times than bad. But she had been lying to herself.

"I think you should go back to AA," she said gently.

"I intend to."

Maybe this time he would.

He looked down into his coffee cup. "I went for a while after you left me. You knew that, didn't you?"

"You told me."

"It would have been easier if I'd had your support."

Laura bit her lip and looked away from him.

"I was feeling sorry for myself because you had withdrawn. Our sex life had gone to hell." He shrugged. "You know the story. At AA I found out everyone had withdrawn spouses. Nobody had a good sex life. It was my fault, not yours."

There was no way to know if he really meant what he was saying, or if he was admitting the crash of their marriage was his fault because he wanted her to lie for him.

She reached for her purse and put it in her lap. "I honestly don't know what I'll do," she said slowly, "but whatever I decide, I want you to know I deeply resent your putting me in this position. It isn't fair and it isn't right."

They were replaying a record that had worn out long ago. She had said the same thing over and over.

"I know. I'm sorry, Laura. If there was anyone else I trusted . . ."

She said goodbye, then felt him watching her all the way to the ladies' room door. Once inside, she leaned over the sink and splashed cool water on her face, hoping it would clear her head. All it did was smear her mascara.

Damn him.

Lifting her head, she looked at herself in the mirror. Good bones, firm chin, clear eyes. How did it happen that strong people were manipulated by weak people? Or was that a stupid question? Weak people had been depending on strong people for safety and protection since time began. Manipulation was their strongest weapon. They used guilt, pity, whatever was at hand.

Angrily she opened her purse and set her mascara and lipstick on the countertop. Dave hadn't missed a trick. He had reminded her of the good times, of a time when she had loved him. He had made her feel pity for his situation, made her feel partly responsible that he was still drinking. She knew she would feel guilty if she didn't help him.

So. What was she going to do?

Because she couldn't deal with that question quite yet, she concentrated on repairing her makeup, then she read a placard placed in front of the mirror.

Win a year's free membership at the Sleek Chic Spa. If your name is drawn in our grand-prize drawing, you will win 52 weeks' full-membership benefits at your nearest Sleek Chic Spa.

A pad of entry blanks was in a Lucite box beneath the placard.

Well, why not? If she won, the day would not have been a total loss. And maybe it would motivate her to lose five pounds. She filled out a form and dropped it in the Lucite slot, then smiled at her foolishness. She had never won anything in her life. On the other hand, maybe this would be the time.

She thought about doing some shopping as she was near Southwest Plaza, then realized she was too upset by the conversation with Dave to enjoy looking at the new spring fashions. Instead, she decided to go home and spade the area near the fence. Gardening usually relaxed her and cleared her mind. Maybe a way out of this would come to her.

SHE LIVED in a modest area, not far from Columbine Elementary School. In good weather she could walk to work. The house was small but perfect for her, set back from the street and surrounded by mature cottonwood trees and aspens that were shady now and glorious in the autumn.

A car was parked at the curb and, when she turned the Subaru into her driveway, she saw a man standing on her porch.

Not just any man, she thought, as she opened her car door. A very handsome man. Tall, with dark hair and eyes, he was in his early thirties, and dressed quietly but well.

"Are you Mrs. Penn?" he asked, smiling. His teeth were as white as any she had seen. When she nodded, he removed a badge from his breast pocket and showed it to her. "I'm Detective Max Elliot, Littleton Police Department. I'd like to speak to you for a few minutes."

Laura stopped as if she had run into an invisible wall. It hadn't occurred to her to ask Dave how soon the police might want to question her. Damn. She wasn't going to have time to think this out.

Realizing he must think she was behaving strangely, she made herself smile. "Yes, of course," she said, digging in her purse for her house key. Stepping past him, she opened the screen door and fit her key into the lock. Today everyone looked familiar. She had an idea she had met Max Elliot previously, but she couldn't place him.

The door opened onto a small foyer, then a short hallway led past the kitchen door into her living room. She waved a hand toward the living room, but he paused before the portrait of her cat, R.C., that hung in the foyer.

"Did you paint this?"

Laura smiled. "One of my students did. I teach fifth grade at Columbine Elementary. Would you like some coffee?"

"Thank you. With milk if you have it."

Her kitchen featured a pass-through, which opened the kitchen to the living room, and she watched him as she put a pot of coffee on to brew.

"Nice place," he said.

"It's small, but I like the openness." Suddenly she noticed the clutter. Pieces of a jigsaw puzzle covered her coffee table, a basket of mending sat on the fireplace hearth, a stack of books spilled over one end of the sofa. Usually she thought of clutter as homey—until she had a visitor. Then it just looked like clutter.

Dave. What on earth was she going to do? A dozen thoughts ran through her mind. What if the police discovered she had lied? What would they do to her? Could she go to jail? But if she didn't back up Dave's alibi, would they arrest him? Could they pin Ruby's murder on Dave based on circumstantial evidence? If they did, she would feel like it was her fault for betraying him. Dammit, dammit!

Only now did she notice the pot of flowers on her kitchen counter.

Surprised, she blinked twice. The pot was circled by a gold bow enclosing a beautiful bouquet of blue chrysanthemums. There was no card.

How on earth? she thought, frowning. Then she had it. Dave. This was probably why he had been late to the restaurant. He had let himself inside and left her the flowers. He had always given her flowers after an argument.

Tears of anger stung her eyes. It was so unfair. He had no right to put her in this position. She was going to feel terrible if she lied for him, and terrible if she didn't.

She stayed in the kitchen until her hands steadied, then she carried a tray into the living room and set it on top of the jigsaw puzzle spread over her table. "You said milk, right?"

"Right." He pushed aside a couple of pieces of the jigsaw puzzle and accepted the cup of coffee. "This is going to sound a little strange," he said, smiling at her. "But your maiden name doesn't happen to be Trainer, does it?"

Laura straightened and stared at him. "Yes. It is."

"You went to college in Greeley. University of Northern Colorado."

"Wait a minute." She looked at him, her mind spiraling backward. No wonder he had looked familiar. "Economics. You were in Professor Gehard's class."

"I'll be damned. Small world, isn't it?"

She remembered now. Max Elliot. A smile lit her face and they beamed at each other. "You played football," she said. "And weren't you voted the man most campus women would like to be marooned with?"

He laughed, the sound deep and pleasant. "Some sort of nonsense like that. It seems I remember you were engaged, weren't you? To Dave Penn?"

As smooth as glass, he brought the conversation back to the point. Laura released a breath and nodded.

"Laura—may I call you Laura?"

"Of course."

"I assume you know this visit has to do with the murder of your ex-husband's fiancé, Ruby Alder."

"Yes." What was she going to say?

He laid a notepad over the jigsaw-puzzle pieces. "We'll begin with some background information if you don't mind. Most of it I already have. I think we can cover the rest quickly. You married Dave Penn after college?"

Laura wet her lips. She wished to heaven there had been time to think this mess through.

"Yes. Shortly after graduation."

"And you moved to the Denver area immediately afterward?"

"Yes."

"How long have you been divorced?"

"About two years. We were divorced in 1988."

"I apologize for the personal nature of this question, but I have to ask it." He gave her a smile intended to put her at ease. "What was the reason for the divorce?"

Laura carried her coffee across the room and stood beside the French doors that opened onto a covered patio. "That's not easy to answer," she said finally. "Are you married?"

"I was. I'm divorced."

"Then you probably know marriages end for a variety of complex reasons. It's hard to point to one thing and say, this is what caused the divorce." Max Elliot was good at what he did. By saying nothing, he forced her to continue. Laura returned her gaze to the patio windows. "I don't know. Dave drank too much and I wasn't very understanding about it. We discovered we didn't have much in common. Didn't like the same things, didn't have the same value systems, didn't look at the world the same way." She shrugged. "I suppose Dave thought it was my fault. I thought it was his fault."

His pen scratched across the notepad. "When you say he drank too much . . . do you feel he had a problem with alcohol?"

"Yes," she said softly, watching a robin light on the lawn. "I understand he started going to AA after the divorce."

"Was he ever violent? Maybe when he had been drinking?"

"What do you mean?" she asked, hedging.

"Did he throw things? Threaten you? Strike you?"

Turning from the window, she faced him. "Why are you asking these questions? Do you think Dave killed Ruby Alder?"

Max tasted his coffee. "Right now we're just gathering information. Trying to learn about the people nearest Miss Alder." He paused, met her eyes. "Did he ever strike you?"

"I...yes." The admission came hard. She had never told anyone. "It only happened once. At the end of our marriage. I'm convinced it wouldn't have happened if Dave hadn't been drinking."

"Were you injured?" He made a notation on his pad.

"Bruised. Not really injured." The memory of the last night sprang into her mind and she raised a hand to her cheek. In a way she was almost glad Dave had struck her. Otherwise their marriage might have limped along for another year before she divorced him, as she should have done much sooner.

"Is there anything else you want to tell me about that period?"

"I...no."

"Have you seen your ex-husband often since the divorce?"

They were moving nearer the crucial question. "I've seen him several times, but not often, not really. Oddly, I think we like each other better now that we're not married."

Max smiled. "Makes sense to me," he said lightly. Then he looked at her. "When was the last time you saw your ex-husband?"

There it was, the question she was dreading. She knew what he was asking, but she chose to stall.

"Would you like more coffee?"

"No, thank you."

"I think I would," she said, moving past him into the kitchen. She flicked a look at the pot of blue chrysanthemums, scowled, then filled her cup. "Actually, I had lunch with Dave today," she said.

"Were you with him Wednesday between three-thirty and six o'clock?"

He lifted his head and looked at her over the counter. Laura touched a petal on one of the chrysanthemums. If Dave had been standing before her, she would have been tempted to throw the pot at him. Damn him for doing this to her. For making her think he would be arrested for murder if she didn't lie for him.

A sigh lifted her shoulders. "Yes," she whispered.

"You're sure?"

"Yes." So he wouldn't see her expression, she turned and moved around the end of the counter. By the time she reappeared in the living room, she had arranged a pleasant smile on her lips. "So. Do you have any clues?"

A frown drew his brows together. "Not as many as we'd like. There never are."

"Is it true there were no signs of forced entry on Ruby's door?"

He nodded, then regarded her curiously. "Did you know Miss Alder?"

"I met her once or twice, but I can't say I knew her. I knew who she was if I passed her in the grocery store—that kind of thing."

He closed his notebook and replaced it in his jacket pocket. "How did you feel about your ex-husband planning to remarry?"

The question was placed in a conversational tone as if it wasn't particularly important. But Laura sensed that it was. Suddenly her palms felt damp and a chill traced down her spine.

"Good God," she whispered. "Do you suspect *me*?"

"It couldn't have been you," he said, standing. A light smile touched his lips. "You were here with Dave Penn when the murder was taking place."

Abruptly, Laura sat down on a chair. It had not occurred to her that *she* might be a suspect. Her mind ran the thought through like a newspaper heading: Jealous Wife Murders Ex-husband's Fiancé. Oh my God! It seemed she needed an alibi as much as Dave did.

"Look. There's nothing between Dave and me anymore. I didn't care one way or another about him planning to remarry. If you're thinking I was jealous or upset or something, you're wrong."

"I'm glad." Something in his eyes suggested he wasn't speaking in his official capacity. But the look was gone before she could be sure. Then he was moving toward the door. "That should do it for now," he said in the foyer.

"If there's anything else I can do..." she said, leaving an implication she didn't really mean.

"Thanks. I'm sure there'll be a few more questions as the investigation progresses."

"You know where to find me," she said faintly.

When she closed the door, she fell against it, only now noticing that her heart was banging against her ribs.

MAX ELLIOT PAUSED beside his car door and looked back at Laura Penn's house. It was an interesting coincidence running into her again like this. He supposed he had a crush on her in college. Nothing serious, nothing he considered pursuing after he noticed her engagement ring. But strong enough that he had spent a lot of hours thinking about her, regretting she wasn't free to date.

She hadn't changed all that much in ten years; he had recognized her at once. Shiny dark hair, trim curvy figure, a wholesome girl-next-door expression. He bet that all her fifth graders were in love with her. Smiling, he slid into his car and pushed a Neil Diamond tape into the cassette player.

Before returning to the station, he drove around Laura's block, then cruised down West School Avenue and parked across the street from Ruby Alder's town house. The units were ultramodern, lots of wood and odd-shaped windows, uneven roof lines. The appearance suited what he knew of Ruby Alder. He would have been surprised if she had lived in a quiet section like Laura Penn, in a conventional homey house.

Flipping open the file on the seat next to him, he studied Ruby Alder's photograph, a photograph found in her bedroom. She had been a flashy number. The photograph showed her dressed in a low-cut black sequined dress. She had dyed-blond hair, wore too much makeup. A challenge stared out of the photo, daring the world to disapprove. There was something a little sad about her, not obvious, but there.

Whoever she was, she had not deserved to die brutally, violently.

Staring at the strip of police tape crossing her door, he leaned back against the car seat and gripped the wheel. Someone had appeared at Ruby Alder's door about four o'clock on Wednesday and she had opened the door to him. Someone with a knife.

Lifting the file folder, he flipped over to the next photo, the one taken at the scene. One thing he knew. No woman had committed this crime. The attack had been almost frenzied, committed by someone with brute strength, someone out of control and boiling with hate.

After closing the file, he eased the car from the curb and rolled past Ruby Alder's door. His thoughts returned to Laura Penn.

Why had she lied to him?

Chapter Two

Laura's Sunday routine was wrecked. Normally she would have slept in, then curled into the corner of the sofa next to a pot of coffee and a basket of muffins, and she would have read the Sunday newspaper until it was time for *Dr. Who* on PBS. After the *Dr. Who* episode, she might have met friends for tennis or golf, or worked in her garden or gone cycling. After dinner, she usually reviewed her lesson plans for the upcoming week.

This Sunday she couldn't concentrate on anything. Not the newspaper, not *Dr. Who*. She canceled a tennis date. The full implication of what she had done weighed on her like a slab of marble.

She had lied to the police. The enormity of it staggered her.

She, who had never defied authority in her life, had lied to the police. Shaking her head, she stood at the French doors and stared at the sprinkler spraying water over her lawn.

Seeking justification when in her heart she knew there was none, she reminded herself that if she had not lied, Max Elliot's prime suspect would have been Dave. And, like Dave had said, if the police focused on him they would stop looking for the real killer.

The real killer. The phrase repeated itself in her mind.

After a while, she poured her by then cold cup of coffee down the sink and dialed Dave's number on the kitchen phone.

No answer. She hung up and stood tapping her fingernails against the counter, looking at the trash bin. After a moment, she sighed and retrieved the blue chrysanthemums. It was dumb to throw them away. She might as well put them out and enjoy them. It was a grim thought, but she had earned them.

Because she had to do something, and because she was too restless to remain indoors, Laura decided to go for a drive. She told herself she had no particular destination in mind. But when she pulled her city map from the car's glove box and studied it, she understood that wasn't true.

Forty minutes later, she turned her Subaru past twin brick pillars and a sign that read: Welcome to Willow Hills. Driving slowly over the speed bumps placed throughout the subdivision streets, she wound through an area that was perhaps ten years old. The houses were modest and well maintained. It was a young neighborhood. She noticed house after house with skates or tricycles in the yard or on the porch, basketball hoops above several garage doors. Each street was heavily populated with kids chasing across the lawns and adults working in their yards.

A sinking feeling sent her heart plummeting toward the gas pedal. All right, she thought, trying to give Dave the benefit of the doubt. Maybe the subdivision was made up of two-family incomes. Wives who worked outside the home and kids who spent the weekdays in school. Maybe Willow Hills resembled a ghost town during the week and only came alive after five o'clock and on weekends. Maybe

Willow Hills was—what did they call it?—a bedroom community. Deserted by day, populated only at night.

She had an uneasy feeling she wasn't going to sleep well tonight.

WHEN THE LAST BELL RANG on Monday, Laura stuffed her papers into her briefcase and was out of the school building almost before the kids were. A few minutes before four o'clock, she was driving into the Willow Hills subdivision. According to Dave, it should have been quiet and deserted.

It wasn't.

There weren't as many adults in evidence as there had been yesterday, on a weekend, but Laura saw children everywhere, home from school. Presumably, their mothers were also home. Or sitters. The point was, if Dave had been here at four o'clock on a weekday, there would have been about fifty people—albeit most of them children—who saw his car. Surely there would have been a sitter or a mother who remembered him coming to the door to ask about a real-estate listing.

Street after street, it was the same thing. Children playing outside and here and there a woman on the porch with a toddler. Moreover, the adults took a good look at Laura as her car passed. The looks were friendly, but this was a neighborhood that noticed strangers.

Willow Hills should have provided Dave an excellent alibi.

If he really had been here.

A headache started behind Laura's eyes and spread to the back of her neck.

"HI."

"Where have you been?" Laura flicked off the TV with

the remote-control button and leaned back on the sofa, holding the telephone tightly against her ear. "I've been calling you for two days!"

"I needed to get away. I went to Keystone. Did the police contact you yet?"

Trust Dave to go out of town and leave the mess in her hands, supremely confident that she would handle it. Laura closed her eyes and pressed her fingertips to her forehead.

"I can't tell you how angry I am. There aren't words strong enough." When he didn't say anything, she drew a breath. "I spoke to Detective Max Elliot. I confirmed your alibi."

"Thank God. I knew I could count on you, Laura. Thank you. I owe you one."

"No, you don't. If I'd had more time to think about it, I would not have lied for you, Dave." Her voice hardened. "I don't ever want to see you again. I mean it. This is the worst thing you have ever done to me."

"I know, and I'm sorry."

He didn't sound sorry; he sounded relieved. She could hear him smoking and there were voices in the background. "Where are you? It sounds like you're at a party."

"A few people dropped by." A verbal shrug sounded in her ear. "Life goes on."

Disgust silenced her for a moment. "I drove through Willow Hills yesterday," she said finally. "There were lots of people on the street at four o'clock. Someone should have seen your car."

"You're checking up on me?"

"I think I have that right, don't you?"

"What are you trying to say, Laura?"

She wasn't certain. "Just that Willow Hills is full of young families. Someone should remember seeing your car."

"Maybe I wasn't in Willow Hills. I'm not sure. I thought it was Willow Hills, but maybe it was the next subdivision over. Are you saying I lied about it?"

That was exactly what she was saying. "You told me that you were knocking on doors in Willow Hills."

"So I made a mistake. Look, Laura, forget it, okay? It's over now. Put it out of your mind."

She heard the annoyance in his voice, heard his defenses click into place. Now that she had done as he asked, he didn't want to discuss it anymore, didn't want to hear about it again. His callousness outraged her.

"One more thing," she said between her teeth. "I want you to return your key to my house. You can mail it to me."

"I don't have a key to *your* house."

"Come on, Dave. I locked the front door when I left to meet you Saturday, and I unlocked it when I returned."

"So? I don't know what you're talking about."

"The flowers. I'm talking about the chrysanthemums."

"The chrysanthemums?"

If he was irritated, so was she. "Why are you playing dumb about this? I'm talking about the blue chrysanthemums you put in my kitchen!"

"I didn't send you any flowers. I thought about it, then I got busy and . . . you know how it is."

She drew a breath, seeking patience. "You know I'm not talking about flowers delivered by a florist. I'm talking about the flowers you put in my kitchen!"

"I did not go into your kitchen and leave flowers there." He sounded pained. "One of your neighbors must have done it."

"Dave, I told you. The Ackersons moved to Florida. Their house is vacant. Vacant as in no one lives there, as in I have no neighbor on that side. The house on the other side is a rental and I don't know who lives there. Why are you denying that you left the flowers?"

"Because I didn't, dammit."

"All right," she said at length. There was no point fighting about it. If he didn't want to admit he had come into her house without her permission, arguing was a waste of time. "Just send back the key."

"I told you, I don't have a key anymore. I lost it or threw it away a long time ago."

"Goodbye, Dave." Furious, she hung up the telephone and glared at it. He was a pathological liar. He lied even when the truth was better. Why did she insist on thinking he could or would change?

Tomorrow, before she left for school, she would call a locksmith and have her locks changed.

WHILE SHE WAITED for the locksmith to finish, Laura sat at the table and pushed around a couple of the jigsaw pieces. But she kept looking at the chrysanthemums on the end of the kitchen counter.

Suppose Dave was telling the truth. Suppose he hadn't put the flowers in her kitchen? If she wanted to be fair, it was a possibility she had to consider. But if Dave hadn't given her the flowers . . . then who had?

She pushed a hand through her hair and frowned at the piece of puzzle in her fingers.

It wasn't possible for anyone else to have placed the flowers in her house. Laura had grown up in a small town and she wasn't as careful about locking her door as she should have been, but the door had been locked on Saturday. She was sure of it. She remembered unlocking it when she returned and found Max Elliot on her porch.

But why would Dave lie about leaving flowers?

Why would he lie about Willow Hills?

After paying the locksmith, she hung one of the new keys on the key hook in the foyer and dropped the other into her purse.

Before she left for school, she glanced around the living room, feeling uneasy that someone—that Dave—had been inside her home when she wasn't here.

She hated this whole thing. The lying, the wondering, the uneasiness. She hated herself for getting involved. With a sigh, Laura thought she would be very glad when the police solved the Ruby Alder case.

MAX ELLIOT had been thinking about Laura Penn off and on for several days while he conducted a discreet inquiry into her background.

She had taught at Columbine Elementary for seven years, was well thought of, had won the Teacher of the Year award twice. None of the people he talked to indicated in any way that she was dishonest or ever fudged the truth. She was one of those special teachers who seemed to genuinely enjoy children and who loved to teach. Everyone on the faculty liked and respected her; she saw several faculty members socially, as well as professionally.

He discovered she had never been in any legal trouble, except for a traffic ticket two years ago, about the time of her divorce. Her car had slid on a patch of ice and smacked into a tree. Merely a fender-bender.

The divorce seemed straightforward enough. She had filed; Dave Penn had not contested the proceedings.

Property and indebtedness was split down the middle. Dave Penn was not one of those men who could claim his ex-wife took him to the cleaners.

As near as Max could determine, Laura Penn lived a quiet, well-ordered life. She wasn't the type of person he would have associated with murder.

Leaning back from his desk, he tapped a pencil against his chin. So why had she lied to him? He had been with the force long enough to sense when someone was lying. And she had shown all the signs. The hesitation in her voice, the avoidance of eye contact, a slight tremble in her fingers. That she was lying, he didn't doubt. What she was lying about, he didn't know for certain. Or why.

She could have lied about Penn's propensity toward violence. Maybe Dave Penn had been more violent than she had admitted. From what he knew about the man, that was a definite possibility.

What worried him most was wondering if she had lied about Penn's alibi.

Raising his glance, he looked at his partner, Eric Ashbaugh, seated at the desk facing his. "Any luck tracking down the other guy Penn thinks Alder was seeing?"

Eric shook his head. "The guy's a phantom. The neighbors didn't see any other guy. She never mentioned another man to her friends or the people she worked with." He shrugged and pulled a hand through his hair. "We're hitting a brick wall with this one."

Max nodded. They were hitting a brick wall everywhere they turned.

"Too bad Penn's alibi checked out," Eric said, throwing down his pen.

"Yeah." He thought about it.

After Eric left for the day, he reached for the telephone and called Laura Penn.

"It's Max Elliot," he said when she answered. "With the—"

"Littleton Police. I remember."

"It's six o'clock. I was wondering if you'd like to have dinner. There's a pretty good steak house not far from you."

"The A-1. I know it." She hesitated. When she spoke again her voice sounded artificially bright. "Is this an official request or a social request?"

"A little of both." When he realized how that sounded, he made an amendment. "More social than official. You won't be arrested if you refuse," he added, smiling. "Actually, I'm hoping you can tell me what happened to Joe Everly. Did you know Joe? Or Whitey Mobler?"

"Not well. I think Whitey is a politician now, isn't he? Somewhere in Iowa or Ohio. Joe Everly married—"

"Wait. You can tell me over dinner. That is, if you don't mind having dinner with a tired detective."

She hesitated a beat, but he heard it. "It sounds great. I'll put my TV dinner back in the freezer. You've saved me from something that looks like steak but wouldn't have tasted much like it."

He laughed. "Good. I'll pick you up in thirty minutes. Okay?"

"Fine."

The minute she hung up the phone, Laura felt a wave of panic. Placing her hands flat on the kitchen countertop, she dropped her head and drew several long deep breaths.

If he had discovered she had lied about being with Dave, he would not be asking her to dinner, he would be at her door to arrest her. There was no reason to panic. This was simply what it appeared to be. Two long-time acquaintances meeting again over business.

Except the business was murder.

SINCE SHE DIDN'T WANT to make too much of it, she wore
the same outfit she had worn to school, a camel-colored
skirt and a green silk blouse. When the doorbell rang, she
ran her palms over her skirt and checked her hair in the
foyer mirror, then opened the door.

"Hi."

"Would you like a drink before we go?" He didn't really
look like the TV detectives. His hair was on the longish
side as if he didn't have time to have it cut, sort of like Don
Johnson on *Miami Vice* but not as long. But he didn't
dress like Don Johnson. He wore a well-tailored jacket and
dark slacks. She guessed he had put on a fresh shirt and tie
after leaving the station.

"A scotch and water would hit the spot if you have it."

When she carried their drinks from the kitchen into the
living room, he was standing beside her dining table,
studying the jigsaw puzzle.

"I thought you would have finished this by now," he
said.

Laura smiled as he took his drink. "I work on it a little
while I'm watching TV. But this one is particularly hard."

"I hate these things." Giving her an apologetic smile, he
fit a piece into the puzzle. "I can't leave them alone until
they're finished."

"Not surprising for a detective," she said lightly. "Help
yourself. That's been sitting on my table for about two
weeks. I'd love to have it finished and back in the box."

He sat down. "My mother used to set out a jigsaw puzzle every year at Christmas. Members of the family would
work on it for a while then drift away, and someone else
would sit down in their place. A lot of family problems
were talked out and solved over the Christmas puzzles."

"That's a nice tradition."

He fit a piece of sky into the border. "Except these damned things are addictive. Other members of the family came and went, but I couldn't leave until the puzzle was finished."

"You make it look easy," she commented, watching him fit another piece into place. She decided there was something rather charming about a man in a coat and tie bent over a jigsaw puzzle. Relaxing a little, she smiled. "Is your family large?"

"Two brothers and a sister. How about you?" With a triumphant expression, he tapped another piece into place. "Where's the lid to the box? To do this right, you have to have the lid on the table where the puzzlers can see it."

Laura laughed, then reached to the chair next to her and lifted the box lid to the table. Max studied it, then examined the pieces strewn across her table. "You started to tell me about your family?"

"I have a sister who is married and lives in Chicago," Laura said. "My brother owns a restaurant outside Vincent, Colorado, where we grew up."

"Ah, a small-town girl."

"You've heard of Vincent?"

"Between Boulder and Estes Park." Frowning, he turned a piece of puzzle in his palm, then tried it in the upper corner before he set it aside. A helpless smile curved his lips. "We should get out of here while we still can. Five more minutes and you won't be able to tear me away."

"If I wasn't hungry, I'd insist you stay right there until it's finished," she said, grinning. "I'm tired of dusting around that thing."

"We could send out for something..." With reluctance, he stood, still studying the pieces scattered across the table.

"Not a chance." To her amazement, she found it easy to talk to him. She didn't know what she had expected, but she hadn't expected this rapport. "Could it be that you're a bit of a compulsive type?" she asked, teasing him.

"Could be." After a final glance at the puzzle, he followed her to the door, then led her down the porch steps and across the lawn to a black Monte Carlo. "I hate loose ends. Unfinished things."

He smiled when she suddenly remembered who he was—a cop—and hastened to fasten her seat belt. During the drive to the A-1, she discovered she was stealing glances at his profile, waiting for the next time he looked at her.

When she realized what she was doing, she straightened and faced squarely ahead. Max was an attractive man. He was single; she was single. But he was also a man she had lied to, a man investigating a murder that skirted very close to her ex-husband. And to her.

Once they were inside the restaurant and had given their order, Laura decided to put the worst behind them.

"How official is the official part of this dinner?" she asked in a light voice, hoping her smile didn't look as phony and nervous as it felt.

"Just a couple of questions."

"Shoot."

"How did you know, or rather, meet Ruby Alder?"

There was nothing threatening about the question or his tone of voice. Only his dark eyes indicated they were discussing something of more importance than the weather.

"I had her stepson in my class last year. Ruby came to a couple of parent-teacher meetings. Usually Bobby's father came, but Ruby accompanied him two or three times. About this time last year—before the end of the term—Bobby said his father was getting a divorce and he and his father were moving to California."

"Then you didn't see Mrs. Alder socially?"

"No." She and Ruby Alder were wildly divergent types. Ruby had laughed too loudly, dressed too loudly—everything about her had been overdone. Except her attitude toward Bobby. Toward Bobby she had displayed an affectionate indifference. It hadn't surprised Laura when she learned Bobby's father was divorcing his stepmother. Ruby hadn't impressed her as a woman likely to welcome being tied down by a child.

She blinked when she discovered Max was watching her.

"Did it surprise you when you learned Dave Penn planned to marry Mrs. Alder?"

"As a matter of fact, it did for a while." She tore a corner off her napkin and rolled it into a little ball. "Actually Ruby seemed nice enough, but..." Heat rushed into her cheeks. "I don't know. I guess I expected Dave to choose someone more like me instead of someone directly opposite. But when I thought about it, I could see why he would be attracted to Ruby Alder. In many ways, she was all the things Dave wanted but didn't find in me."

"Like what?"

She lifted her shoulders in a shrug. "From what Dave said, Ruby liked to party. I don't. Not the kind of parties where there's a lot of drinking and craziness. And she was..." The heat deepened in her cheeks. "She was very sexy. She wore low-cut blouses even to the parent-teacher meetings."

Good Lord. She had just said in so many words that Ruby was sexy and she was not. She glanced up in time to see Max flick a glance toward her high-necked silk blouse then smile. She would have given a lot to know what that smile meant.

She managed a smile of her own. "So. How is the investigation proceeding?" Leaning back, she watched the waiter place a salad before her.

Max looked at her, then laughed. "My ex-wife would have passed the meal in total silence rather than discuss a murder."

"Really?" She gave him a look of curiosity. "How long have you been divorced?"

"Three years. Linda wasn't comfortable being married to a cop. Some women aren't."

"Do you have children?"

"No." He lifted an eyebrow. "I'm a little surprised that you don't. Being a teacher, you must like children."

She put down her fork. "You know I do. Patty Selwick told me you had been by the school asking questions about me." Her heart was beating like crazy beneath her blouse. "May I ask why?"

"Laura, I'm investigating a murder case." He paused and pushed at his salad. "In any murder case, there is a set of dynamics involving the people around the victim. Like ripples connecting outward from a stone tossed in a pond. Once we understand the dynamics, the relationships, it's easier to understand what might have happened."

Two dots of color burned high on her cheeks. "Are you saying I am one of the ripples in this particular pond?"

"Yes." He looked at her across the candlelight. "Your ripple seems a long way from the stone, but it's there. How much did Penn tell you about the fight he had with Ruby Alder the night before she was murdered?"

"Enough that I know he said some stupid things."

"I have three people willing to swear they overheard Dave Penn threaten to kill her."

It sounded so stark and terrible. Laura felt the color retreat from her cheeks. She pressed her hands together in her lap and didn't speak.

"Penn struck her. Once on the chin. Once on the shoulder."

Laura tore another piece of her napkin and wadded it into a ball, unaware of what she was doing.

"The only thing standing between Dave Penn and an ideal suspect, Laura . . . is you."

She wet her lips and fervently wished she had never, never gotten into this. "So. Do you have any other suspects?"

"Not at the moment."

"Maybe it was one of those nuts—you know, a random killer . . ." God, she loathed this. She had a feeling she was twisting herself deeper and deeper into a black mess.

Max studied her a moment before he cut into his steak. "There are very few genuine random killings. Most killings happen for a reason. Maybe the reason doesn't make sense to you or me, but there usually is one."

Laura spread her hands. "Maybe Ruby had some enemies no one knows about."

"Maybe."

"And what about her ex-husband?" She felt bad asking about Robert Alder. He had seemed like a nice man, a concerned father.

"We checked it. Robert Alder was in a business meeting at four o'clock last Wednesday." Max tilted a dark eyebrow. "Look, are you really interested in this? We could change the subject . . ."

If she hadn't been involved, she would have found the conversation fascinating. To some extent she did anyway. After all, the quicker he solved the Ruby Alder case, the sooner she would breathe easier again and be out of this mess.

"I'm interested. I've never known a detective before." After a moment, she looked up again. "What about the weapon? Did you find it?"

He grinned at her. "I think I could like you a whole lot. Any woman who can discuss a murder weapon without missing a bite is my kind of woman."

She gave him a weak smile.

"As a matter of fact, we don't know what the weapon was. It was a knife, but an unusual type of knife." He smiled as Laura glanced at her steak knife. "We haven't pinned it down yet."

After that, the conversation drifted away from Ruby Alder's murder. They discussed college, people they had known and what had become of them. There were long moments when Laura forgot how and why she had run into Max Elliot again.

When they returned to her house, she invited him inside for a nightcap after a brief inner struggle. On the one hand, she was playing with fire. On the other hand, she would have invited anyone else inside with whom she had enjoyed a pleasant evening. While he telephoned the station and checked in, Laura poured two snifters of brandy.

"Thank you." After accepting the drink, he gave her an apologetic look, then seated himself at the table and fit a piece of the puzzle together.

"It's almost annoying how easily you do that," Laura said with a mock scowl. After a minute, she asked in a casual tone, "What happens next on the case?"

"We keep digging. Keep looking for a knife that matches the pathology. We hope for a break." He glanced up and smiled. "Annoying? Could that be envy speaking? I haven't seen you put one in place."

"Absolutely it's envy. This thing defeated me a week ago."

"The light isn't very good over the table. There's a glare. Do you mind if I move the table nearer the kitchen pass-through?"

Laura smiled as he loosened his tie. "Help yourself."

After sliding the table nearer the light falling through the kitchen pass-through, he frowned. "I'm being pushy, aren't I? You invite me in for a nightcap and I rearrange your furniture and take over your puzzle."

"No problem. Seriously, go ahead."

"You're sure?"

"If you don't finish it, that puzzle is just going to sit there gathering dust for another week or two. Then one day I'll get tired of eating on top of the pieces and tired of looking at it, and I'll pick it up and put it away."

"Without finishing it?" He looked appalled and Laura laughed.

"The only hope for this puzzle is you."

She sat across from him and they sipped their brandy and worked on the puzzle. They talked about books and movies, restaurants they liked or didn't. They talked about growing up—Laura in Vincent, Max in Denver—and they talked about college and politics. When Laura got up to let in her cat, she realized Max was still wearing his jacket.

"Would you be more comfortable if you removed your jacket?"

"Are you sure it won't make you uncomfortable?" He looked at her curiously.

She couldn't think why it would. "Of course not."

Standing, he removed his jacket and folded it across the back of his chair. Immediately Laura understood what he meant. He wore a .357 revolver in a shoulder holster around his left shoulder. She swallowed and tried not to stare. Not once had it occurred to her that he was wearing a gun.

"I didn't realize you wore a gun to dinner," she commented, fixing her eyes on his face.

"I'd hate to get a call and have to tell the captain I'll be there as soon as I go home and get my piece."

"Yes, of course. I hadn't thought of that."

"If it makes you uneasy..."

"It was just a surprise." It required a moment to adjust to the sight of a man wearing a gun, sitting in her living room, putting together a jigsaw puzzle. "I grew up around guns. My dad and my brother hunted. My sister and I used to do some target practicing."

"Do you own a firearm?"

"I bought a .38 after the divorce." She gave him an embarrassed smile. "To tell the truth, I'm not sure where I put it. I haven't thought about it in more than a year."

Over another brandy, they talked about gun control, then Laura stood and stretched. "My back is aching from leaning over the table." Since Max was absorbed in the puzzle, she wandered to the sofa and picked up the books she had recently received from the Mystery Book Club. Absently, she moved a bookend and pushed the books onto a shelf. Then she did a double take. "That's odd."

"What's odd?" he asked, looking up.

"This bookend." Reaching for the shelf, she removed the bookend and turned it over in her hand, frowning. "This isn't mine." The bookend was heavy, made of gold-painted metal, and shaped like a reclining lion. The bottom was padded with green felt.

"Who does it belong to?"

"I have no idea. I've never seen it before."

As bookends came in a pair, she raised her head and peered at the bookcase. Most of her shelves were filled.

There was only one other set of bookends, and they were definitely hers—two bricks painted like bears that one of her students had made for her. There was no gold lion to match the one she held in her hand.

"This is very strange," she said, looking at the lion. "I wonder how long this has been here?"

She tried to recall when she had last paid any real attention to the bookshelves. Frowning, she tried to recall if the lion had been on the shelf last weekend when she had dusted. For the life of her, she couldn't remember. It was possible she had been thinking about the lunch with Dave and finding Max on her porch, and she had dusted the gold lion without really noticing it.

"Max?"

"Hmm?"

"Have you ever heard of anyone putting things *in* someone's house?" The pot of blue chrysanthemums came to mind and she glanced toward the kitchen counter.

He looked up and grinned. "The kind of people I deal with usually take things *out* of people's houses."

"That makes more sense," she agreed, smiling absently. She balanced the lion between her hands. "I don't understand this. I honestly don't know where this came from. I have no memory of it at all."

"It will probably come to you."

"Probably." Sitting on the sofa, Laura closed her eyes and tried to remember if she had ever purchased lion bookends and what might have happened to the second one if she had....

The next thing she was aware of was a hand gently shaking her awake.

Blinking, she sat up and rubbed her eyes. "Good heavens. I fell asleep." Embarrassment flamed on her cheeks. "Max, I'm sorry. We had drinks before dinner and the brandies here... I'm not much of a drinker. And I haven't been sleeping very well lately." A stricken expression tightened her mouth. "What time is it?"

He looked as embarrassed as she was. "It's a quarter after three."

"In the morning?"

"I apologize. I was working on the puzzle, thinking about the Alder case, and the time got away from me. But I finished it."

"You solved the case?"

"No, the puzzle."

"You've been working on the puzzle all this time?" Suddenly it struck her as funny. Her smile widened into a grin that burst into laughter. Max, smiled, then he was laughing, too. He sat beside her on the sofa and shook his head. "I don't know what to say. I should have gone home hours ago."

"I hope you never see the dresser I'm refinishing in my garage," she said. "If you hate unfinished projects, you'd be here for a week."

He groaned and covered his eyes. "I don't want to hear about it."

"I pass it every time I get out of the car. I try not to look at it."

He opened his hand. "Here. I saved this for you. It's the last piece of the puzzle. I thought you might like to put it in."

"That's nice, but you finish it. The pleasure of the last piece should belong to you."

His expression told her he agreed. "You're sure?"

"No question." Yawning, she followed him to the table and watched him tap in the last piece. "Nice job."

"Now I'm going home and I'm going to try to pretend I didn't put you to sleep with boredom."

"I wasn't bored, honestly. I enjoyed the evening."

She followed him to the door and watched him walk down the steps. At the bottom of the porch he turned and looked up at her. "I'd like to tell you this kind of thing doesn't happen often, but it does. I start thinking about a case and I forget everything else."

"I didn't mind. Really." She would mind in a few hours when she had to get up and go to work, but right now she was telling the truth.

"I'd like to see you again, Laura." He smiled. "I'll try not to think about work."

She laughed. "And I'll try to stay awake for the entire evening."

"Agreed." He looked at her a moment and Laura wished with all her heart that she had not lied to him. She wished they were meeting on a purely social basis.

She stood in the doorway and watched him cross the deep shadows spread over her front lawn then reappear at the curb. He waved and got into his car.

After she closed the door, she stood against it for a moment wondering if it had been a good idea to agree to see him again. Then she wondered if his interest in her was social or professional.

She moved through the house turning off the lights. Before she snapped off the lamp beside the sofa, she noticed the gold lion lying on the floor where it had slipped from her fingers. Lifting it, she replaced it on the bookshelf.

It was very strange.

Dave must have put it on her shelf when he brought the chrysanthemums. But why? It didn't make any sense at all.

Chapter Three

Eric Ashbaugh lit a cigarette and leaned back from his desk to cross his ankles on top of the papers scattered across the desktop. He ran a hand over his thinning hair and looked at Max. "If Laura Penn is lying about Penn's alibi, then Penn's back on deck."

Max nodded and frowned. "It's a gut feeling."

"So what's her involvement?"

"Accessory after the fact, if Penn did it."

"That's not what I'm asking, Max." Eric exhaled and looked across the desks through the smoke.

He lifted his head. "I know this woman, Eric." Lifting her file, he looked at it a moment then let it drop. "Laura's not involved with Ruby Alder's murder. She wasn't part of it. And I don't think she would lie for Penn if she thought he was involved. If she lied, he sucked her into it somehow."

"Okay. Let's assume for a moment that she alibied him and it's a lie. So where was he at four o'clock on that Wednesday? Why is *he* lying?"

"You think he did it?"

Eric shrugged and lit a fresh cigarette from the end of the old one. "The guy's strictly small change. One of those types who feels powerless in life so he takes it out on women. A hitter. Maybe went too far this time."

Max opened the file on Dave Penn and glanced through it. "I'd buy it if Alder was beaten. But she was knifed. Dave Penn is probably paranoid and he has a lousy temper, especially when he's been drinking. We've got evidence from two women saying he smacked them around—Laura and Aline White, the woman he dated before Ruby Alder—and there were a couple of marks on Alder's body. He hit them, but he didn't injure them. No broken bones, no cracked ribs, no need for a hospital visit. Just a lot of bruising. On the face of it, it looks like he's merely putting on a show. Enough to intimidate them into doing whatever he wants. Or maybe it's some sick macho way to establish who's boss. But the violence stops short of anything life threatening."

Eric made a disgusted sound. "We've got motive on him—he thought Alder was seeing another man—and we've got sworn statements that he threatened her. If Laura Penn is lying, then we've got opportunity. No alibi." He heaved a massive sigh. "But ... I don't buy that he's a murderer, either. I could be convinced, but right now ... dammit, I don't see it."

"So where does that leave us?" Max said. The question was rhetorical. He knew where it left them.

"Zip. We've got zip." Eric sucked on the cigarette. "Beneath it all, Ruby Alder was a pretty decent person. Too flashy, maybe. And she liked to party. But we haven't turned up a single hint that anyone hated her. No enemies. No other man. No secrets. If Dave Penn didn't do her in, then we're looking at a phantom killer."

Senseless killings were the worst kind. And the most difficult to solve. "Before we settle in that direction—"

which was about the same as shelving the case, Max knew "—let's do some more digging on Dave Penn."

"Okay," Eric agreed sourly, dropping his feet to the floor and reaching for his jacket. "Maybe we'll get lucky. Maybe we'll discover he put someone in the hospital, or he collects knives, or is certifiable."

Max laughed. "You've been doing this too long, partner. You're getting cynical."

"No, I just want to solve this damned case. It's frustrating me to death. Everywhere we look there's a dead end. We can't identify the knife. No one saw the killer go to her door. He left no prints. Nobody hated her. The best suspect has an alibi." He swore.

Eric was right about everything but Dave Penn's alibi, Max thought as they left the station. His gut feeling told him Penn had no alibi. If Laura Penn was the woman he thought she was, eventually she would tell him the truth. If he was right, it was only a matter of giving her the opportunity and waiting it out.

MAX INVITED HER out to dinner Wednesday night. Having discovered they both loved Italian food, he chose Little Peppina's in North Denver. Classical music drifted over starched checkered tablecloths, candlelight flickered atop wax-dripped bottles. The waiter had just served platters of lasagna that smelled like heaven when Max's beeper sounded.

"I'm sorry," he apologized, eyeing the lasagna. "That must be Eric. He wouldn't page me if it wasn't important."

"Go ahead, Max. I'll be fine."

Swearing under his breath, he left her at the table and located a pay phone in the restaurant lobby. Dispatch patched him through to Eric's car. "This better be important, pal," he said when Eric came on the line. He could see Laura through the archway. Tonight she was wearing a soft silk blouse and a rose-colored skirt. Candlelight glowed in her short dark curls. "A great-looking woman is in the next room watching a plate of lasagna get cold. What's up?" His face sobered as he listened. "Repeat the address. Okay, I'll meet you there."

Laura looked up and her eyebrows rose when he returned to their table. "Something's happened."

He studied her a moment. "There's no nice way to say this. There's been another murder. It looks like it could be the same guy."

She made a small sound, but she didn't gasp or turn pale as his ex-wife would have. "It's the same M.O., then?"

"M.O.?" He smiled. "It's too soon to tell. But there are enough initial similarities that the Wheatridge force thought they should bring us in on it. It sounds like there are some significant differences, too."

"Like what?"

"This woman was married. She didn't live alone. It's a different area of town. That kind of thing." Pushing back his jacket sleeve, he glanced at his watch, then at the platters of lasagna.

"Oh," she said. "You have to leave. Of course. I'm sorry, Max, I wasn't thinking." Hastily, she laid aside her napkin and started to rise.

"This case is outside Littleton's jurisdiction. If I don't get there immediately, it won't cause a problem. Eric is on his way. We're only being invited to observe. Finish your dinner, then I'll take you home."

A thoughtful look darkened her eyes to a deeper blue. "Be honest. You're dying to get out of here and up to Wheatridge, aren't you?"

"Not at all. I'm..." He had never been an accomplished liar and he could see she wasn't buying it. "All right, yes. I'm sorry, Laura, but if there's any chance this killing was committed by the same man..." Before he finished speaking, she was on her feet, pushing the check into his hand.

Once in the car, she turned on the seat to face him and said quietly, "Wheatridge is only a few minutes from here. If you take me home then come back, it will take an hour or more."

She was right. He tapped his fingers on the steering wheel and thought about it. "You'd have to wait in the car," he said finally.

"I don't mind."

The situation was not that unusual. A detective's wife or girlfriend occasionally found herself waiting outside a crime scene. It was unavoidable. Crimes didn't always occur at the policeman's convenience.

"All right. I owe you a lasagna dinner." This time he glanced openly at his watch, his thoughts leaping forward to what he would find at the address Eric had given him.

The scene on Nelson Street was no more chaotic than any crime scene. There were three black-and-whites, four private cars, a Channel Nine TV van and crew. A few porch lights burned along the street although full darkness hadn't yet fallen. A dozen or so people milled about the lawn in front of the murder house. Knots of neighbors had congregated in the street.

Eric spotted Max's car and hurried forward as his partner eased the Monte Carlo against the curb behind a black-and-white.

"Eric Ashbaugh, this is Laura Penn."

Eric smoothed a hand over his hair, touched his tie, then leaned into the car window to exchange greetings with Laura. He gave Max a look that said *wow*.

"Have you been inside yet?" Max asked, stepping out of the car. The spring night was warm.

"Not yet. I was waiting for you."

Max bent to the window. "I have no idea how long this will take."

She was looking at the lights blazing inside the house, at the people standing on the lawn. "Don't worry about me. Take as much time as you need."

"Great-looking woman," Eric commented as they walked toward the police tape surrounding the perimeter of the property. He looked at Max from the sides of his eyes. "Are you sure your interest is purely professional?"

"I don't recall claiming it was." They ducked under the police tapes and entered the house. The front door opened directly into the living room. "Who found the victim?"

"The husband. Ralph James and Gene Sage have him in the backyard talking to him. It happened in the kitchen. Same as the Alder case."

"What's the story on the husband?" Max asked Bill Ridley from the Wheatridge force as Ridley came out of the kitchen.

Ridley shook his head, shaking Max's hand at the same time. "Nothing there. We have four witnesses who all say they saw the husband pull into the driveway at six-thirty. He was inside the house less than three minutes, then he came running outside. He didn't have time to do it and there was no blood on him. He says he was at work all day and has people who will swear he was. My gut says it'll check out." He gestured Max and Eric into the kitchen and asked the coroner's assistant to lift the sheet covering Diane Gates.

"Nasty," Eric observed.

Ridley nodded. "Anything look familiar to you guys?"

Kneeling, Max studied the wounds. Diane Gates had been about Laura's age, a pretty woman. "Could be. If our guy did this, forensic is going to turn up a wound consistent with a blade that's smooth on one side, serrated on the other. We've found blades that are half and half, but we haven't found one to match the pathology yet. Any sign of the weapon?" he asked, standing.

"We're still looking." Ridley gazed at the sheet-covered body and scratched his jaw. "We'll test everything, of course," he said, indicating the kitchen knives a lab man was dropping into bags.

"What have you got so far?" Eric asked. They moved out of the crowded kitchen and stood in the small neat living room.

"Not much. Mr. and Mrs. Gates own a motel on West Colfax. One or the other of them is on the desk every day but Sunday. Mrs. Gates took Mondays and Wednesdays off. A neighbor telephoned at noon today, so we know she was alive then. Looks like she was killed sometime between noon and six-thirty when the husband arrived home. We'll try to pin it down tighter, but that's all we have now. I've got a half-dozen uniforms talking to the neighbors."

"There's a full pot of coffee on the kitchen stove, and two cups set out on the counter," Max commented. He stepped closer to a shelf above the television set. A short row of books took up most of the space on the shelf. A Michener novel, an Erma Bombeck book, a school annual and a book of household cleaning tips about the same size as the annual. The Gateses hadn't been big readers. But that wasn't what caught his attention.

"Yeah," Ridley confirmed. "Looks like she was expecting whoever killed her. Or he gave her time to make coffee."

One of the bookends enclosing the short row of books was a paperweight shaped like an apple. The other was a metal reclining lion painted gold.

"What have you got?" Eric asked, following Max's gaze.

"An odd coincidence. Laura has a lion bookend like this one. She can't recall where it came from."

Eric's smile dismissed the bookend. "I can't say I'm surprised. I've got a pair like that, too. Look around your place and you'll probably find a set. A couple of years ago gold lion bookends were as common as VWs. Everyone who reads probably received a set of gold lion bookends for Christmas that year. You can still find them around. They're a staple item in any junk shop."

Everyone who reads. Max glanced at the shelf again. The Gates were not big readers.

While Eric talked to Bill Ridley, he walked through the small house. Everything was tidy, well kept. Max didn't notice anything out of the ordinary. He also didn't notice more books or another gold lion to match the one on the living-room shelf. Of course, if there had been a matching bookend, logically it should have been at the other end of the row.

Logically it shouldn't matter at all. Lots of people owned mismatched bookends—he had a couple himself. It was the type of bookend, he thought, returning to the living room to have another look. This lion bookend was identical to the bookend that had mysteriously appeared in Laura's house.

Ralph James and Gene Sage entered through the back door, following the husband inside. This was the part Max hated. He shook hands with Tim Gates, knowing the man would not remember him, then he stepped back, thrust his hands in his pockets and listened to the two officers. There wasn't much that Bill Ridley hadn't already reported. He and Eric had turned toward the front door when Ralph James asked if they had any questions for Tim Gates.

Max hesitated, then nodded toward the bookshelf. "That lion bookend—do you remember where and when you got it?"

Tim Gates stared at him from red-rimmed blank eyes. "What?" Turning, he looked up at the shelf as if he had never seen it before. "No, I don't remember. Diane must have...I...no, I don't know."

"Usually bookends are a set. Is there another lion to match this one?"

Gates covered his face and made a motion that might have been a shrug. "It must be around here somewhere." His anguished gaze flicked toward the kitchen then quickly away. "I don't know."

"What was that all about?" Eric asked, when they had stepped outside. Stopping on the porch, he lit a cigarette.

"I'm not sure. Nothing, probably. It's just a peculiar coincidence. And I don't like coincidences."

Eric exhaled and studied the people milling in the street beyond the police tapes. "Now who's been a cop too long?" he asked, smirking.

"Two people show up in less than a week with one bookend. The same one bookend." He, too, ran an eye over the people gathered in the street. It was now too dark to see their faces clearly. "So, what have we got?"

"Same day of the week. Same approximate time of day. No sign of robbery or forcible entry. Same brutality, same nasty type of wounds. Missing weapon. My gut reaction? This is our guy."

"Diane Gates was married. Younger than Ruby Alder. No physical similarity. On the face of it there doesn't seem to be many personality similarities. Alder was a cocktail waitress, worked nights, and she read everything. Books all over her house. She liked a good party. Ridley says Diane Gates was friendly and outgoing, but definitely not a party type. The Gateses lived quietly. Plus the murders are in widely separated locations."

Eric grinned. "And you think the murders are connected, too."

Max smiled. "We've worked together too long." Then he spotted Laura Penn and his smile vanished. He swore. She was standing in the street across from the house, talking to a small group of Diane Gates's neighbors.

Eric rocked back on his heels and gave him a smile. "Appears you've come full circle, old son. First you get Linda, who wouldn't discuss so much as a traffic ticket, now you've got a lady willing to throw herself into the middle of a murder investigation."

Still watching Laura, Max pushed his hands into his pockets. "Do you want to meet at the office and kick this around a little more?" The office he referred to was the last booth at the Denny's Restaurant on Wadsworth.

"Are you going to bring Laura with you?"

He thought about it. Maybe hearing about the case would nudge her toward the truth. "Yes," he said. "If she's willing, I'll bring her along."

As he walked across the street toward Laura, his thoughts turned backward. Maybe he had been too protective with Linda, his ex-wife, in the beginning. Maybe he had frightened her by suggesting she remain distant from the dark and often ugly world he dealt with. If he had done that, then he had no right to blame her for later refusing to comment when he needed to talk about his work.

As he walked toward Laura, he saw her face suddenly freeze and turn pale. Her expression surprised him to the extent that he turned to see what she was looking at, but by the time he did, whatever it had been was gone. He saw nothing but a group of people, none of whom appeared familiar, talking and looking toward the Gates's house.

"Laura?" She jumped when he touched her and turned wide eyes up to him. "What's wrong?"

"Wrong? I...nothing's wrong." Her gaze slid away from him and she fumbled with her purse strap. "I was just talking to some of Mrs. Gates's neighbors," she said, falling into step beside him as they walked toward the car.

He said nothing, frowning, trying to figure it out. Maybe she thought he would be angry that she had left the car. But that didn't explain her strange expression. Maybe he had imagined it. The light from the street lamps was not particularly good.

"Did you discover anything?" he asked after he helped her inside the car.

"Probably nothing you don't already know." She looked as if her thoughts were a hundred miles away.

"I thought we'd meet Eric for coffee at Denny's. But if you'd rather I took you home first..."

"No. I could use a cup of strong coffee." For the first time an uncomfortable silence opened between them. Then she seemed to make some kind of effort and she turned on the seat to face him. "Tell me about Eric Ashbaugh."

"First I'd like to know what happened with the bookend you discovered the other night." He didn't see how there could possibly be any connection between Laura's bookend and the Gates's bookend; most likely it was merely an odd coincidence. If you believed in coincidence. "Did you remember where it came from?"

"No, it's a real mystery." A flush of embarrassment tinted her cheeks. "Well, not a *real* mystery, not like the mysteries you're used to..."

He gave her a distracted smile, still thinking about the bookends. "Do me a favor, will you? Keep your doors locked."

"So, tell me about Eric."

"We've been partners for nine years. He and Sarah are good friends. Practically family." He had time to relate a couple of anecdotes before he turned the car into the parking lot in front of Denny's. But he wasn't sure if she was really listening.

Eric was waiting in the last booth. "I didn't know if you took cream or sugar," he explained to Laura as she and Max slid into the booth across from him. He waved a hand at three cups of coffee already waiting on the table.

"I like it black," she said.

"Good girl. Only sissies adulterate a good cup of coffee," he added, grinning at Max.

"Sissies, huh?" Max said, then stretched his arm across the back of the booth. He touched Laura's shoulder lightly. "Okay. Do you want to tell me anything you found out?"

She ducked her head and tore off a piece of her napkin. "Not much. Except...it's a second marriage for both the Gateses. Tim Gates has a son who visits in the summer. Diane Gates seldom talked about her first marriage, apparently."

"A jealous ex?" Eric suggested. He and Max looked at each other, then shook their heads. "It doesn't fit with the Alder case. Won't wash."

"One of the neighbors said Diane Gates came from a small town, somewhere here in Colorado, and wasn't as careful about locking her doors as she might have been."

"No forcible entry. But it looks like she might have been expecting whoever it was," Max said. "So. Was she careless enough to let a stranger inside? And offer him coffee?"

"If the stranger seemed safe, she might have," Eric observed, thinking out loud. "Like maybe one of those religious folks who solicit door to door."

Laura stared at him. "You can't be serious. Surely you don't think—"

"No, I don't. That's just an example of strangers who appear harmless. A safe stranger. Someone you wouldn't feel uncomfortable about inviting inside."

"I don't think so, Eric." Max stirred another container of milk into his coffee. "My gut—" he looked at Laura "—my stomach tells me Gates and Alder expected whoever came to their door. Laura, did any of your sleuthing turn up a witness?"

"What?" She was looking out the window, a frown between her eyes. "Oh. No, no witnesses. No one I spoke to saw a stranger in the neighborhood."

"Hopefully one of Bill Ridley's uniforms will turn something up." Lifting his wrist, Eric checked his watch. "Sarah will be wondering what happened to me." After sliding from the booth, he leaned across Max and shook Laura's hand. "Make this boy buy you the biggest dinner in the place. I understand he owes you."

"I like Eric," Laura said, watching through the restaurant window as he walked to his car.

"You'd like Sarah, too. She barbecues the best steaks you ever tasted. Plus, she taught school years ago." He could have moved to the side of the booth Eric had vacated, but he didn't. "Speaking of food, are you hungry?"

She glanced at her watch then toward the parking lot as if she were eager to leave.

"The truth? I'm starving. But it's getting late, and this is a school night...."

"They serve the fastest cheeseburgers in the west here. I'll have you home in less than an hour."

He watched the struggle behind her eyes before she nodded agreement. Again the curious silence he had noticed in the car opened between them. Something had happened to alter her mood while he was in the Gates's house.

"Laura—" he touched her shoulder with the tips of his fingers "—is something wrong tonight?" She bit her lip, tore another piece off her napkin and rolled it into a little ball. When she didn't respond immediately, he apologized. "I shouldn't have taken you to a crime scene."

"No," she said quickly. "That isn't it." He lifted an eyebrow and waited. After a moment her shoulders dropped and she looked at him. "I'm sorry, Max. There's something I'm wrestling in my mind..."

"Do you want to talk about it?"

"Not yet. I don't have it worked out. I'm not sure what the right thing is." She spread her hands. "That isn't entirely true. I know what the right thing is, it's just... Look, I'm sorry. I really don't want to talk about this."

He tried to hide his disappointment. He had a feeling she was very close to telling him something about Dave Penn. Maybe how she had lied to give Penn an alibi. If that was what she had done.

"Look at that!" she said, deliberately changing the subject. "One of the waiters just entered the ladies' room."

Thinking about what she had said earlier, Max watched the ladies' room until the waiter emerged. He propped open the door, then pushed a woman in a wheelchair inside. Returning outside, the waiter leaned against the wall and waited.

A sheepish smile curved Laura's mouth. "Since meeting you, I'm starting to be suspicious of everything."

"That's not a bad quality. When you spoke about Diane Gates being from a small town and not being consistent about locking her doors, I remembered you're from a small town, too. I asked you to make sure you always lock your doors. Do you usually?"

"Most of the time."

His eyebrows soared. "Most of the time?"

"Small towns look at these things differently, I guess. My family lived two miles outside of Vincent, on the South Saint Vrain river. I don't remember my parents ever locking our door and we never had a problem. I didn't grow up as security conscious as you big-city kids. We didn't spend a lot of time worrying about crime. We didn't have to."

"Crimes occur in small towns, too."

"I suppose, but . . . you know something? I just remembered. You're right. We did have a burglary once." She smiled. "We came home from dinner out one night and discovered someone had been in the room I shared with my sister."

"Why do I feel like this is a setup?" he asked grinning.

"It was a terrible crime. Someone actually stole—" she paused, drawing it out "—a framed photograph of me...and my diary." Max groaned. "In fact, Vincent had a real crime wave that year. The same thing happened to two of my friends. Someone stole their photographs and diaries, too."

"Could this crime wave have been instigated by a couple of curious boyfriends?"

"I don't think so. At least Dave never admitted to it." Her expression softened as she remembered the story.

"Losing the diaries was the worst. High trauma. Those diaries contained scathing comments about everyone we knew." She laughed. "We worried for weeks that the thief would pass our diaries around school and everyone would read what we had written about them and we wouldn't have a single friend left." She looked at her cheeseburger. "It's sad, isn't it? The good friends you make in school then lose track of? Everyone scatters. Gets married. Moves to other parts of the country."

It occurred to Max that he should have moved to the other side of the booth. He was very conscious of her sitting next to him. The perfume she wore reminded him of summer nights and the scent of lilacs after a rain.

"Would you like some dessert?" he asked, clearing his throat.

"I don't think so." She glanced at her watch and the distracted expression returned to her eyes. "I really have a long day tomorrow. I'm giving a test in the morning. We're coming up on the end of the term...."

Before they left the restaurant, Laura ducked into the ladies' room. The Sleek Chic Spa was advertising their drawing here, too. Seeing the forms reminded her of the day she had met Dave for lunch and this whole mess had started. Grimly she studied the Lucite box filled with the forms of hopeful entrants. Maybe they would draw her name and something good would come out of that much-regretted lunch with Dave. Meanwhile, she badly needed to talk to him.

She and Max didn't speak again until he eased the car to the curb in front of her house. He helped her out, then walked her across the dark lawn.

"You need a new porch light," he observed. "It's black as pitch out here. The bushes between your house and that one cut off all light from the street lamp."

"The porch light burned out a couple of nights ago. I keep forgetting to put a new bulb in." She paused and looked at him in the light falling through the panes on the door. "I'd invite you inside for a nightcap, but..."

He smiled down at her. "I know. It's a school night."

For an instant he wondered if it would be ethical to kiss her, then decided the time was not yet right. He was seeing her because he was attracted to her and because he liked her. A lot. But he was also seeing her because he hoped to keep the pressure on her to tell the truth. He really didn't know what her involvement was in the Ruby Alder murder—if any. But he experienced enough unease on that point that he turned away and made himself walk down the porch steps.

"Good night," he said.

"Good night," she called after him.

Dammit. It was going to be tough to take if he discovered she was protecting a murderer.

LAURA WENT DIRECTLY to the telephone near the sofa without pausing to remove her jacket or put her purse in the closet. Dropping onto the cushion, she dialed Dave's number and listened to the signal sounding in her ear. On the tenth ring, she replaced the receiver in the cradle and struck the sofa arm with her fist.

"Rats!"

She had to talk to Dave. She had to know why he had been standing outside Diane Gates's house. Because she had seen him. Just before Max returned, Laura had glanced toward a group of people and she had seen her ex-husband standing in the shadows just behind them.

For the first time she let herself face the thought that had been pressing at the back of her mind trying to push past the block she had raised.

What if Dave Penn really was the killer? What if he had murdered Ruby Alder?

A chill traced down her spine. Bending forward, she placed her elbows on her knees and covered her face with her hands.

She remembered Max saying something about the only thing standing between Dave and his being a prime suspect was her. What if she had lied to protect a murderer?

Anguish clouded her thoughts.

No, it wasn't possible. Dave Penn was a lot of things, but he wasn't a murderer. Still...she knew he was capable of violence. And she knew he often didn't remember what he had done. She knew the alibi he had given her didn't hold up.

And he had been at Diane Gates's house tonight.

Reaching for the telephone, she tried his number again, then gave up when no one answered after a dozen rings.

Standing, she looked at the blackness beyond the panes of the French doors. Everything that had happened was starting to have a spooky effect on her. She had an unpleasant feeling that someone was standing in her yard watching her through the windows. The skin on the back of her neck prickled.

Frowning, annoyed by her foolishness, Laura walked firmly to the French doors and reached for the drapery pulls to draw the curtains.

A face loomed out of the darkness directly in front of the window.

Her heart leapt in her chest and a tiny scream caught in her throat.

It was Dave. "Let me in," he demanded, pointing to the door.

Her heart was still pounding. "You scared me to death!" she said, fumbling with the latch. Immediately she smelled the liquor on his breath and regretted opening the door. Turning away from him, she started toward the kitchen. "Why didn't you come to the front—"

He caught her by the wrist and spun her to face him. "Did you tell that detective you saw me?"

Strong fumes flowed over her face and she made an expression of distaste. "Let go of my arm," she said quietly. "You're hurting me."

When he released her she backed toward the fireplace, then smothered a gasp of fear when he followed and leaned over her, speaking in a menacing tone. "I asked a question, Laura. I want an answer!"

Now she understood the primary reason she had lied for him. She was afraid of him.

Having admitted the truth, she understood it was time to confront her fear and put an end to it. Easier thought than accomplished. On the positive side, two years stretched between this moment and the last time he had tried to intimidate her with roughness. Plus, this time she wouldn't have to deal with him tomorrow. He was no longer part of her life.

"Back off, Dave," she said, speaking as quietly and calmly as she could. "I don't have to put up with this any more. If you raise your hand to me, I'll call the police. I'll file charges. I mean it."

"All I want is a goddamned answer! Did you tell the detective you saw me?"

She met his eyes and spoke in a firm voice, sounding a lot braver than she felt. She absolutely would not allow herself to think that she might be confronting a murderer. "I want you to leave, Dave. I won't talk to you when you've been drinking."

He stared into her unwavering gaze, and when she did not look away, the hands he had placed on the wall on either side of her dropped away.

"Hell, you'd drink, too, if your wife thought you murdered someone. That's what you believe, isn't it? You think I killed Ruby."

"Did you?"

"No, dammit! I did not kill her! I was going to *marry* her." Stumbling backward, he tripped over the edge of the coffee table and sat hard on the end of the sofa. "And I didn't kill Diane Gates, either, if you're thinking that!"

"What were you doing there?" Carefully she edged along the fireplace wall until she stood next to the poker set. She let her fingertips rest on the handle of the poker, taking a measure of comfort from the touch of the heavy metal.

"You won't believe me."

"Tell me anyway."

"I was showing houses in the Wheatridge area to an out-of-state buyer. Afterward, I saw the commotion on Nelson Street and stopped to see what it was all about. I swear to you, that's all there is to it. I saw your face when you spotted me and I knew what you were thinking. Then I saw you go off with that detective and I figured you told him you saw me. Now I'm in trouble again."

"I didn't tell him," she admitted, watching him.

He lifted his head. "God. Thank you."

"But I think I'm going to, Dave." Her fingers curled around the handle of the poker and she saw that he noticed. "I don't want to be involved in this. I don't want to lie to the police. I wish I hadn't done it."

"Laura, for God's sake. Do you know what will happen to me if you tell them I lied about being here with you?"

Briefly she closed her eyes and pressed her lips together. "I'm sorry. I have to get out of this mess, I . . . I'm sorry." He looked frantic. "You have to trust the system," she added in a low tone.

"You've got to be kidding! Trust the system? Laura, I'm not so drunk that I can't figure this one out. Think about it. I threatened Ruby and I don't have a decent alibi for when she was killed. Then I was unlucky enough to blunder onto the scene of another murder. How is that going to look?"

Like he was involved up to his eyebrows. Biting her lip, she looked away from him.

"And what am I supposed to do while you're making up your mind whether to tell them or not? Hide out? Skip town?" Dropping his head, he swore into his hands. "Laura, I didn't do it."

"Then who did? You knew Ruby. You knew her life. Who could have killed her?"

He shook his head. "I don't know. Don't you think I've been racking my brain trying to come up with someone, anyone, who might have done it? There isn't anyone."

"Yes, there is. Someone did it." She raised a hand. "Did she ever mention anyone she didn't like? Who gave her trouble or something?"

"You didn't know Ruby. She liked everyone. The only person I ever heard her put down was her dentist, for God's sake. She thought there was something screwy about him."

"Do the police know about him?"

"Laura, come on. Ruby's dentist didn't kill her because she decided to take her business to someone cheaper and closer to home."

"What was screwy about him?"

"I'm the one who's screwy for having mentioned the poor bastard. Trust me, Ruby's dentist is not a suspect. I wish he was, but there are no suspects except me. Hell, if I was Max Elliot, I'd think Dave Penn did it, too. When you confess all, Elliot's going to be sure of it."

Laura hated herself, but she was wavering again. If Dave was telling the truth, then he was in a hell of a mess. The problem for liars was not telling lies. It was telling the truth. When a liar told the truth, no one believed him.

Her shoulders dropped and she released the handle of the poker.

"All right, Dave. I'll hang in a little longer." She let her head fall back against the fireplace wall. "I hate this. I really hate it. You don't know what this is doing to me." She drew a breath. "Let's both pray they catch the real killer soon."

After he left, she pulled the draperies and checked to make sure she had locked the doors. Before she snapped off the lights in the living room, she realized she had forgotten to ask him about the gold lion bookend. It probably didn't matter. Most likely he would have denied putting it on her bookshelf. Just like he denied putting the chrysanthemums in her kitchen.

She glanced at them on the end of the counter. The flowers were starting to fade. The tips of the leaves were turning brown.

Sighing, she entered her bedroom and hung up her clothing, then put on her robe. In the bathroom, she looked into the mirror and released another sigh. Her face was unnaturally pale. Faint blue circles ringed her eyes.

She longed to tell Max Elliot the truth. She had a sus-
picion he had guessed some of it anyway. Lying was hard
enough. But in the beginning, when she had agreed to lie,
it had been to an anonymous government body. But now
the police had a face and a name. She was lying to Max
Elliot, a man she was attracted to and enjoyed. A whole
lot. That made a terrible situation a thousand times worse.

For a moment she remembered that strange instance on
the porch when Max had looked into her eyes and she had
thought he was going to kiss her. She had hoped he would.

After a minute, she sighed again and tried to put the
thought out of her mind.

Chapter Four

After nine years on the force, Max had learned to trust his instincts even when he could not justify or completely define or explain them.

"Okay, we're here," Eric said, looking around Ruby Alder's ultramodern living room. The draperies were drawn and the interior was dim and silent. A thin layer of dust had accumulated on the glass tables and uncomfortable-looking chairs and furnishings. "So. Do you want to tell me why we're here?"

"We're looking for a gold lion bookend." Standing in front of a Lucite shelving unit, Max scanned the rows of books.

"What is it with you and that lion bookend? I don't get it."

"I don't, either," Max said absently. The bookends in the wall unit were replicas of *The Thinker*. One row of books was held upright by a short stack of novels lying on their sides.

"Okay," Eric muttered. "That's good enough for me. I'll take the guest room. You check the master."

Neither man considered confining the search to the bookshelves. One assumed nothing on a homicide. They searched Ruby Alder's town house carefully and methodically, looking into drawers, peering under furniture.

"Find anything?" Eric asked, emerging from the kitchen.

"Nothing." An odd sense of relief loosened the tension bunching Max's shoulders.

They took a final walk through the rooms then returned to Max's car, but he didn't immediately switch on the ignition. Eric lit a cigarette and they both looked across the street at Ruby Alder's unit.

"This one feels peculiar," Eric said at length.

Max nodded. "We're running out of ideas and places to go. Did you finish checking the names in her address book?"

"They all check out. Nothing there. How about her aerobics class?"

"Nothing."

"Shall we try the lounge again? See if any of the employees have remembered anything?"

Max considered the suggestion then shook his head. "We've been there three times. We've talked to everyone she worked with. I think we've gotten all we're going to get."

"And none of it goes anywhere."

They continued to stare at Ruby's door.

"If we start with the premise that Dave Penn is not involved in the murder, who else might have had a motive?"

Eric frowned. "Nobody. Are you suggesting a random hit?"

"It can't be random. The similarities between Alder and Gates are too concrete. That would confirm both hits were deliberate and both done by the same guy."

"You, me, Ridley—we've all tried to establish a link between Ruby Alder and Diane Gates. Max, old son, it flat does not exist. These two women did not know each other. Their paths never crossed. Tim Gates says he's never heard of the Merry Cherry Lounge where Alder worked. He's positive his wife never went there. Alder and Gates lived in different parts of town. They could not have run into each other at the grocery, the cleaners, a neighborhood event. We've compared their address books and no names match. None of their activities coincide or intersect.

"Let's take the Gates case. We've got the same set of problems. No apparent motive. Everything Ridley is turning up says the Gateses' marriage was on solid ground. He's located the first round of spouses, and there's nothing there. Gates's ex-husband is in Florida. The husband's ex-wife was at a bridge tournament at the time of the murder. Gates had no enemies. What we're looking at is two apparently motiveless killings."

"With a hell of a lot of similarities," Max said. "The hit happened on the same day of the week at about the same time. No sign of forcible entry in either case. It was the same or a similar weapon, and both times the killer took the weapon with him—he didn't leave it at the scene. Both of the victims were women, both were killed in the kitchen. And nobody saw a damned thing. The guy's invisible.

"There should be a connection, so why isn't there? These murders are related. You believe it, too."

Nodding, Eric flipped his cigarette into the street. "It's the same guy." He squinted at Alder's door as Max pulled the car away from the curb. "Okay, let's take Alder. Without Dave Penn, there is no motive for killing her. But we're agreed this isn't a random hit. So what the hell is it? Where does that leave us?"

"Maybe we're focusing on the wrong thing. Maybe we're taking too narrow a view. Suppose Alder isn't the real target. Suppose it could have been anyone. Maybe it's the way she was killed. Maybe her death is supposed to be some kind of crazy message."

"Okay, let's go with it. All right, our killer is sending a message. So what is the message and who is supposed to receive it?"

Turning the corner slowly, Max cruised past Laura's house. He wondered if she had remembered to lock her front door. Small-town thinking might work while you were in a small town, but it didn't work if you moved to a city.

"The message," Max repeated, thinking out loud. "Okay, suppose Ruby Alder's death is intended as a warning to someone else. A threat." Driving aimlessly, he turned again at the next corner.

"Gates is the most logical someone else, but so far we can't establish that the two women ever met. If Alder's death was intended to warn Gates about something, Gates didn't get the message."

"Maybe Diane Gates's death is a message, too?" Even as he said it, Max knew he was stretching the idea too far. "All right, that's no good. Is there anything about Alder's death that could be significant to Diane Gates even though they didn't know each other?"

"Like the method?"

"Maybe, but that doesn't feel right. And it can't be the weapon, or the killer would have left it behind."

An hour later Eric flipped another cigarette out the car window. "Both women were a little overweight. Is there anything in that?"

"Neither of them had a serious problem. They could have dropped ten pounds, but . . ." They let the idea die.

"Let's drive up to Wheatridge," Eric suggested. "See if Ridley has turned something over."

As always at this stage of a case, when things seemed to have gone stagnant, Max felt a frustrating sense that he was seeing something without comprehending what he was seeing. It was like holding a piece of a jigsaw puzzle in his palm, unable to envision the entire picture from one small piece. Unable to move forward until that piece fit into another. Unfortunately, instinct warned him they had all the pieces of the Alder puzzle they were going to get.

Unless Laura told him the truth.

For perhaps the hundredth time, he wondered if possibly he was imagining things. Maybe she wasn't lying. Maybe the case had truly hit a dead end.

PATTY SELWICK turned in the car seat and looked at Laura. "I thought we were going to lunch. I didn't know you were going to drag me up to Wheatridge to look at a house where a murder occurred." She made a face, then shifted to look at the Gateses' house. "What are we doing here, anyway?"

"I'm not really sure," Laura admitted. Like the Willow Hills area, this was a young neighborhood. The houses were older, but the residents looked to be young families. On the night Diane Gates had been murdered, Laura had noticed several children. The killer had taken a big risk of being seen.

"Are we looking for something particular?"

Laura's glance swung toward the spot where she had seen Dave standing.

"No, not really. I'm trying to make my mind up about something. I guess I thought coming here might help."

Patty rolled her eyes. "You are getting weird. I'm not sure dating a homicide detective is a good idea, Laura."

"I'm not dating him. Not exactly."

"Call it what you want. But I think I liked it better when you were reading mysteries instead of getting involved in them."

Laura's head jerked around. "What do you mean, getting involved?"

"Rushing off from dinner to the scene of a murder. Talking to the neighbors. Dating a homicide cop. What did you think I meant?"

Laura looked back at the Gateses' house. There was something sad about it, sitting quietly in the May sunshine. It was the only house on the block with the draperies drawn. Already the house looked vacant, as if no one lived there anymore.

"A woman died there," Laura whispered. "Someone killed her."

"Laura, think about this. A month ago you were a normal person living a quiet normal life. Your most pressing problem was whether or not to fail that rotten kid, what's his name, Gene McTavish. Now look at you. Now you're sort of involved in two—count 'em, two—murders. Doesn't this strike you as a bit peculiar?"

"Two murders?"

"Oh, come on, don't sound so edgy. You know what I'm talking about. You're on the scene of this one. And you knew Ruby Alder. Dave was engaged to her, for heaven's sake."

Laura was glad she had not told Patty about the alibi.

"And how about this Max Elliot? You're dating a guy who wears a gun. And he takes you to a murder on the second date."

"Patty, it wasn't a date."

"Then what was it?"

She thought about it. "Maybe it was a date."

"Okay. You tell me this Max is great looking and he has a heart-stopping smile. And you're bright, curious, and you like mysteries. So far so good. But this is not your average everyday guy, Laura. Other guys go home and empty their loose change on the hall table. This Max goes home, puts a gun on the table and for a little light reading leafs through some mug shots."

"I think I'm falling for him."

"Oh, God." Patty stared at her. "Do you know what life with a cop would be like? You would worry yourself to death every day when he went to work. Wondering if he would come home at night."

"I know." She reached for the ignition. "Forget I mentioned it. I doubt anything will come of it."

"Well," Patty said, "people can't choose who they fall in love with. And, looking on the bright side, police departments offer retirement benefits, so we can assume some policemen do live to retire."

"Thanks. You're a real ray of sunshine," Laura said. "I don't want to talk about Max Elliot over lunch." She had a feeling she had already said too much about him. "I want to talk about blue chrysanthemums and a gold lion." She laughed at Patty's expression, then explained.

When she finished, Patty stared at her. "You're saying someone is putting things *in* your house?"

"It looks that way. At first I thought it must be Dave. But now I'm not so sure. Any ideas?"

Patty threw out her hands. "Not even a glimmer."

After lunch they walked out to the restaurant parking lot together, and Patty paused beside Laura's car. "I don't know if I envy you or pity you. But one thing is certain— your life is getting bizarre."

"It's better than worrying about Gene McTavish. Did I tell you he set off a stink bomb in science class last Thursday?"

Laughing, Laura waved and drove home. She let herself into the house through the garage door and tossed her purse and jacket into the hall closet, then put a pot of coffee on to brew.

She walked into the living room intending to open the French doors to the patio, then stopped abruptly. A paper crown sat in the middle of her coffee table.

For an instant she was so surprised she could only stare. Then, approaching slowly, she circled the coffee table and studied the crown from all angles. Sitting on the sofa, she lifted it in her hands. The crown was made of heavy paper covered with foil. By prying up the foil she discovered an advertisement for a local burger drive-through underneath. In the back of her mind she recalled seeing a TV ad featuring a giveaway crown with every two burgers, or something of that sort.

Turning the crown in her hands, she wondered who on earth had bothered to cover it so carefully in silver foil, then place it on her coffee table. Her brow furrowed.

Eventually she stood and went to the front door and tried the handle. It was locked. So, she had remembered. Next she tried the French doors. Locked.

After going into the kitchen for a cup of coffee, she leaned on the pass-through counter and frowned at the paper crown.

There was no other explanation. Someone had unlocked her door, come inside and put the crown in her living room. A tiny chill of fear raised bumps on her skin.

"Don't be silly," she said out loud, annoyed with herself. "Think it through."

The first problem was the lock. The only person besides herself who had a key to her house was her brother in Vincent. She had sent him a new one after the visit from the locksmith. John had a key in case there was ever an emergency and he had to get inside her house.

Feeling utterly foolish, but unwilling to leave any possibility dangling, she lifted the kitchen phone and dialed long distance.

After exchanging family news, she drew a breath and looked at the crown on her coffee table. "John, this is going to sound a little silly, but . . . have you given anyone the key to my house? Or maybe a copy?"

"Of course not. Is something wrong?"

"No, no. Nothing to worry about. I was just wondering, that's all."

After mutual promises to get together soon, she hung up and stepped out onto her porch. The Ackersons' house on the west was vacant. So she went to the rental house on the east side and knocked on the door.

"Hi," she said brightly when a young woman opened the door. "I'm Laura Penn, your neighbor on that side." She pointed to the row of tall thick bushes that entirely obscured her house. "I'm sorry I haven't stopped by before to say hello and introduce myself."

"I'm Holly Ames. Come on in."

"Just for a minute." Inside, the house was even smaller than it looked from the outside. Holly Ames's clutter made Laura's look like the work of an amateur.

"My roommate is in Chicago right now. We're flight attendants. Not home much," Holly Ames explained with a dimpled smile.

"Holly, I won't keep you. I was just wondering . . . did you happen to see anyone at my door today?" Immediately she realized that was a stupid question. Holly Ames could not see Laura's house, let alone her front door. "All right, let's try this another way. Did you see anyone in the neighborhood in the last couple of hours? Any strange cars, maybe?"

"An Avon lady stopped by earlier. And some guy selling magazines. Is that what you mean?"

"I'm not sure." Feeling like a fool, she asked Holly to describe the Avon lady and the magazine salesman. Neither sounded out of the ordinary.

"Just a sec. The Avon lady left a card." In a minute Holly returned and gave the card to Laura. The name meant nothing to her. "And here's the receipt for the magazines I ordered. Does any of this help?"

Not much. Laura doubted her intruder would leave a calling card with her next-door neighbor. A sigh touched her lips. "Well, thanks. I'm sorry to have bothered you."

"It was no bother. Come over for coffee sometime."

"Thanks, I will."

Laura stopped on the sidewalk in front of her house. The house to the west was empty. The heavy shrubbery on the east cut her off from Holly and her roommate. A fence and a row of poplars secluded her house from the unknown neighbors on the back side. Turning, Laura frowned at the vacant lot across the street directly in front of her house. Occasionally the kids in the neighborhood used the space for sandlot ball. But today the lot was deserted.

It occurred to her that her house was as isolated as if she lived alone in the country instead of in the heart of a thriving suburb.

Feeling uneasy, she let herself inside her door, then checked to make sure her spare key was hanging on the key hook in the foyer. She even tried it in the lock to make certain it was the right key. It was. No one had stolen it and hung another in its place.

"The plot thickens," she muttered, returning to the kitchen for the coffee she had left on the countertop.

Since she was getting exactly nowhere with the problem of how her intruder had gotten inside, she turned her attention to the peculiar items he or she had left. Sipping her coffee, she studied the pot of chrysanthemums. It was time to throw the flowers away. This time for good. They were wilted and sad looking.

But first, she carried the flowerpot into the living room and placed it beside the silver crown on the coffee table. She took the lion bookend from the shelf and placed it beside the other two items. Then she leaned back on the sofa and drank her coffee and studied the three items, pondering the mystery.

By now she had decided Dave was probably telling the truth. At least on this point. Certainly he could not have put the crown on her coffee table. If he still had a key to her house, it was the wrong key.

So. Did the items have anything in common? Besides their mysterious appearance? Not that she could see. Laura swallowed another sip of coffee.

Were they supposed to mean something? A pot of flowers, a bookend, and a paper crown. If they meant something, she wasn't grasping it. The only similarity between the items that she could think of was that someone wanted her to have them.

Ten minutes later, she finished her coffee and gave up. She suspected she could stare at the items for ten years and not be any closer to understanding. As far as she could tell, there was no connection, no meaning, no message.

Nuts to it. Annoyed, she changed into shorts and a T-shirt and got her gardening tools out of the garage, then carried a flat of bedding plants out to her garden. Bending, she dug a hole and pressed a petunia into it.

Blue chrysanthemums, a gold lion and a silver crown. What did they have in common?

Think about it. If this were a mystery she was reading, what would the items mean? She pressed another petunia into a hole and pushed dirt around it. Did the colors signify anything? She didn't think so.

Trying another angle, she tried to figure why in the world someone would put things in another person's house. Straightening abruptly, she stared at the back fence.

Someone might put things into another person's house if they wanted to hide those things. But why would they want to hide something?

Pushing to her feet, she took off her garden mittens and dropped them in the grass, then sprinted toward the French doors. Once inside, she looked at the items on the coffee table and her shoulders drooped in disappointment.

No. There was no way to smuggle anything inside a pot of flowers or a paper crown. But just in case...

Taking the pot back into the kitchen, she eased the flowers out of the pot, then dug her fingers into the dirt. There was nothing there but soil and roots.

Next she got a nail file from the bathroom and pried off the felt base beneath the lion and peered into the cavity. Nothing. The lion bookend was hollow inside, but the hollow was empty.

So much for that idea. She lifted an eyebrow at R.C., her cat, as he strutted through the living room toward the patio. "Too bad you can't talk," she muttered as the telephone rang.

"Hi." Max's deep voice filled her ear. "How would you feel about inviting a cranky frustrated detective over for some take-out pizza? I'll pick it up on the way."

She hesitated only a moment. "Good idea. As a matter of fact, I could use a detective's viewpoint. I have a puzzle that needs solving."

"Say it isn't so." He groaned. "I don't have the energy for another three-in-the-morning puzzle marathon."

"It's not that kind of puzzle," she said, smiling. "I'll tell you about it when you get here."

After dumping the old coffee, she put a fresh pot on to brew, then freshened her lipstick and changed into a pair of slacks and a plaid blouse.

When Max arrived, he was carrying a steaming box, which he carried into her kitchen.

"Is this a business or a social call?" Laura asked in a light voice.

"Strictly social. Do you mind?"

"Good. In that case, take off your jacket and check your gun. Do you mind?" She pointed to a peg on the wall, where she usually hung her aprons.

Max tested the weight of his holster on the peg then winked at her. "When a woman installs a gun rack, it usually means the relationship is progressing."

Laura laughed, feeling a flush of pink heat her cheeks. Turning, she opened the pizza box and stared inside. "Anchovies? Ick!"

"What? Are you saying you don't love anchovies?"

"I hate anchovies." She picked them off the slices she placed on her plate.

He blinked. "Seriously? You really don't like anchovies? I thought you would."

"Next time get half and half—half anchovies, half pepperoni." When she realized she was assuming a next time, the color in her cheeks deepened.

"I can't believe you don't like anchovies." He scooped up the anchovies she'd picked off and tipped them onto his plate.

Laura laughed, liking him a lot. "Come on. Bring your pizza and beer into the living room. I want to show you my puzzle." They sat on the sofa and Laura pointed to the three items on the coffee table. "There it is. Now tell me, how are those items connected?"

"This is great pizza." Max placed his glass of beer on the coffee table and studied the items. "Okay, what have we got here? A pot of wilted flowers, a bookend, and a kid's crown. What happened to the bottom of the bookend?"

"I pulled the felt off to look inside. There's nothing there. And I looked under the foil on the crown. It's a giveaway item from a local burger place, if that means anything."

"All right, I give up," he said after a minute. "What's the answer?"

"I don't know the answer. I was hoping you might see something I missed." She explained that each item was like the lion bookend, it had appeared in her house when she was out. "It's a real locked-door mystery," she finished with a humorless smile.

There was no humor at all in Max's expression. "Who has a key to your house?"

His frown deepened as she traced the history of her keys. When she finished, he took her plate from her hands and placed it beside the items on the coffee table. Then, still holding her hand, he led her to the front door. First he checked to make sure the door wouldn't lock behind them, then he guided her outside and closed the door.

"Look through the window and tell me what you see."

Curious, Laura peered through the small window set in the upper half of her door. It was small, approximately five inches by four inches wide.

"I see the top two or three feet of the wall and part of the ceiling. What am I supposed to see?"

He studied her with a tilted eyebrow, then clasped her around the waist and lifted her until her head was level with his. "Now tell me what you see."

"Good heavens. I can see into the living room." Her next observation emerged more slowly. "And I see the key hook next to the foyer mirror."

"Right," he said in a grim voice, setting her on her feet. "Laura, when you said you remembered to lock your door most of the time, does that mean there are occasions when you don't remember to lock your door?"

"Sometimes," she admitted reluctantly. She could guess where this was leading. They went back inside and picked up their plates of cooling pizza.

"Making an impression of a house key is ridiculously quick and simple," Max commented, looking at the three items on her coffee table. "I'm not saying that's what happened. But it could have. Someone tries your door and finds it unlocked. You could even be home when it happens. They see the key hook from the window, step inside, make an impression and go. The whole thing wouldn't take two minutes."

She stared at him. What he was saying was frightening.

"If you've accounted for all your keys and none are missing, and if you are absolutely certain your door was locked on the days the items appeared, then you have to consider that someone may have a key you aren't aware of."

"And that key could have been made from the foyer key," she said slowly.

"Laura, there's no way to know for certain if that's what happened here, but it's possible. No one has tampered with your lock, I can tell you that much. I checked it. Did you check the rest of the house for any signs of entry?"

"I thought I did." She considered for a moment. "Wait." Rising, she returned to the foyer and went down four steps to the cellar door. It opened easily. "Oh boy," she said, raising her eyes to Max. "This is usually locked."

Without speaking, Max lifted the flashlight hanging beside the door and stepped past her onto the cellar steps. The flashlight beam swept over the furnace and water heater, then up to a small window above the potting table. The window was hanging open.

"How he got in isn't the mystery we thought it was," Max said in a tight voice. After he closed the window, they returned to the living room and sat on the sofa.

"I walked around the house, but I didn't notice the cellar window was cracked open," Laura said, looking at the slice of pizza in her hand. She drew a breath. "I don't know when the lion bookend appeared, so I can't say for certain the door was locked that day. But the doors were definitely locked when the flowers and the crown appeared."

"Well, it apparently didn't matter," Max muttered.

"But . . . why? If someone is going to all this trouble to get inside my house, you'd think it was because they wanted to steal something. But nothing is missing."

"You're sure?"

"Yes. Max, I'm having trouble accepting the idea that someone is putting things inside my house. This would be a lot easier to figure if things were being taken out."

They ate their pizza and studied the items on the coffee table.

"Laura, are you absolutely certain none of these items rings a bell? Either singly or collectively?"

"Nothing I can think of."

"None of the items has any personal meaning for you?"

"I like flowers. A lot of people know I enjoy gardening. It's no secret that I read a lot. Readers can always use another set of bookends. But the same statements would apply to millions of other people. The crown doesn't make any sense at all, except for the child connections and my teaching." Max's expression concerned her. "You're worrying me a little," she said, trying to make light of it. "There's nothing to be concerned about, is there? I mean, nothing has been stolen, and these items are harmless enough."

"Laura, listen to me," After setting aside her plate, he took her hands in his. "Anytime someone comes into your home uninvited, without your permission or knowledge, it's cause for serious concern."

"I know you're right...." Then she told him about Holly's Avon lady and the magazine salesman, and gave him the card and magazine receipt. "It's probably nothing..."

"Probably," he said, frowning at the card and receipt. "But I'll check it out tomorrow."

"Oh, I just remembered something else you might check out. I almost forgot to tell you." Realizing how silly it sounded when she said it aloud, she told Max what Dave had said about Ruby changing dentists.

"Hey, don't apologize. Sometimes something that doesn't seem important in the beginning turns out to be crucial. Did Dave say why Ruby thought this guy was screwy?"

"No, he didn't."

Max finished his beer. "When did you see Dave?" he asked casually. "Recently?"

"Yes," she admitted uncomfortably. "He...he just dropped in for a minute." Jumping to her feet, she cleared the pizza plates and took them into the kitchen.

After Max left, Laura loaded the dishes into the dishwasher, then poured a cup of coffee and carried it into the living room. Standing over the coffee table, she gazed at the chrysanthemums, the bookend and the crown. The items themselves were not threatening, but she felt uneasy looking at them. Her intruder was telling her something, but she couldn't figure out what. And she didn't like the way he was doing it—by coming into her house. On the other hand, her mystery items were intriguing—a small mystery to take her mind off Dave and larger, more serious mysteries.

Perhaps she was making more out of the items than they actually merited. If she really thought about it, the pot of chrysanthemums had probably come from Dave even though he denied it. It would have been like him to give her flowers at that point, and despite what he claimed, it was possible he'd still had a key to her house. And she didn't really know for a fact that the bookend had just mysteriously appeared when she was out. Patty Selwick or someone else might have left it behind when they were visiting. And the crown—one of her students could have made it for her then crawled through the cellar window to put it inside if she wasn't home when they came to deliver it.

Laura was in bed and almost asleep before she admitted she was fooling herself. Dave would have been the first to claim credit if he had left the flowers. Patty Selwick hadn't been carrying around one bookend, which she then put on Laura's shelf and forgot. And no child put the crown on her coffee table.

MAX DROVE TO THE END of Laura's block, made a U-turn, then cut his lights. After driving back toward her house, he parked across the street and switched off the ignition. Leaning forward, he studied the situation. Her house was an ideal target. Screened by shrubbery on two sides and fronted by a vacant lot. The only house from which there was a view of hers was vacant.

Moreover, as long as it was possible that someone had a key to her front door, Laura Penn was vulnerable to that someone. She might as well be sleeping with the door wide open.

Leaning his head back against the headrest, he folded his arms across his chest and sought a position that was comfortable yet allowed him an unobstructed view of two sides of her house.

For a time he thought about the Alder case and the Gates case, ran various scenerios in his mind, wondered if the information about the dentist would amount to anything. Eventually he turned his curiosity back to the items on Laura's coffee table.

The items appeared harmless, and he knew that Laura didn't attach any particular significance to them. But someone did. Someone had chosen those items for a reason.

And managed to place them inside her home. That's what worried him.

Chapter Five

"It's a new book," Eric said, thumbing through the address book they had found beside Ruby Alder's phone. "No erasures, no strike-throughs." A mournful expression tugged his mouth. "All cops hate new address books."

"So if a dentist is listed—"

"Two are listed."

"It's probable neither one is the old 'screwy' dentist."

"Maybe she mentioned his name to the new dentist?" Eric suggested hopefully.

"It's worth a phone call. While you're tracking that down, I'm going to check out an Avon lady and a magazine salesman."

"Have you got the Friday crazies, or are you going to explain that?" Eric asked, reaching for the telephone.

"I'll tell you about it later."

After Eric had spoken to both dentists listed in Ruby Alder's address book, he rubbed his eyes then tilted his head toward the ceiling. "The new dentist is Dr. Morgan. He says Alder wouldn't tell him her old dentist's name. Thought she'd get him in trouble or something."

"This is sounding more interesting," Max said, looking up. "What kind of trouble?"

"Dr. Morgan got angry talking about it. He says he doesn't know anything about Alder's previous dentist having a screw loose, but he says the guy did the worst dental work he's ever seen. Says even a first-year student could have done better. The longer Morgan talked, the madder he got. He was saying things like 'ought to be run out of town on a rail.' Stuff like that."

"How long was Ruby a patient of Dr. Morgan's?"

"About six months. So if she had a blowup with the previous dentist, it happened before then."

They both looked disappointed. "Still, this is the only fresh piece of information we've got."

"I hear you, partner." Eric didn't look happy. "We need to find dentist number one." He flipped open the yellow pages and heaved a sigh. "I had no idea there were so many dentists in the Denver area. There must be one, two million listings in here."

"Okay. I'll take A through L. You take M through Z. Let's find the guy."

Max hit the jackpot about three in the afternoon.

"Yes," a bored female voice said, "Mrs. Alder is one of Dr. Latka's patients."

"I'd like to speak to Dr. Latka."

"Sorry, the doctor is out of town. He won't be back until a week from yesterday. That's next Thursday."

"This case is shot full of frustrations," Eric said, when Max relayed the conversation. "Well, at least we have Thursday to look forward to. It's better than sitting around wishing and hoping on nothing."

MAX APPEARED on Laura's doorstep on Saturday morning dressed in crisp jeans and a plaid work shirt, and carrying a cardboard box filled with tools and cans.

"What on earth?" Blinking, Laura opened her door, embarrassed that he had caught her still in her robe. Her hair was tousled and she wore no makeup.

"You know something? You look great in the morning."

"Liar." Laura peeked at herself in the foyer mirror, then groaned and pushed at her hair.

Stepping past her, Max carried the box into the kitchen and murmured happily when he noticed she had already brewed a pot of coffee. He poured two cups, gave her one, then leaned against the counter. "Seriously, you look terrific. All scrubbed and tousled and sorta sunshiny."

"Sunshiny? That's a nice word."

"It's for a nice lady."

"What's all the stuff in the box?"

"Tools, stripping compound and stain." Max took a screwdriver from the box and unscrewed Laura's apron peg. When she lifted an eyebrow, he grinned and explained. "We need to anchor your gun rack."

"Good idea." It was a positive sign they would continue to see each other. If only she hadn't lied to him. If only she could turn back the clock and have that moment again.

"What's the stripping compound and stain for?"

"Well, I've been thinking about your unfinished dresser. The one you ignore when you go in and out of the garage. I thought—if you don't mind—that I'd work on it a little. That is, unless it's a project you've been looking forward to, saving for yourself . . ."

Laura laughed. "I'm starting to think you really are compulsive about finishing things. If you're willing to finish my dresser, help yourself. I'd be grateful." She continued smiling. "I have a feeling you're following behind me cleaning up loose ends."

"Could be. How many more are there?" he asked, not looking at her. Stepping backward, he studied the anchored peg. But he was waiting for her answer.

Laura had an idea the conversation had undertaken a subtle shift. And suddenly she wondered if their deepening friendship was all a sham, some kind of police tactic. Maybe Max was seeing her only because he suspected the truth, that she had lied. Maybe he hoped if she felt close to him, she would confide in him.

And wasn't that exactly what was happening? Each time she saw him she felt guilty and felt worse about the lie. Every time they discussed the cases, she experienced the horror of wondering if she was protecting a murderer. A dozen times the truth had hovered on her lips.

When she realized he was watching her, waiting for her to answer, she wet her lips and tried to smile. "Not at the moment," she said. "Well. Are you ready to see what you're up against?"

"Lead on."

One side of her two-car garage was occupied by her Subaru. The other side had become a storage catchall. The shelves were stacked high with boxes of tax records, old lesson plans, a couple of tennis rackets, skis, a carton of photo albums and school mementos, a collection of flowerpots and gardening equipment, a bicycle.

"It could stand some organizing," Laura commented when Max heaved an exaggerated sigh.

The dresser sat against the back wall. In a burst of early enthusiasm, Laura had stripped the finish from the top and one of the drawer fronts. Then her enthusiasm had waned, and eventually she had dragged the dresser into the garage to await a fresh infusion of interest.

"It's a nice piece of furniture," Max observed, wiping the dust away.

"It belonged to my grandmother. You know, we have a problem here." She drew a breath. "This dresser matches my bed and vanity. If you finish the dresser, then the bed and vanity are going to look shabby."

Max looked at her and their eyes held. Then he bent to the box and began setting out cans of stripping compound and stain. "Better get used to me, then. This looks like a long-term project."

Any other time the warmth in his eyes would have given her a shiver of pleasure. But it seemed to Laura that the lie took on tangible form and she imagined she could see it standing between them.

"By the way," he said. "I checked out your Avon lady and the magazine salesman. They're both legit."

"Thanks, Max."

"Both said they knocked at your door, then left immediately when no one was home. Neither saw anyone near your property."

"I appreciate your checking. How about Ruby's dentist? Did you locate him?"

"It took some doing, but yes, we found him. He's out of town, but we'll talk to him Thursday."

She thought about the warmth in Max's eyes as she left him with the dresser, then went back into the house to dress and go about her Saturday chores. The lie was looming larger than ever. It was terrible, awful, a possible obstruction of justice. Now a personal element was part of the equation, equally as distressing. Aside from whatever would happen to her legally when the lie was discovered, she wondered what Max would think of her.

Pausing, she leaned against the washing machine and closed her eyes. When he looked at her the warmth in his gaze seemed special and just for her alone. What would happen to that special warmth when he learned what she had done?

And she had to tell him. She knew that.

She couldn't live with it anymore. Didn't want to. Stepping backward, she leaned against the folding table and rubbed her forehead.

Although Dave Penn was a liar and he could be violent, she really didn't believe he could murder anyone. She didn't believe that, did she?

If she thought he was guilty, then she truly was obstructing justice by maintaining the lie. But she honestly wouldn't have agreed to the lie if she had believed he was guilty. She couldn't bring herself to think that someone with whom she had lived for four years could murder anyone. Maybe they hadn't known each other as well as she would have liked, but she thought she knew *that* much about Dave Penn.

If he wasn't guilty, then he was right about being in a lot of trouble. But Laura believed in the system. The system didn't send innocent people to jail for something they didn't do, did it?

Once she confessed what she had done, things would look bad for Dave for a while. But in the end justice would win and the real killer would be caught and punished. She had to believe that.

Having decided to do the right thing, she felt a tremendous relief. If Max was so disgusted with her that she never saw him again, that would be sad and hard to live with. But even losing Max was a price worth paying to be out of this terrible mess that was robbing her of her sleep and her self-esteem.

But she owed it to Dave to tell him what she was going to do. After checking to see that Max was still occupied in the garage, she went into the living room and used the phone by the sofa to dial Dave's number. The phone rang and rang.

Frustration pinched her expression when she hung up. She wanted to end this now, today. Instead, she would have to wait.

"I don't believe it!" she exclaimed when she took a cold beer into the garage for Max. The dresser project had progressed further in a few hours than in the last year.

"Remember that song?" he asked, referring to a song playing on her car radio. He had the radio tuned to a station that played "Oldies but Goodies" on the weekend.

"It dates back to high school," Laura remembered with pleasure. "I danced a few miles to that one."

"Me, too." Grinning, Max bowed before her then caught her hand and danced her around the empty bay.

Laughing, Laura threw back her head and gave herself to the music and the warm spring sunshine falling past the open doors of the garage. "Where were you when I was in high school?" she asked when he released her. "No one I dated could dance like that."

"Not even Dave?"

Somehow their conversations always came back to Dave. "We only dated occasionally in high school. Things didn't get serious until we were in college," she said, her voice reluctant. "Actually I didn't date much in high school."

The warmth she liked filled Max's eyes as his gaze flicked over her shorts and T-shirt. "That's hard to believe."

"I had a crush on Dave, but he hadn't really noticed me yet. Most of the other guys I might have dated were already going with someone else. The ones who were left were twerps. There was one guy, he used to call Bets and Bumper and me all the time..."

"But you and your heartbreaker friends wouldn't give the poor guy the time of day, right?"

She smiled. "Frank wasn't bad looking, but he was sort of weird. Every school has a few weirdos and we seemed to have more than our share," she said, remembering. "Maybe if we'd known some of those guys better, we would have liked them. Who knows?" Kneeling, she examined the area of the dresser Max was scraping. "That was a long time ago. Do you keep in touch with any of your old school friends?"

"I did for a while. But not anymore."

"Me, neither. I swore I would, but it didn't work out that way. Maybe I'll go to my ten-year class reunion. I received a notice last month."

"If you're feeling even the slightest urge to hurl yourself into this project, I have an extra scraping knife."

"I wouldn't dream of pushing myself into your territory," she said, grinning and backing toward the car. "I think I'll run to the grocery store and pick up a couple of steaks. Does that sound like a suitable reward for doing all this work? Barbecued steak, baked potato and a green salad?"

"Laura." He paused and looked at her. "What did you and Dave talk about that Wednesday?"

Her mouth suddenly went dry. "Can we discuss this later? The fumes are getting strong in here." She dropped her eyes.

"If you'd rather," he said lightly.

"I'd rather." She slid into the car, biting her lip, wishing things had been different. "I like you, Max." She hadn't meant to say it, but she did.

"I like you, too."

They looked at each other for a moment, then she backed the car out and drove to the grocery store. Before she went inside, she stopped at a phone booth beside the entrance and dialed Dave's number. No answer.

"Dammit."

When she returned from the store, Max helped her carry the bags inside, then opened a cold beer while Laura sorted the groceries and put them away.

"Is there anything new on the Alder case?" she asked in what she hoped was a casual tone. She prayed he would tell her they were onto a strong suspect.

"Aside from the dentist bit, we've hit a dead end. And the Gates case doesn't seem to be going anywhere, either. Wheatridge is still running down loose ends, but there's nothing promising." He shrugged and frowned.

"I should have bought more steak sauce," she said peering into the cabinet. "There wasn't much in the newspaper about Diane Gates's murder."

"Tim Gates wants it that way. He refused to give the media a photograph of his wife. That's fine with me. We don't want the media creating a panic."

Startled, Laura turned from the refrigerator. "A panic? Max, do you think the murderer will kill again?"

"The truth? Probably." Max leaned against the counter, speaking more to himself than to her. "The motive isn't apparent in either of the cases, but that doesn't mean there isn't one. Whoever killed Ruby Alder and Diane Gates had a reason. Until we know that reason, we can't assume he's finished."

"That's—" Laura broke off and stared into the foyer. "Good heavens. Will you look at that?"

"At what?"

"At the picture next to the garage door. In the foyer."

Puzzled, Max looked into the foyer than back at her. "I'm not following you."

"I don't believe this. The picture of my cat is gone!" A different picture was hanging where her cat picture had been.

"I remember. You had a picture one of your students did for you."

"Not anymore." What she had now was a framed photograph of the Fortrell Museum for Classic Cars. Laura stepped closer and peered at it. The photograph showed the front of the building and one car parked near the steps.

Max looked at it, his frown pulled at his eyebrows. "You're saying this isn't yours?"

"No. I don't know anything about cars. I've never particularly cared about them. As long as I have a car that runs..." She stared at the photograph. "I don't even recognize what kind of car that is in the photograph."

"It's a Chevy. A 1976 or 1977 model. Don't touch it," he said quickly when Laura reached to remove it.

"You want to fingerprint this?"

He leaned close to the photograph. "Was this here earlier today? Or did you still have the picture of your cat?"

"I don't know." Closing her eyes, Laura tried to remember. Finally she spread her hands in a frustrated gesture. "I've walked past this door half-a-dozen times today, and I think I would have noticed if... but I'm just not sure."

With a serious expression, Max tried the lock on the front door, a few feet away. "It's not locked," he said in an expressionless voice.

"You were in the garage. I was in the house. I didn't think—"

"Laura. This isn't a small town." His voice was low and deliberately patient. "You need to get into the habit of always keeping your door locked."

"Max, this is a weekend. The neighborhood is filled with people working in their yards, playing outside."

"No one can see your house."

That was true. "Look, if I can't feel safe when a detective is standing in my garage, when can I?"

After a moment he released a breath and nodded, dropping an arm around her shoulders. "I'm worried about you, that's all. And I sure as hell don't like what's happening around here."

He lifted her chin and kissed her lightly on the lips. "I'll be back in a few minutes," he said, stepping outside before the surprise had faded from her expression.

It outraged him to think someone might have switched the pictures while he was standing a few feet away, working in her garage. He couldn't be certain the switch had occurred in the past hour, but instinct told him it must have. Laura had noticed the Fortrell Museum photograph the minute she turned in that direction after returning from the store. If the switch had been made earlier, he guessed she would have noticed during one of the times she had gone into the garage or had passed the door.

He swore beneath his breath. He had been concentrating on stripping the dresser. He had not heard the front door open, had not heard a damned thing. In point of fact the switch wouldn't have required even a minute. Open the door, step inside, make the switch, step back, then leave.

The likelihood that anyone had seen anything was minute. As he stood on Laura's porch, a group of eleven- or twelve-year-old boys ran into the vacant lot across the street carrying a bat and ball. But a moment ago it had been deserted. The shrubs concealed her house to the east. He saw no movement near the vacant house on the west, but he walked around it and looked in the windows, tried the doors, just in case. Nothing.

He walked around the shrubbery on the east and met the flight attendants who rented the nearest house. To his amusement, they flirted with him. But they hadn't noticed anyone who looked suspicious. One of them said they hadn't seen any strangers. The other one said she had never met a stranger in her life and winked at him.

The neighborhood was bustling with weekend activity, but he saw immediately that the shrubbery blocked a view of Laura's house. Someone could have spray painted the front of her property and no one on the block would have seen a thing.

"Those shrubs should be cut down," he said when he returned.

"They're on the rental property. If they were mine, I'd cut them to about three feet."

While Laura put the steaks on the barbecue, Max studied the photograph of the Chevy. A 1976 or 1977 model didn't really qualify as a classic. That was puzzling. Also, the car in the photograph didn't have a license plate.

He continued to look at the photograph, focusing on the car. It was green. There was a pair of oversize dice hanging from the rearview mirror. Once upon a time this car had been every teenager's dream. What was it supposed to mean now?

"The steaks are ready," Laura called in a subdued voice.

They ate dinner outside on the patio, neither speaking often. After dinner Laura served coffee and they watched the sun slip behind the poplars toward the mountain peaks.

"All right," Max said, "let's run this through. Do you know anyone who drives a 1976 or 1977 Chevy?"

"I can't tell one kind of car from another," she said apologetically. "I don't know if I know someone who drives that kind of car. I can tell a station wagon from a VW, but that's about it. I couldn't tell you what kind of car my friend, Patty Selwick drives. For that matter, I'm not sure what kind of car you drive. It's black, but beyond that...." She gave him a weak smile.

"You hate anchovies and you don't know a Monte Carlo when you ride in one?" He clicked his tongue, teasing her.

"I'll admit I'm not the most observant person in the world. I probably wouldn't make a good witness." She spread her hands. "I can't tell you how long the bookend was in my bookcase before I noticed it, or how long the sketch might have been hanging in the foyer. My self-esteem is taking a beating on this."

"Is it a fair assumption that you never owned a 1976 or 1977 Chevy?"

"Right."

"So that car has no personal meaning to you?"

"I'm not sure." When he looked at her, waiting for an answer, she ducked her head and looked into her coffee cup. "I'm not sure, I couldn't swear to it, but Dave may have had a car something like that in high school."

A silence opened, then he asked gently, "Laura, is there anything you want to tell me?"

She bit her lip, looked away from him. "Not yet. Soon, but . . . not yet."

If he pushed her it could go either way. Maybe she would tell him now, or maybe she would dig her heels in and never tell him. He was patient, he could wait. Meanwhile, the prudent thing was to back off and keep the conversation within the context of her mystery rather than the larger issues.

"Do you think Dave Penn is putting these items in your house?"

She chewed her lip, then raised her head to look toward the sunset. "I don't know. I felt certain the chrysanthemums came from him. But he denied it." Frowning, she turned to look at him. "I just can't believe Dave would do this, Max. He and I were finished a long time ago. I mean, what's the point? If Dave wanted to tell me something, he'd just tell me. He wouldn't leave a bunch of things for me to find and try to figure out."

If he assumed she was right and her intruder wasn't Dave Penn, he still had to assume the intruder was male. Until now, that instinct had been only a hunch, now Max felt it as a certainty. The photograph of the car seemed more personal to the intruder than the other items, although that was only speculation.

"I have that feeling, too," Laura said. "This car was or is important to whoever hung its picture in my foyer." She bit her lip. "What about the dice draped over the mirror? Is that supposed to be a message, too?"

"You mean the numbers on the dice."

She nodded. "One of the dice shows the number two. The other shows one. Do you think the number three has some special meaning?"

"Go with that a minute. What does the number three signify to you? Anything special?"

Laura thought a minute then shook her head. "Not that I can think of." She touched her temples. "Dammit, this whole thing is so frustrating."

Instinct and experience told Max the dice and/or the numbers showing on them were significant. In the intruder's mind, the number three referred to something, something he probably expected Laura to recognize.

"I'm going to telephone Dave and ask him about the car," Laura said, standing abruptly.

His patio chair was placed at an angle that he could watch her as she went into the house and dialed the phone beside the sofa. Two things impressed him. Her suddenly furious expression. And the fact that she knew Penn's phone number by heart. She didn't have to look it up.

"He's not home," she said when she returned to the patio, scowling. "He's probably in Keystone. Sometimes he goes to Keystone for the weekend."

He didn't ask how she knew that because he wasn't sure of his motives for wondering. Instead, he asked if she had a cleaning lady.

"Oh, I see. Maybe a cleaning lady... No, I don't have one. I am solely responsible for the dust and clutter." After a moment, she sighed. "Do you really expect to find any fingerprints on that photograph?"

"Probably not. But it's worth a try. I'll drop it by the station on my way home."

She started to pick up the dirty dishes. "I think I'll go by Fortrell's Museum tomorrow."

Following her, he carried in the butter dish and the salt and pepper shakers. "I'll go with you."

"Do you have time?" After opening the door to the dishwasher, she looked up at him.

A shrug rolled his shoulders. "Nothing is happening on the Alder case, especially not on a Sunday. Why not?"

Maybe Laura couldn't think of anything significant about three, but he could. Ruby Alder, Diane Gates, and Laura Penn. There was no apparent connection between the three women, and aside from a nasty gut reaction he had no legitimate evidence, no reason to tie Laura to Alder or Gates. So why had that been his first thought?

When he realized how close they were standing and how much he wanted to kiss her, not a quick brush across the lips but a real kiss, he stepped back.

Before he left he reached a hand to her cheek and let his fingertips rest lightly against her throat. "Whatever it is you want to tell me, Laura, make it soon."

There was anguish in the eyes she turned up to him. "Soon," she whispered. "I promise."

He thought he knew what they were talking about, though he couldn't be sure. But he sensed she was holding some kind of key. In her eyes he saw that she needed to be free of it as badly as he needed to have it.

Once outside, he paused for a moment and looked back through the window on the door. He saw her spin away and march into the living room and lift the telephone. Feeling uncomfortable spying on her, nevertheless he continued to watch until she slammed down the receiver and covered her face in her hands.

He would have bet the farm that the number she dialed belonged to Dave Penn. Stepping off the porch, he crossed the lawn to his car then sat inside for a moment before he took the photograph to the station.

He had broken his own cardinal rule. He was falling in love with a woman involved in a murder case.

WHEN ERIC ASHBAUGH learned about the photograph, he insisted on accompanying them to check it out.

"I don't mind," he told Max. "Like everyone involved in this case, I'm restless as a cat waiting for a storm. Laura's mystery gives us something to do."

Max and Laura had driven to the Fortrell Museum and discovered it was closed on Sundays. Monday afternoon she had a faculty meeting; Tuesday she'd had parent meetings after school. It was Wednesday. And Wednesdays were the worst. Both the murders had occurred on Wednesdays. He and Eric had stuck close to the phone all day, waiting for a call they hoped would not come.

"We need to get out of here," he said, reaching for his jacket, glad they had something to do that had nothing to do with the case.

They met Laura at the Fortrell Museum after school. When Max saw her waiting on the steps, an unconscious smile curved his mouth. Today she was wearing a red-and-white summer dress made of a light material that seemed to float around her legs. Sunshine gleamed in her short dark hair.

"Did you bring the photograph?" she asked when they came up to her.

"I have it," Eric said. He watched Max take Laura's arm as they climbed the steps and he gave his partner a knowing look.

Max had phoned ahead, so Martin Abrams, the curator, was waiting for them.

"Yes," he said, when Eric showed him the photograph, "we sell these." Asking them to follow, he took them into the back room filled with rows of cross-hatch shelving. There were thousands of photographs in the boxes. "We have photographs like the one you're holding showing just about every make and model parked in front."

"To qualify as a classic," Max asked, "a car would have to be at least thirteen years old and a limited edition, right?"

Abrams nodded. "The cars in the museum fit that description, but the photographs don't. I could sell you a photograph of this year's latest model parked in front of the museum." He smiled and shrugged. "It's a fundraising gimmick."

"If I wanted a photograph of, say, a 1956 Ford Victoria, you would have a photo of that car parked in front of the museum?"

"Oh, yes." Martin Abrams beamed at them. "We can even give you a choice of color. And you could have a photograph of the Ford Victoria showing dice hanging above the dashboard and even a choice of which numbers are showing. Or we could give you a photograph with a Kewpie doll on the dash, or a couple of books, or a graduation cap, or—''

Max interrupted. ''So these photographs can be individualized. Is that what you're saying?'' He and Laura had been right. The number three was significant.

Martin Abrams nodded. ''We get lots of people coming through the museum who had a car they loved in high school or college and they want a photograph of it. Their first car, that kind of thing. We can deepen the illusion that it's a photograph of their actual car by offering a choice of a few common items on the dash. If you were the kind of kid who drove a 1975 blue Olds with a Kewpie doll stuck on the dash, we can give you a photograph of that car.''

Laura scanned the rows of shelving. ''There's no possibility you would remember the sale of one particular photograph, is there?'' The disappointment in her voice indicated she knew the answer.

''We keep track of which models are the most popular for restocking purposes and which dash items are most in demand. But, no. We don't keep a record of who buys them, the names of customers, if that's what you're asking.'' Martin Abrams looked startled as if she were a bit mad to suggest such a thing.

Bypassing the area where rows of classic cars gleamed on display, they turned directly into the museum's coffee shop without speaking. While Eric phoned the station, Laura found a table and Max bought coffee.

''Well, that was a disappointment,'' Laura commented, when Max returned to the table. ''A total waste of time.''

''Did you ask Penn if he ever had a 1977 Chevy?'' Max inquired, stirring milk into his cup.

"I haven't been able to reach him."

"Maybe we're looking at this wrong. We've been thinking about the present for the most part. Think back. Did you know anyone in the past who drove a 1977 Chevy? Maybe when it was new, when you were in school?"

"In 1977, I was a freshman in high school. I knew even less about cars than I do now." Her expression was discouraged. "I was a sophomore in 1978 and no better informed or more interested. This is hopeless."

"How about your friends? Did one of them drive a 1977 Chevy?"

Laura shook her head. "Bumper drove her father's car occasionally. It didn't look like the car in the photograph. Bets didn't have a car. When we went somewhere, Bumper or I drove."

"All right," Max said, as Eric hurried toward their table. "Think about it. Maybe you'll remember something."

"Maybe," Laura said doubtfully. "I wish to hell I could reach Dave."

Max took one look at Eric's expression and pushed his coffee away. He stood immediately.

"Our guy hit again," Eric confirmed in a low voice.

"Oh, my God!" Shock widened Laura's eyes.

"Denver has this one. Southeast. Big-ticket area. This one doesn't have a chance of staying quiet. It's going to hit the papers with a big splash."

Three. Now they had three murders. "Are we invited?" Max asked, looking at Laura. No, if she were on the list, the dice face would show a number larger than three.

Eric nodded and looked at his wristwatch. "So is Wheatridge. Our guy is right on time. What do you want to bet the hit took place about an hour ago?"

Max placed his hand on Laura's shoulder. "I'll call you tonight."

At the exit from the coffee shop, Max looked back at her. She was sitting where they had left her, staring at nothing. He would have given a lot to know what she was thinking.

"You've got it bad, old son," Eric said, smiling.

"She's lying, dammit. I think she wants to tell me, but she hasn't." They got into his car.

"The more I'm around Laura, the more I agree with you. She's special. She's a good person, decent. She'll tell you, Max."

"I hope she tells me before it's too late. If we find proof that she lied before she admits it . . ."

Eric ignored that possibility. "When she tells you, remember that Penn is a hitter. You saw the bruises on Ruby Alder. Laura probably has some pretty good reasons for backing him up."

"I've thought about that. I've worked it out."

"I figured you probably had." Eric looked out the window, lit a cigarette and smiled.

Chapter Six

The scene on Braithwaite Street was chaotic. Neighbors congregated in the street, reporters argued with the uniforms spread along the cordoned-off area. A half-dozen black-and-whites crowded the driveway leading up to the house and were parked along the street curb. The coroner's wagon had backed up to the steps of the house. Max noticed at least three unmarked cars, two of which he recognized. One belonged to Bill Ridley from Wheatridge.

"Ridley beat us here," Eric observed as they flashed their badges then ducked under the tapes. "Denver must have called Wheatridge before they called us."

"I'm beginning to wonder if anyone besides you and me ties Alder to the Gates case."

"Sure they do. What we're seeing is political juggling between departments. But weapon and method ties us in. We've got three women murdered with the same type of knife and in the same frenzied way. Plus all the hits occurred on a Wednesday." They moved up the steps onto a wide porch and Eric leaned over to examine the door lock. "No forcible entry. This was our guy, Max." He gazed at the house and grounds. "Impressive."

Eric's comment was an understatement. Elizabeth St. Marks had lived in a rambling Tudor house that ran toward four thousand square feet. A heated swimming pool sparkled in the back. Manicured lawns swept the house and flanked the gravel drive circling in front.

Max and Eric stepped backward as the coroner's people brought the body of Elizabeth St. Marks past them. After a moment, the coroner's wagon eased away from the steps and moved slowly down the driveway. Grim faced, the two detectives entered the house.

Max had time to take in the expensive tucked paneling and decorator furnishings before Bill Ridley appeared and shook his hand. "I've spoken to Jim Marshall," Ridley said, referring to the Denver detective in charge of the scene. "He said to show you around and fill you in."

"Did it happen in the kitchen like the others?" Eric asked.

Ridley shook his head. "Not this time. He led them into a large sunny living room and pointed toward the body outline chalked on the oak floor. "That's where the neighbor found her."

There were people all over the house. Print men dusting surfaces, detectives methodically checking every item in each room, and others interviewing the gardener and a neighbor.

"Looks like she put up a struggle," Max commented. The coffee table in front of the sofa and the end table had been overturned. A lamp lay smashed across the floor along with pieces of a terrarium that had contained a couple of plants. "Any sign of forced entry on the back or windows?"

"Looks like she let him in. No forced entry."

Max continued to examine the overturned tables, the plants and dirt spilled across the oak floor. "Looks like our boy is getting careless. This one didn't go down easy."

"Jim is hoping she got a few licks in and they'll find something under her nails. The coroner thinks she might have."

"How about the wounds?" Eric inquired.

"Consistent with Gates and Alder," Ridley answered. "Plus it's Wednesday again. And no sign of the weapon."

"Mind if we look around?"

"Help yourself. The print guys aren't finished yet."

Keeping his hands in his pockets, Max wandered to the bookshelves occupying one wall of the two-story living room. St. Marks had read glitz novels, it appeared, but mostly self-help books. There were at least two-dozen volumes targeted to makeup and hair care. "Was she married?" he asked Ridley.

"Divorced. A couple of years ago. She has two kids who are spending the summer with her ex—he lives in Wyoming. Heavy in the oil business. Lots of money. She was a looker." He nodded toward the portrait over the fireplace. "Very social, according to the neighbors. The media is going to be all over this one."

Max glanced at the portrait, then returned his attention to the bookshelves. There were several bookends, most of which looked expensive. If impulse hadn't prompted him to kneel and check the shelves behind a chair pushed up against them, he would have missed the gold lion bookend.

"Ridley? Take a look at this." When Bill Ridley and Eric crossed to his side he reminded Ridley of the gold lion bookend in Diane Gates's house.

"I remember. We have it listed on the inventory. We didn't find a match, by the way."

"That reminds me. We still haven't received a copy of the Gateses' file."

"Really?" Ridley frowned. "Anderson was supposed to send it over to you guys. I'll follow up."

Eric rocked back on his heels. "I'd say that particular bookend is a bit downscale for a house like this."

"And I'd like to know if there are any prints on it," Max added.

"I don't know why you guys think a bookend is important, but—" Ridley waved over one of the print men "—metal takes prints like a dream. Want to put five bucks on it that your bookend is going to be covered with the cleaning lady's prints?"

"You're on." A humorless smile curved Max's lips. "I've got five bucks that says there aren't going to be any prints at all."

Ridley lifted an eyebrow. "Want to explain?"

"I can't. It's just a feeling."

"If that bookend turns up clean, pal, we're all going to be interested."

"Were there any prints on the Gateses' bookend?"

"We didn't dust it. No reason to. If you thought it was important, why didn't you say something?"

"At the time I wasn't sure it was. I'm still not. But now we've got two murders where a lion bookend turns up. It's worth a dusting."

Ridley shrugged and watched the print man coat the bookend.

Eric went one way, Max another. First he inspected the bedrooms. There were two guest rooms that shared a bath. Nothing of interest there. Then a girl's room. He stood in the doorway, looking at a canopied bed, a ruffled vanity, a row of dolls displayed on a shelf unit. A few books, a letter sweater, a set of cheerleader's pom-poms. The photographs, mostly rock stars, stuck around the mirror were what one would expect of a girl in her early teens. Everything was neat and appeared to have been recently cleaned.

The next room belonged to a boy. Again, everything was dusted and tidy except for two chess pieces tossed on top of a desk. There was a personal computer, a stereo, some sports equipment, nothing intriguing enough to tempt Max inside the room.

The master bedroom was at the end of the hallway. It was large and beautifully decorated in shades of rose, mauve and cream. Three detectives were going through the bureau drawers, the closets, checking the connecting bath and exercise room.

He shook hands with Brad Denny, a detective he had known for several years. "Anything interesting?"

"A couple of diaries," Brad said, nodding toward two books lying on the bedspread. "Eat your heart out, Elliot. At least we've got someplace to start." He smiled.

One of the diaries had a locking strap, and it looked as if it had been cut. "Someone was eager to read that one," said Max.

"Yeah, but it was a long time ago," Denny said, without much interest. "It's high-school stuff. But the other one is current." Using the eraser end of a pencil, he opened the diary to a random page. "The last entry was made three days ago."

"Lucky find."

"Don't I know it. We've got the diary and a thick address book. Plus she has a rack of men's clothing in her closet. The neighbor says she had a couple of boyfriends. We've got a lot to work with. How are you and Eric coming on the Alder case?"

"We're running in place."

"Tough," Brad said, meaning it. "Maybe something will break. If we crack one of these, we'll have them all."

Moving around the room, Max looked at the art on Elizabeth St. Marks's walls, examined the items on her dressing table. A pair of big diamond earrings had been dropped next to a hairbrush. Burglary was not a motive. Nor had it been in the Gates and Alder cases. He stood in the door to the bathroom for a moment watching Walt Osburn dismantle the drain under the sink, then he returned to the hallway. Elizabeth St. Marks had enjoyed a taste for luxury. Everything in the house was top quality, very expensive.

Therefore it surprised him to discover a bare picture hook at the end of the hallway. The image he was getting of Elizabeth St. Marks was not that of a woman who would allow a single detail out of place. If she had a picture hook, she would have a picture hanging on it or the hook would have been removed. Stopping, he noticed a rectangle of darker wallpaper—where a picture might have hung.

Brad Denny came up behind him. "Yeah," he said. "I made it, too. The empty hook doesn't fit. You think a painting was stolen?"

"The art in the house is expensive, but not as expensive as the earrings she left in plain sight on top of her dresser. Who would cart off a painting when he could carry away ten grand in his pocket?"

"WELL, WHAT DO YOU THINK?" Max stretched his neck against his hand then tasted his coffee. They were in the back booth at Denny's on Wadsworth.

"One of the victims was married, two were divorced. We're looking at different social strata. Different lifestyles." Eric stared glumly into his coffee. "I'll bet my house we aren't going to find an easy connection between Elizabeth St. Marks and the other two. They never met, they didn't move in the same circles, they didn't live in the same area, they didn't know each other.''

"Did anyone see anything going on at the St. Marks place? Anyone at the door? Were there any witnesses?"

"The Mormon Tabernacle Choir could march down Braithwaite Street singing at the top of their lungs and not a soul would notice. The houses are set back from the street, and most of the residents don't know the names of the people who live next door. It's that kind of neighborhood. The men are at work wheeling and dealing, the kids are in private schools, the wives are out shopping or attending a fashion show or a charity event."

"You're getting cranky, partner," Max commented.

"You can say that again." Eric swallowed a mouthful of coffee and lit another cigarette. "A maid up the street thinks she might have seen a car near the St. Marks place at about the right time. Might have. Can't remember a make, model or definite color."

They finished their coffee in silence, then signaled for a refill. Max loosened his tie. "Did you find a match for the lion bookend?"

"That bookend is worrying you like an old dog with a new bone. No. I didn't locate another one."

"Neither did I."

Eric swore. "We're looking at a rerun here. Same basic everything. Some bastard with a knife is having himself a heyday and we don't have a clue!" He stubbed out his cigarette with an angry motion. "What did you get? Any background?"

"She was twenty-eight. Divorced. The house is the same one she lived in when she was married. She's been there about five years. The divorce was two years ago. The husband is remarried, lives in Wyoming. The kids are his by a previous marriage, but they lived with Elizabeth St. Marks because they don't get along well with the ex-husband's new wife. He takes the kids every summer." Max flipped through the pages of his notebook. "She was dating a guy named Ralph Hepplewhite. There was trouble in that particular paradise—apparently they hadn't been getting along lately. She was dating someone else, too. No name on that one yet."

"It will probably turn up in the diary."

"Brad is leaning toward a jealous boyfriend."

"Hepplewhite?"

"They'll start there," Max said. "Denver has a lot to work with. They've got Hepplewhite, plus the new boyfriend, plus the fact St. Marks was suing her ex for more money. And they have the diary, which might turn up something else."

"Meanwhile here we sit with Ruby Alder and no leads. None of what you just mentioned helps us." Eric glared out the window before he turned back to Max. "You know, your lion bookend is starting to bother me, too. How come it turns up in two of the murders, but not in the first one? And how come you spotted it as possibly important at the Gateses' place?"

Max reminded him about Laura's lion bookend and the other items.

"I forgot about that." He looked at Max. "Are you suggesting Laura is somehow connected?"

Max didn't answer. He had asked himself the same question.

"It must have crossed your mind, old son, or we wouldn't have gone back to Ruby Alder's to search for a lion bookend. And you wouldn't have gotten a bee in your bonnet about it. You're formulating a connection, Max. Like it or not."

"Maybe. I know I sure as hell felt relieved when no lion bookend turned up in Ruby Alder's town house. And nothing else connects. No chrysanthemums or paper crown or car photo has turned up at any of the murder scenes."

"Just for the sake of argument, since we aren't doing anything else, let's play with this a little." After lighting another cigarette, Eric moved his coffee cup about the table. "Suppose, just suppose for a minute that there is a connection. Suppose our three victims each received a pot of flowers, the bookend, the paper crown, and the car photo. Just like Laura, okay?"

"It sounds farfetched when you state it aloud."

"Agreed. But we're just supposing. And we're not worrying about the why of it just now. So, suppose they each find this stuff in their houses. How long would a woman like Elizabeth St. Marks keep a pot of flowers or a paper crown? Okay, chrysanthemums seem to last forever, but she'd toss them at the first sign of wilt. The paper crown would probably hit the trash compactor about five minutes after she found it. Those items would be long gone before we ever got to her. Right?"

Eric wasn't saying anything Max had not already conjectured, but it made him uneasy hearing someone else say it. "It's a fair assumption the same reasoning applied to Diane Gates."

"Okay, now the bookend." Eric had brightened somewhat. "Gates gets the bookend, shrugs, and put it up on the shelf over the TV. This is something she can use. Not a throwaway item."

Going with it, Max nodded. "Supposing St. Marks is having things put in her house. It's possible she didn't even notice the bookend. It was almost hidden on the lower shelf behind a chair."

"I can buy that. Or maybe she discovered it but couldn't decide what to do with it. The bookend isn't disposable like the flowers or the paper crown. It's too substantial to throw away, and maybe she thinks it belongs to someone, but it's not quality enough to put out for show. So she puts it out of sight on the lower shelf until she can make up her mind what to do with it."

"If that's what happened, her prints will be on it. I'm liking this less and less," Max said slowly.

"Just supposition, old son. Brain games to pass the time while we're waiting for a break in the Alder case."

"There was no car photograph in the St. Marks house," Max said, frowning. "But there was an empty picture hook."

"Anybody find the picture that should have been hanging there?"

"Brad Denny was still looking when we left. I have a feeling he isn't going to find anything."

"Okay, how does this play? St. Marks finds the car-museum photo hanging on her wall. So what does she do? I figure she'd take it down and toss it out. What did Abrams say those prints cost? About ten bucks? That ain't great art."

"So she disposes of it." Max stared out the restaurant window. "The painting that hung in that spot is gone. And she's murdered before she has time or opportunity to replace it. But she intended to—that's why she didn't remove the hook. Meanwhile, the killer took the painting he replaced as a memento. Find the killer, and chances are we'll find Laura's cat painting, and maybe a wall hanging from the Gates and St. Marks residences." He paused. "That is, if any of this supposition is on target."

They didn't speak for several minutes.

"Okay, pal. Now I'm worried, too," Eric said finally. "Have you mentioned any of this to Laura?"

"All this is merely supposition. We don't have a single shred of hard evidence."

After a time Eric nodded. "You're right of course. But the whole thing feels nasty."

"The only genuine tie-in is the gold lion bookend. The rest is mind games like you said. We don't have a hint of evidence suggesting that Alder, Gates or St. Marks received any of the other items."

"But they could have."

They looked at each other. Then Max glanced at his watch. "Let's find out."

Eric pushed his coffee away and reached for his wallet. Together they stood, paid the check, then drove to Wheatridge to pay a visit to Tim Gates.

THE MINUTE Laura returned home, she went straight to the telephone. Relief flooded her features when Dave answered on the fourth ring.

"Where the hell have you been?" she demanded, suddenly furious.

"I have been on a bender to end all benders, if you have to know. God. You won't believe this—maybe you will— I woke up last night in Las Vegas. I can't remember going there or what I did. I flew back this morning."

"Where were you this afternoon? About four o'clock. And don't lie to me, Dave. I have to know the truth."

"Four o'clock?" A silence opened. "I'm not sure. I went to an AA meeting. I think I was still there at four. Why?"

"Can you prove that?"

"Laura, I have a headache like you wouldn't believe. I'm in no mood for games. What are you driving at?"

"There was another murder."

He swore, then fell silent again. "Are you sure it happened at four o'clock?"

"I don't know precisely when it happened except it was this afternoon. Before five-thirty."

"You know something, Laura? I'm getting pretty tired of you thinking I'm involved every time something happens."

"Not 'something,' Dave. Murder." A headache had begun behind her eyes.

"Okay, murder. How many times do I have to tell you? I may be a bastard sometimes, but I'm not a murderer. I didn't kill anyone."

She sat on the sofa, leaned forward and covered her eyes. "It isn't me you have to convince, David. It's the police. I wanted to tell you first. I can't go on with lying. I've hated it from the start. I'm sorry I did it. I'm going to tell Max Elliot that I lied. That I wasn't with you when Ruby Alder was murdered."

"Dammit, Laura. Do you know what's going to happen to me if you tell him?" He was shouting.

She drew a deep breath. "That's your problem," she said in a calm voice. Something snapped somewhere deep inside, and she knew whatever slender thread still bound her to David Penn had finally broken. Tears of relief moistened her eyes. "I'm sorry, but that's how it is. You should have told the truth in the beginning."

A snarl sounded in her ear. "You'll regret it if you tell Elliot. I mean it, Laura. Tell him, and you'll wish you'd never been born!"

He was still shouting threats when she quietly hung up the phone. After waiting a minute, she took the receiver off the hook and placed it beside the cradle.

TIM GATES INVITED Max and Eric inside and offered them plastic tumblers of Pepsi. "I've already packed the beer," he apologized.

"Pepsi is fine." Max examined the packing boxes scattered across the kitchen and living-room floors.

Gates followed his glance. "It's too difficult staying here alone. There's an owner's unit at the motel. It was too small for two people, but now..."

"I'm sorry, Mr. Gates."

"Make it Tim."

"Tim, then. We have a couple of questions, then we'll get out of your way. Okay?"

"I don't know what else I can tell you. I've told you guys everything. But sure. Go ahead."

Eric stepped forward. "In the weeks before your wife was killed, did she receive any odd gifts? Items that appeared in the house?"

"Odd gifts?" Tim Gates stared then scratched his head. "I'm not sure I know what you mean. Like what?"

"Anything." Max didn't want to lead him.

"That's hard to say. She might have. You probably noticed all the kids on the block. They were always giving Diane little things. She loved kids." He walked to the back door and stood looking out the window. After a silence he continued. "She baked cookies for them. Made a big deal out of Halloween. Led a Brownie troop. She couldn't have children, you know. So she sort of adopted the kids in the neighborhood. Is that the kind of thing you're talking about?"

"Possibly. What sort of thing did the neighborhood kids give her? Can you recall a recent example?"

"Mostly they were little things. Crayoned pictures, paper chains, a bouquet of flowers. Things like that. Odds and ends they thought she would like."

"What did she do with them?"

"She'd keep them awhile. Then, I don't know, I guess she threw them away."

Max considered the empty picture hooks on the back wall. The questions would have to be more direct. "Did Mrs. Gates ever mention a photograph taken in front of the Fortrell Museum for Classic Cars? Show a car parked in front?"

"A car?"

"Maybe a 1977 Chevy?"

Tim Gates passed a hand over his eyes. "If so, she didn't mention it. But I don't think so. That doesn't sound like something a kid would give her."

"You didn't notice such a photograph while you were packing? It would be framed."

"Diane's family took some of her things—you could ask them. And I told my brother he could take whatever he wanted. The owner's unit at the motel is small. I'm trying to pare things down. I don't remember a picture like you're talking about, but to tell you the truth that doesn't mean much. Maybe there is one. I don't know. You could ask Diane's family."

"Let's try this from another angle. Did you notice if one of your paintings is missing?"

Tim Gates closed his eyes. "I don't recall seeing Diane's graduation photo. It was hung in the bedroom. But Max—it is Max, isn't it?—right now, my car could turn up missing and I probably wouldn't notice. I'm just not thinking as straight as I'd like to."

"Did you ever drive a 1977 Chevy?" Eric asked.

For the first time Tim Gates smiled. "You're talking to a Ford man. A 1977 Chevy is a piece of junk."

Even before Max noticed the almost imperceptible shake of Eric's head, he decided they had pushed it far enough.

"Well, thanks anyway," he said, shaking Tim Gates's hand. "We appreciate your time and we apologize for any imposition."

"If you turn up something, you'll let me know, won't you?"

"Sure thing." Once they were outside, Eric lit a cigarette and stared up at the night sky.

"Sometimes this is a lousy job," Max muttered.

They didn't speak again until they were almost to the station.

"If someone was putting things in Diane Gates's house, she wouldn't have given it a second thought," Max muttered. "She would have assumed it came from one of the kids on the block."

Eric agreed. "Except for the car photo."

"If there was one." But he thought about the missing graduation photo.

"I don't know," Eric said, chewing a thumbnail. "Maybe we're working too hard to build a connection. Looking for something that doesn't exist. If that car photo had appeared on Diane Gates's wall, she probably would have mentioned it to her husband."

"Unless she thought he put it there," Max suggested after a minute. He swore. "We're spending more time on this than we are on the Alder case."

"That's because we have more to go on." Eric's comment was accompanied by a sour laugh.

"Most of which we have personally manufactured." The phenomenon wasn't uncommon. At a certain level of frustration, one grasped at straws. Once a case deadlocked, it wasn't that unusual to begin to imagine connections to unrelated cases. The trick was to recognize and separate a genuinely unrelated case from another that might have a legitimate tie-in. "Bottom line—the Alder case and on the Laura Penn mysterious-items case, look unrelated.''

"Right. We were just indulging in mind games." Eric yawned and looked at his watch. "We're coming up zip all around."

Except for the gold lion bookend, Max thought. Two of the murdered women had one lion bookend. And so did Laura. The coincidence ate at him.

If the lion bookend connected somehow to the murders, it should have turned up in Ruby Alder's town house, not in Laura Penn's house. Assuming there was a connection, was it possible the killer had forgotten the bookend with Alder? Could he have left it at Laura's by mistake? No, not likely. Okay, was the damned bookend significant at all?

Intuitively Max linked the bookend to the killings. Yet except for a gut feeling, there was no evidence to support that idea or to connect the bookend in any way to the murders. Two of the victims had owned one gold lion bookend. Period. Nothing so far suggested it was anything other than coincidence.

He didn't believe in coincidence.

"By the way," Eric said as they walked into the station. "Sarah asked me to invite you and Laura for barbecued steaks. Saturday night if you can make it."

"I'll check with Laura." Max smiled. "Tell Sarah not to be too obvious."

Eric laughed. "She'll be devastated when she hears you saw through her invitation. She says she wants to meet Laura before the wedding."

"Slow down. We're still in the get-acquainted stage."

"Sure you are."

"Max?" The sergeant on the desk called to him. "You have a couple of messages. This one sounded important."

It was from Laura. She said she had to talk to him right away.

"This could be it," he said to Eric.

"Then what are you waiting for? Go see her. I'll wait here. If you're right, call me and we'll pick him up."

SHE PACED THE LIVING ROOM, looked at her watch, paced some more. She tried to eat something but had no appetite, then mixed a drink she ended by pouring down the sink.

When the doorbell rang, she jumped, then ground her teeth. She deserved whatever happened to her.

"Hi," Max said, stepping into the foyer. "I got your message."

She led him into the living room and sat on the edge of the sofa. God, this was tough. "First—was today's murder done by the same person who killed Ruby Alder?"

Max sat at the dining table, turning his chair to face her, and crossed his legs at the ankle. "It looks like it."

She folded trembling hands tightly in her lap and drew a deep breath. "Max, there's something I've wanted to tell you almost from the first." When he didn't say anything, she drew another long breath. "I've done something stupid and terrible. I lied about Dave's alibi. I wasn't with him when Ruby Alder was killed."

"I didn't think you were."

She stared at him. "That's all? You aren't going to arrest me or something?"

"What you did was wrong, Laura. I don't have to tell you that. You know it. If it turns out Dave Penn is the man we're looking for...well, I'll see what I can do, but you're going to need legal assistance."

"The stupid thing is, I'm not really sure why I agreed to do it." She frowned down at her clasped fingers. "I've tried to think how to explain what I did. And, Max, I can't. I could tell you I was afraid of him and that would be true, but it isn't all of it." Tears brimmed in her eyes. "You probably won't believe this, but I'm not a liar. I just..." She covered her face.

He crossed the room and sat beside her, gently guiding her into his arms. "Look, people do things for complex reasons." He stroked her hair, felt her tears on his neck. "I'm not going to minimize what you did. It was wrong. But I'm not going to judge it, either. I've seen just about everything in the past few years, Laura. Believe me, this isn't the worst. Not by a long, long shot."

"Maybe those other women would still be alive if I..." She shook her head and wept harder.

"Wait a minute." Moving back, he eased her away and lifted her chin. "Do you have some reason to think Penn could be involved with the Gates murder? Or the murder today?"

She looked at him, her anguished eyes streaming tears. "I saw Dave in front of the Gateses' house the night it happened. He was standing with the street crowd."

"Christ, Laura! Why didn't you tell me?"

"I wanted so badly to believe that Dave wasn't involved in any of this. That I wasn't protecting a murderer."

Grim faced, he reached across her and dialed the telephone, calling Eric. "Put out a pickup on Penn," he said when Eric answered. "And Eric, you'd better phone Sarah. It's going to be a long night."

"Max?" she said when he hung up the telephone. "I'm sorry. I am so sorry. If I could go back and change what I did, I would."

He touched her wet cheek. "I believe you."

"I hope you do. I can't tell you how much I regret this. If it turns out that Dave..."

Gently, he raised her mouth and kissed her, stopping her words.

Then he was gone.

Eventually Laura dried her eyes and stopped thinking about Max's kiss. She retrieved the sandwich she had made earlier, not wanting it any more now than she had then. She watched the late news. There wasn't much about today's murder, just a few exterior shots of Elizabeth St. Marks's house. Laura turned off the television and leaned back on the sofa, closing her eyes.

She was glad it was over, that she had told Max the truth. Whatever happened, she was glad. She only wished she had done it sooner.

Because she couldn't bear to think about whether or not she would see Max again, she leaned forward and concentrated on the items still on her coffee table.

The only item that made sense was the photograph taken in front of the Fortrell Museum for Classic Cars. Obviously, at least she thought it was obviously, the car meant something to whoever had hung the picture in her foyer. But why had he given the photograph to her?

She thought about it until her head ached, but no solution presented itself. Maybe there wasn't a solution. Maybe the items spread across her coffee table were just what they appeared to be. Silly unrelated items.

Giving it up, she ran a hot tub and stepped into it. She glanced at the bathroom clock and wondered if the police had picked Dave up yet.

She wiggled her toes in the water and sighed. And she hoped to God he was more convincing with Max and Eric than he had been with her. She prayed he had told her the truth.

THEY BROUGHT HIM IN about one in the morning. Max and Eric waited in one of the small interrogation rooms while the preliminaries were completed. They both stood when Sergeant Dickerson brought Penn into the small room.

"I remember," Penn said, cutting short the introductions. He had been drinking, but he wasn't drunk. "Just one beer," he said as if he had read their minds. "Maybe two." Sitting down, he leaned back in the chair and looked at Max. "Laura told you I wasn't with her."

"Yes."

"It wasn't her fault. I made her do it."

"You're entitled to have an attorney present."

"They gave me the whole speech outside. I don't need an attorney. I haven't done anything wrong."

After offering Penn a cigarette, Eric lit one. "So. Let's try again. Where were you when Ruby Alder was murdered?"

Dave Penn drew a breath and spread his hands. He looked hopeless. "You aren't going to believe this. And I can't prove it." He went through the story about Willow Hills. Or maybe he had been in an another subdivision altogether. He couldn't remember.

They spent about an hour on it, then Max asked, "Want to tell us what you were doing in front of Diane Gates's house the day she was murdered?"

Penn leaned forward and gripped the sides of his head in his hands. "I know how this looks. No alibi for Ruby's murder. Then I show up in front of another one. You guys think you have me placed at the scene of two murders." He told them about the out-of-town clients and explained being in the area.

"What are your clients' names and how do we run them down?"

"Mr. and Mrs. Charles Whitcomb. From St. Louis, I think. Yeah. St. Louis."

Max looked at Eric, and Eric nodded and left the room. "Where were you today? This afternoon."

"I went to an AA meeting. And before you ask, yes, there were other people there. But, no, I don't know their names or how to find them. You only give your first name at an AA meeting."

"Where was it?"

"At the downtown center. On York Street."

Max made a note on his pad. "We'll check it out." He looked up as Eric came back into the room.

"This isn't your lucky day, pal," he said to Penn. "There's no listing for a Mr. and Mrs. Charles Whitcomb in the St. Louis directory. Want to try again?"

Penn spread his hands. "Hell, I don't know. Maybe they have an unlisted number."

"Wrong. No listing at all."

He rubbed his eyes. "Maybe they lied to me. Maybe they told me they were from out of town so no real-estate agent would bother them."

Maybe it was true, thought Max, but it sounded unlikely.

At eight in the morning, Max sent out for coffee and he and Eric went outside to stretch their legs.

"What do you think?" Eric asked. He took another cigarette out of a crumpled pack, looked at it and made a face, then threw it away.

"We've got enough to book him. He threatened to kill Alder and he can't account for his whereabouts when she was hit. We can put him at the scene of the Gates hit."

"There's a couple things wrong."

"I know." Max pushed his hands in his pockets and kicked a pebble off the station's front step. "It's all circumstantial. We can't put him inside either of the houses. We don't have a witness to put him at the scene at the right time.''

"The D.A. would laugh himself sick if we tried to take this one in with what we've got right now.''

Max nodded, kicked another pebble off the step. "Well, at least we've got something to work with.''

"Yeah.'' Speaking around a yawn, Eric looked at his watch. "Well, let's go home and get a few hours' sleep. We've got enough to hold Penn for a while.''

"Yeah.''

"Sleep fast,'' Eric called over his shoulder. He looked happier than he had in days. "We have a lot of work to do.''

Max's smile faded before he reached his car. If Dave Penn's story checked out, they would lose their prime suspect. If it didn't, and if they could tie him to the murders, Laura would be partially responsible for the deaths of Diane Gates and Elizabeth St. Marks.

Chapter Seven

Eric poked his head inside the interrogation room and asked Max to step outside for a moment. When Max was in the hallway, he leaned against the wall and pushed his hands in his pockets.

"Not only am I getting nowhere on the murder cases, Penn says he never owned a 1977 Chevy. He drove an MG in high school and college. Upgraded each year from that point. Now he drives a Lincoln." He raked a hand through his hair. "I don't know how much longer we can hold him. So far he's been cooperative. But he asked to use the phone an hour ago. I have an idea he's going to start screaming for an attorney."

"We had a call from Brad Denny."

"Bad news?"

"It is, if we're positive the same guy committed all three murders."

"The coroner's report."

"Right on target, old son." Eric handed him a sheaf of stapled papers. "Elizabeth St. Marks had human tissue under her fingernails. Whoever did her should look like a cat got to him. She had long nails. She broke a couple of them on the guy."

After looking through the report Max returned it to Eric. "Dave Penn doesn't have a scratch on him."

"Right."

"We haven't been able to find anyone at the York Street AA meeting who remembers him...but it looks like he probably wasn't at St. Marks's place." A sigh came up from Max's chest. "Where does that leave us on the Alder case?"

After a silence, Eric said, "He's still our number-one suspect on that one, but it's starting to look unlikely. Possible, but unlikely. Not if the same guy did all three."

A balding man in a three-piece suit walked toward them. "Are you Elliot and Ashbaugh?" he asked pleasantly.

They stood away from the wall and glanced at each other. "Who are you?" Max asked, even though he had guessed.

"Millard Clinton." He gave them his card. "Mr. Penn's attorney."

Eric swore.

"You've had my client for two days, gentlemen. He's been the soul of cooperation the way I hear it. But enough's enough. Either charge him and arrest him and let's get going on a bail hearing, or say bye-bye." He smiled. "Where did you say he was? In here?"

"Well, that's that." Glaring, Max watched Millard Clinton step inside the interrogation room. "We don't have enough to charge him. It's all circumstantial. Not a single piece of solid evidence."

"Yet." Eric tapped a cigarette out of the pack with a savage motion. "If it's out there we'll find it. Meanwhile," he said, glancing at his watch, "we've got our dentist, whom we've been neglecting. We've got time, let's pay him a visit."

SINCE THE TERM was ending, Laura graded final papers, scheduled parent-teacher meetings, and began sorting and clearing out the contents of her desk and locker. Columbine functioned on a year-round system, and so the building would be vacant for a week of cleaning and preparation before the beginning of the summer session.

"Lucky you," Patty Selwick said as they carried bulging briefcases toward the faculty parking lot. "Two weeks from now you'll be on vacation. What I'd give to have the summer off..."

"But you can ski every day come winter, while I'm at work," Laura said, tossing her briefcase into her car.

"What are your plans? Are you doing anything exciting this summer? While your friends are working?"

Laura grinned. "I usually spend a week or so with my folks in Vincent, when it starts to get hot here. But I don't really have anything exciting planned."

"What about Max Elliot? Doesn't he count as exciting? And, yes, I'm prying. Friends have that right."

The smile faded from Laura's lips and she slid into her car. "We'll see," she said after a moment. Waving, she backed out of her space and pointed the Subaru toward home.

She hadn't heard from Max since she confessed the lie. Two days without a phone call, without a word. Her chest tightened and she felt a dull ache as she turned her car into the garage.

Well, she had known the possibility existed that he might be seeing her only to elicit the truth. That he might disappear from her life once she confessed and he had what he wanted from her.

It was also possible that the warmth in his eyes had been genuine, but that he couldn't forgive what she had done.

For a moment she sat in her car in the garage, looking at the dresser he had been working on. Heaven only knew when it would get finished now. Feeling the tears behind her eyes, she picked up her briefcase and carried it inside in time to hear the phone ring.

She snatched up the receiver on the fourth ring and answered in a breathless voice.

"Laura? It's Max. We stopped to grab some take-out, and I only have a minute. I just remembered that Eric and Sarah invited us to a barbecue tomorrow night. Did you have other plans?"

"You want to see me again?"

"Why wouldn't I?" He sounded surprised, and her shoulders dropped with relief. "Laura, you sound peculiar. Is everything all right?"

"Yes. More all right than you can guess." A wide smile lifted her expression. She didn't even swat R.C. off the kitchen counter.

"About tomorrow night—"

"Yes! Tell Eric we'll be there."

"Good. I'll see you then. About six."

She was disappointed that she wouldn't see him sooner, but elated that she would see him again. It was going to be all right. "Do you hear that, R.C.?" Picking him up, she hugged him close to her cheek. "It's going to be all right!"

After changing clothes, she carried a glass of iced tea to the patio and opened the newspaper she hadn't had time to read that morning. So far the media hadn't connected Diane Gates or Ruby Alder to the St. Marks killing, but Laura supposed it was only a matter of time.

She shook open the newspaper and studied a photograph of Elizabeth St. Marks positioned on the front page. It was a head-and-shoulder glamour shot, professionally done.

Immediately Laura thought of Bets Kosinski, one of her best friends from high school. She stared at the newspaper photograph. Elizabeth St. Marks could have been Bets's sister. The resemblance was primarily in the eyes and something in Elizabeth St. Marks's expression. Her nose and chin were not remotely reminiscent of Bets's. Bets had had a large nose, rounded at the tip; Elizabeth St. Marks had a thin sharp nose. Bets had despaired of a receding chin; Elizabeth St. Marks had a firm, perfectly proportioned chin. Bets had dark brown hair; Elizabeth St. Marks wore a cloud of golden curls.

Still, looking at Elizabeth St. Marks made Laura think of an older, much prettier Bets Kosinski.

Leaning backward, Laura adjusted her sunglasses and sipped her tea, remembering Bets Kosinski and Bumper Bumperton, wondering what had happened to them since high school. Where were they now? What were they doing? Had life worked out as they had hoped? Did Bumper have a dozen kids? Had Bets gotten the mink coat she used to long for?

The three musketeers, that's what they had called themselves. One for all and all for one. Smiling, Laura wondered if they ever thought of her as she sometimes thought of them.

"I'll go," she decided aloud.

The tenth-year high-school reunion was scheduled for September. She would attend. She would ask the alumni committee for Bets's and Bumper's addresses and she would write and urge them to attend, too. It would be great to see them again and catch up and laugh about the silly things they had done together, the pajama parties, the pranks, the boys they had adored and the boys they had scorned.

Oddly, Laura recalled high school with greater affection and clarity than she recalled college. But maybe that was not so surprising. The high-school years, the teen years, were impressionable years of high intensity, unlike the years before or those that followed.

Bodies changed and awakened during the teen years, and with the changes came a rush of new, intense and confusing emotions. Events that would seem trivial a few years later assumed massive importance during the teen years. A pimple was cause for despair. A glance could be bliss. Rejection caused a level of devastation that was unimaginable. And Saturday nights were the irrefutable measure of personal success. It all happened within an atmosphere charged with searing intensity.

Yes, it was decided. She would attend the reunion. It would be so good to see Bets and Bumper again.

DR. BRUCE LATKA'S dental office was near the Cherry Creek Shopping Center—a good address, centrally located. But his office was small, and Max noticed that the furniture in the waiting room was of poor quality, beginning to show signs of wear as did the woman sitting in a cubbyhole behind a window opening.

He showed her his badge. "We'd like to see Dr. Latka."

"What's this about?" the woman asked, staring hard at the badge.

"Please just tell the doctor we're here."

Slowly the woman rose from her chair and stepped through a door at the back of the cubbyhole.

Eric shoved his hands in his pockets and read a framed diploma hanging on the wall. "This smells wrong," he said in a low voice. "Maybe this isn't such a long shot, after all."

Leaning through the window opening, Max turned Dr. Latka's appointment book to face him and swiftly paged to the days of the murders. "No appointments on the Wednesday Gates was killed. One appointment on the Wednesday that Alder was killed." Speaking in a low voice, he read the client's name to Eric who entered it in his notebook.

"How about the St. Marks Wednesday?"

"A notation saying he's out of town, returns Thursday."

The receptionist opened the door to the waiting room. "Dr. Latka will see you in his office," she said stiffly.

Bruce Latka was standing behind a cluttered desk when they entered his small office. A half-dozen framed diplomas decorated the wall behind him, and the facing wall was entirely covered by books, most of them novels.

The man touched his tie and grimaced. "What can I do for you?" A tic jumped under his right eye.

Picking up on his nervousness, Max did not answer immediately, using the time to study Dr. Bruce Latka. His hair was dyed, a do-it-yourself job that had resulted in a flat muddy color that fell short of matching the pencil-thin reddish brown mustache on his upper lip. He was medium height, medium build. And growing more nervous by the second. Max decided he wouldn't want this man within ten feet of his teeth.

"What happened to your cheek?" Eric asked.

Latka's hand rose to a deep scratch running down his left cheek. "This? It's silly really. I was cleaning a client's teeth and the instrument slipped. Damned thing flew up and got me." His smile faded when neither Max nor Eric returned it. "Well. Sit down, gentlemen."

Something was wrong here, Max felt it in his stomach. Latka was talking too fast. Max had an idea the man was almost holding his breath, waiting for something.

"We'd like to ask you a few questions about Ruby Alder."

Latka nodded, more wary than surprised. "That was a terrible thing. I read about it in the papers."

The hunch came like a bolt from the blue, and it felt right. "And Diane Gates, she was also your patient, wasn't she?" From the corner of his eye, he saw Eric look at him.

"I knew it!" Latka crumbled abruptly. He bent over the top of the desk and covered his face with his hands. "You think I did it, don't you? Well, I didn't!" He looked up, his eyes pleading for understanding. "Look, it's not my fault that two of my patients were murdered."

"Bingo," Eric said softly. "There's the connection."

"No, wait. You guys have this all wrong." Latka wet his lips. "Okay, I did some dental work on both those women, but I didn't kill them. Why would I?"

Max stood. "I think we'd better continue this discussion at the station."

"Latka is looking better with every passing minute," Eric said happily after putting a rush on Latka's prints.

They had spoken to the woman listed as Latka's appointment on the day Alder was killed. She had canceled.

"He can't account for his whereabouts on the afternoons Alder and Gates died. Says he can't remember where he was."

"Brad Denny is checking the airlines," said Max, "to see if Latka returned to Denver on Thursday, like he said he did."

"He didn't." Eric was firm. "You can bet on it. You only have to look at that sleazeball to know he's lying.

Want to bet five bucks that Latka was in town when St. Marks was hit?''

"Did Brad Denny know who Elizabeth St. Marks's dentist was?"

A frown deepened the lines between Eric's eyes. "St. Marks used a society dentist, a guy named Millard Gold. She'd been seeing him for about three years. He did extensive dental reconstruction on her. But if Latka is our guy, we'll find a connection somewhere."

"He's no novice to the system. His lawyer is on the way. Do we have enough to hold him?"

Eric glanced toward the interrogation room where Latka was waiting for his attorney. "Right now all we've got is a connection between two of the murdered women—finally—and the guy's got no alibi for the time of their deaths." With reluctance he added, "But no hard evidence. A fact of life that's turning into a depressingly familiar refrain around here." He brightened. "But we've got something to work with."

"Hello, gentlemen. I'm Rad Burnes, Dr. Latka's attorney. If you don't mind, I'd like a private word with my client."

After showing Rad Burnes into the interrogation room, Eric returned to stand beside Max, who had just dialed a number on the phone. He lit a cigarette and said, "Anybody with an attorney named Rad has to be guilty of something."

Max laughed. "You mean besides the dyed hair?" He returned his attention to the phone. "Laura? Who is your dentist?"

"Hello to you, too." He sensed her smile. "I go to Dr. Eugene Pontly. Why?"

"Have you ever gone to a Dr. Bruce Latka?"

"I've never even heard his name. Is it important?"

No connection to Laura. "I'll tell you about it when I see you tomorrow night."

Before midnight they had a print match on Latka. Except his name was not Bruce Latka; it was Jimmy Smyth. And Jimmy Smyth was wanted in six states by the FBI.

Max shook his head and stared at the sheet. "Take a look at this. The guy is an impostor. He practiced law in Iowa and Washington, sold bogus insurance in Texas and Oklahoma, played dentist in California and Nevada."

"Now in Colorado," Eric said, reading over Max's shoulder. "All those fancy diplomas must be the kind you buy through the mail."

"The question is—is he a murderer?"

"That's what we're going to find out. Meanwhile he isn't going anywhere," Eric said smiling. "You and I can go home and get some sleep." Reaching for his coat, he shook his head. "Hell, no wonder Ruby Alder changed dentists."

ON SATURDAY, they questioned Latka again, then read through the files on Gates and St. Marks and reviewed the updates. Max fed data into his desktop computer, looking for another link between the victims, something that would connect all three.

"Too bad Elizabeth St. Marks wasn't one of our good doctor's clients," Eric said before returning to the files. He had questioned Latka's receptionist and checked the office files. He hadn't expected anything on St. Marks to turn up and it hadn't.

Max stared at his computer. None of the three victims had a criminal record. They were born in different states, had different birth dates. Gates and St. Marks were approximately the same age; Alder was a couple of years older. No connection showed up on the screen.

"This case connects back and forth, but not in a way that makes sense." Frustrated, Max crumpled a paper coffee cup in his hand and lobbed it toward an overflowing wastebasket. "Gates and Alder shared the same dentist, but St. Marks doesn't tie in. St. Marks and Gates have the bookend in their houses, but Alder doesn't. I hope you're having better luck than I am."

"I am." Sitting up straight, Eric stared at the file in his hand with a grim expression. "They should have called us." He looked up. "The St. Marks bookend came out clean."

Max stared. "No prints?"

"Nothing."

"That means St. Marks didn't touch it." Max swore softly. "It's a definite possibility she didn't notice it at all, didn't even know it was on her shelf." Picking up the telephone, he jabbed at the buttons. "The killer put the bookend on the shelf, then wiped it clean. It couldn't have happened any other way."

"You're phoning Jim Marshall? I'll take Ridley."

When Max had Jim Marshall on the phone, he confirmed the lack of prints on the bookend, then asked, "Okay, when did the cleaning lady last go to the St. Marks place?" He hoped to get an approximate fix on when the bookend had appeared in the house.

"Brad Denny talked to the cleaning lady an hour ago," Marshall said. He sounded tired. "She cleaned the St. Marks house every Friday. First she swore she never missed a single item in the place. When Denny pointed out he could write his name in the dust on the lower shelf, she admitted she'd been under the weather lately and she might have missed dusting that shelf for a week or two. There was no dust under the bookend, and it left a distinct outline when it was lifted. That bookend was there for a while."

Max covered his forehead and swore.

"Right," Jim Marshall continued. "I was going to call you today, Max. How come you made the bookend? Why did you think it was important enough to be printed? And what the hell does it mean? No one down here has the foggiest how this fits into anything. Except it's obvious someone deliberately wiped it clean. So talk to me, pal. What have you got that we don't?"

After Max explained Laura Penn's situation, Jim Marshall paused, then asked, "Someone is putting objects into Mrs. Penn's house? And a bookend exactly like the St. Marks bookend is one of the objects?"

"Yes."

Marshall was silent a moment. "Let me see if I have this right. Laura Penn connects to Dave Penn, who connects to the Ruby Alder case. If there is anything to this bookend business, then Laura Pen also connects to Gates and St. Marks."

"That's about it," Max said uneasily.

"Is there any chance . . . ?"

"Laura Penn was with me at the time of those murders."

"Too bad." Marsh sighed. "Does Bill Ridley know any of this?"

"Eric has him on the other line. The Gates bookend was not dusted. Tim Gates doesn't know when it appeared. He can't place any of the other items Laura has received."

"I hear you. We've got three bookends, but we only got to one of them in time to discover it was clean."

"Right."

"The St. Marks bookend could be isolated, not connected to the bookends at Gates's and Laura Penn's. It's a common item, Max. One of our guys in forensic has a set just like it."

"A set. Not just one."

Marshall sighed. "Yeah, the bookend's part of it. Who the hell knows how or why, but there's some kind of connection. No one wipes something clean without a reason. But we have to consider the possibility the bookend is an overlap. We couldn't prove anything in court with it."

Suspicious items or events frequently turned up in a homicide investigation, which later turned out to be of secondary importance and unrelated to the primary crime. "I don't think the bookend is an overlap. Somehow it's part of the case. I'd bet on it."

"You have any ideas how a bookend figures in a murder case? We know it wasn't the weapon, so what is it?"

"Maybe a message of some sort."

Marshall was silent for a moment. "Are you saying Laura Penn is also a target?"

Max thought about the dice face on the car photograph. Three. They already had three murders. And no proof whatsoever that Alder, Gates or St. Marks had received any of the mystery items that appeared in Laura's house.

"I think it's a possibility," he said finally. "I've put extra patrols in her area. I sure as hell don't want her alone on Wednesday."

"How strong do you feel about your dentist? We're going to want to question him."

"He's the only link we have between Alder and Gates. He can't account for his whereabouts on the days of the hits. He has a facial scratch. I've already talked to Brad Denny. Brad is checking with the airlines to verify when Smyth returned to Denver."

"We also heard you picked up Dave Penn. You got anything there?"

"Penn's looking thinner all the time. He had no scratch marks, and he's sticking to his story. So far we can't prove him wrong. He walked out of here yesterday—we didn't have enough to hold him. But we're not ruling him out."

When Max hung up, Eric lit a cigarette and leaned back in his chair, not looking happy. "Ridley says he owes you five bucks. After he heard about the St. Marks bookend, he picked up the Gates bookend and had it dusted." He shrugged. "The only prints they picked up belong to Tim or Diane Gates."

"A lot of prints or a few?"

"About what you would expect if she picked it up, looked at it, then put it on the shelf. And a few of the husband's prints from packing and unpacking."

"Clean otherwise? So it fits both ways. She finds it in her living room—wiped clean—and picks it up. Or, she bought it somewhere and brought it home. No help."

"If she bought it, there should be some unknowns. Print smudges from the salesman, or other shoppers maybe. But there should be something. What's Jim Marshall working on?"

Max tossed his pencil in the air. "Denver has more leads than they can follow. St. Marks's regular boyfriend, Hepplewhite, has no alibi for Wednesday afternoon. Neither does the new boyfriend. They're each trying to incriminate the other. St. Marks's house was broken into three months ago—there may be something there. They've got a lot to work on. Plus, they're very interested in our bogus dentist with the scratch on his face. They'll be asking for a tissue sample."

"Are you and Laura coming over tonight?" Eric asked twenty minutes later. When Max nodded, he added, "That bookend is worrying me, Max. A lot."

"Tell me about it."

"I can't pin it down. It should track back to Ruby Alder. Not to Laura Penn. You said she changed the locks at her place?"

"I checked them myself."

"I'll tell you this. I'm glad we have the dentist locked up."

THE PHONE RANG while she was getting dressed.

"You bitch," Dave Penn shouted when she answered. He sounded very, very drunk. "You put me through hell!"

Uneasily Laura glanced toward the bedroom windows. The draperies were pulled. "David—"

"They still think I did it!" His voice was slurred. "They got a tail on me. They think I don't know, but I know."

"Dave, if you're innocent—"

"You'll pay for this!"

Her hand was shaking when she hung up the telephone.

LAURA LIKED Sarah Ashbaugh immediately. Sarah was marching into middle age with grace and good cheer. The years had added a few pounds and a few gray hairs, a few laugh lines around her eyes and mouth. But the overall impression was of a generous woman who enjoyed people and enjoyed life.

"Eric teases me about taking on too many causes," Sarah explained cheerfully. They were in her large homey kitchen setting food on trays to carry into the backyard. "The truth is, I like to meddle." She laughed, the sound full and robust. "Causes are made for meddlers. Finding out how they function and what they're all about." She added garlic bread to the tray. "Which brings us to you, my dear Laura. I want to know all about you and how you managed to captivate our Max."

A flush of pink heated Laura's cheeks and she glanced out the window. Max and Eric were playing lawn darts, trading affectionate insults.

"Do you really think he's captivated?"

"Good Lord, yes! Haven't you seen the way he looks at you? I can tell you, he didn't look this smitten with Linda."

It was the kind of statement Laura longed to hear but felt embarrassed to hear. Which didn't make a lot of sense.

Sarah studied her expression. "If you've wondered whether Max is carrying some kind of torch for Linda—honey, you're wrong." She poured two glasses of wine and pushed one toward Laura. "Let's talk a minute. I've been married to a cop for twenty-three years. I won't gloss it over. Sometimes it's difficult. Some women can't handle the worry, the late hours, the interrupted schedules, meals and all the rest that goes with it. Linda was like that. Linda is a nice woman, but she wasn't a good cop's wife."

"I don't know if I would be, either."

"Eric thinks you would. He says you aren't squeamish, you aren't an alarmist. You don't resent Max's job."

Laura watched Max through the window, thinking how handsome he was, how much she had begun to care for him. "We're having a little problem right now—I lied."

"I heard about it," Sarah said, nodding, "but I don't think it's going to be a problem unless Dave Penn turns out to be the killer."

"I lied because—"

"Honey, you don't have to explain anything to me. Eric told me all about it. People make mistakes." She shrugged and smiled. "You made a doozy. What you need to remember is that cops see and hear a lot of ugly things. Your lie seems mountainous to you, but to Max and Eric, it's one small piece of a large puzzle."

"I don't know, Sarah...."

"I'm not trying to minimize it. I'm just advising you not to let it mushroom into something larger than it is. I guess I'm trying to say, if Max tells you he's worked it out and it's okay, believe him."

"Thanks," she said in a whisper.

"Good heavens, why did you let me run on like that? I've been preaching, haven't I? Eric would have a fit." Laughing, she stood and handed Laura a platter. "I'm right behind you with the salad. Just one more thing—I like you, Laura Penn. And I think you're just right for our Max. I'm trying to decide what I'll give you for a wedding present."

Laura blushed and laughed. "Don't spend your money too soon. We're a long way from that point."

"You two look smug," Eric commented while they were placing the food on the picnic table. "What plots have you been hatching?"

"We're planning the wedding," Sarah announced with a wink.

Max rolled his eyes. "I should have warned you, Laura. Sarah is the world's most dedicated matchmaker."

"Not this time," Sarah said. "You did fine all by yourself. I'm only meddling at this point to show my approval."

"YOU WERE RIGHT," Laura said later. "I do like Sarah Ashbaugh." She crossed her ankles on top of her coffee table and smiled at Max, who sat next to her on the sofa.

"Sarah's blunt and funny and for all her talk about meddling, no one works harder for the Detectives' Wives Association, the Heart Fund, and a dozen other projects."

"She told me a little about Linda," Laura admitted, swirling the brandy in her snifter.

"Really? What did she say?" He stretched his arm along the back of the sofa, letting his fingertips touch her shoulder. When she had repeated the conversation, he nodded. "That's a fair assessment. It just didn't work out. No hard feelings on either side."

Laura was very conscious of his nearness. "Max, we have to talk about my lying to alibi Dave."

Shifting on the sofa, he lifted her chin until she had to look at him. "That's done, Laura. Finished. We can't change it. We can only hope it doesn't have any long-range ugly implications. And we can decide whether we let it become a problem, or if we want to put it behind us and go forward. I only have one question." His gaze searched her eyes. "Did you lie for Penn because you still care for him?"

"No. Whatever I felt for Dave ended a long time ago."

"I'm glad."

She looked into his warm dark eyes. "For a while I wondered if you were seeing me just because you suspected I was lying."

"Maybe that was part of it in the beginning."

"And now?"

He kissed her then, a kiss that began softly, then deepened in intensity. His arms tightened around her body and pulled her close to him.

"You don't know how long I've wanted to do that," he whispered against her hair.

"Oh, Max, I've wanted you to."

He kissed her again, his mouth urgent and possessive, and Laura felt her heartbeat accelerate against her ribs. When his hand slid to cup her breast, she gasped then tightened her arms around his neck.

He whispered her name, then lifted her off the sofa as if she were weightless. She pressed her face into his neck and inhaled the after-shave she loved. "That way," she murmured, pointing down the hallway.

Max carried her to the bedroom and placed her gently on the bed. It would have been perfect, except something was digging into her back.

"Just a minute," she said, feeling foolish. Rolling onto her side, she slid her hand across the spread, searching in the darkness for whatever was there. A chill raced down flesh that had heated a moment before. "Max," she said, as her fingers curled over an object, "turn on the light, please. Next to the bed."

"What is it?" He snapped on the light and Laura leaned forward.

"It's a chess piece." Before he could make a response, she looked up at him, her eyes dark. "It's not mine. I don't own a chess set. It's another mystery item."

"Stand up a minute." Bending, he ran a hand over the bedspread. "There's another one." He examined the piece in his hand and swore. "Stay here."

But she couldn't. She followed him to the kitchen where his holster was hanging. With wide eyes, she watched him remove his gun then begin a methodical search of her house.

By the time he stepped back inside from the garage, she had made a pot of coffee. She silently handed him a mug.

"Nothing," he said, returning his gun to the holster. "He must have been here while we were at Sarah's and Eric's." Which ruled out Latka/Smyth as Laura's intruder. The dentist was in jail. Was Marshall right? Were the bookend and the other items merely overlaps? He couldn't believe it. "Laura, where are your house keys?"

"In my purse." Going to the hall closet, she removed her purse and handed Max her key ring.

He opened the front door and stepped outside. The key scraped in the lock and he returned inside. Without speaking, he passed her, walked through the living room and repeated the process with the locks on the French doors.

"Your key will not lock or unlock the French doors."

Laura's mouth dropped. "Max! That's impossible."

"It's possible if the lock has been changed," he said grimly.

"What? But . . ." The blood rushed out of her face and her hands trembled. "Are you suggesting someone who isn't me had the locks changed on *my* house? Can someone do that?" The words stumbled over one another, shocked and sputtering. "That's terrible! Appalling. If that can happen, then how can anyone feel safe?"

Stepping past her, Max entered the kitchen, found her broom and brought it into the living room. He pushed the broomstick through the handles of the French doors.

"Keep the broomstick in place, Laura, even when you're in the house. At least until we get this cleared up."

"Max, I'm starting to get frightened," she spoke quietly, but her hands were unsteady. Dropping to the sofa, she looked at the items on her coffee table.

After finding sandwich bags in her kitchen, Max disappeared into the bedroom. When he returned, he had the chess pieces in the bags. "A black queen and a white pawn."

"You're going to have them printed?"

"I predict the only prints we'll find are yours and mine. But it's worth a try." After looking at her for a minute, he dropped onto the sofa next to her and took one of her hands. Speaking in an even tone, he updated her on the lion bookends in the Gates and St. Marks houses, told her he recalled seeing a couple of chess pieces in the St. Marks house. "They could mean something—or nothing."

"Wait a minute." Gazing into his eyes, she thought about what he had told her, putting together the implications. Speaking slowly, not looking away from him, she followed the direction in which he had pointed her. "Are you saying Diane Gates and Elizabeth St. Marks had things put into their homes, too?"

"I think it's possible. It's been nagging at me since I saw the bookend in the Gates house. Then it turned up again at St. Marks. Now we have the chess pieces. The next step is to take a look at the St. Marks pieces and discover if Tim Gates recalls any loose chess pieces."

"And if he does?" she asked in a whisper.

"Two coincidences in a murder case are no longer coincidence."

A shudder passed over her skin and her eyes widened. "Are you saying I could be in danger?"

"The situation is dangerous." Indecision darkened his gaze. "Laura, I don't want to frighten you. What's happening here—" he waved a hand toward the items on the coffee table "—may be unrelated, what we call an overlap. It's possible none of this has anything to do with the murders."

"But you think it might."

"It might," he agreed, stroking her cheek. "The evidence is definitely soft. I can't justify what I'm feeling with proof. But I'm feeling more and more uneasy. Whether or not your intruder is connected to the murders, something is going on here that has me concerned. Laura, I want you to stay with me until this is over and we have some answers."

"Dave is back on the street." She told him about her telephone call.

"I know. All the more reason to get you out of here."

She covered her eyes with her hand. "I just can't believe it could be him. I'd rather think it's your bogus dentist. You know, when the items started appearing, I thought it was intriguing. Maybe I even thought it was a little flattering. Like they were coming from a secret admirer or something like that." She gave him a sheepish smile before a tremor rippled down her body. "But it's different now. Knowing there is a possibility these items may have turned up in the homes of two women who have been murdered . . ."

Max held her until the trembling eased, then he cupped her face between his hands. "Put some things in a bag and let's get out of here. Okay?"

After she left the living room, Max leaned forward on the sofa, elbows on knees, hands clasped under his chin. He stared at the items on the coffee table. Point one: each item was intended as a message—he no longer doubted that. Point two: the items as a whole were possibly a second message. Point three: what the hell was the message? And who was sending it?

Standing, he moved to the hallway and called to Laura. "You said you don't own a chess set, but do you play chess?"

"I've played once or twice, but I wouldn't say I'm a chess player, no."

Returning to the sofa, he separated the items on the table. The flowers and the crown impressed him as female items, and he pushed them to one end of the coffee table. The photograph of the car and the chess pieces in the sandwich bags he pushed to the other end of the table. They impressed him as male, personal to the intruder. The bookend he placed in the middle. The bookend was the key that unlocked everything else, he suspected, feeling his frustration mount.

Finally he shifted his frown to the chess pieces. Why a queen and a pawn? Why not two pawns, or a knight and a castle?

"I'm sorry about . . . you know," Laura said in the car.

"Me, too," he said, looking away from the road to give her a rueful grin. They both understood the mood had altered.

When he parked in front of his condo unit, Laura got out of the car slowly. Max was removing her bag from the back seat when another car pulled into the space next to his and the doors opened.

"Mrs. Penn! Look, Mom, it's my teacher, Mrs. Penn."

Laura spun on her heel and blinked. "Hello, Gene." She lifted her head with a weak smile. "Mr. and Mrs. McTavish."

"We saw *The Terminator* with Arnold Schwarzenegger at the drive-in. It was great!"

Lena McTavish cleared her throat self-consciously. "We don't usually take Gene to such violent movies," she said uncomfortably. "But...oh, hello, Max." Now she seemed to make the connection between Max, standing beside the driver's side of the car, and Laura, standing between the cars on the passenger side. A slow smirk spread over her lips. "Well, come along, Gene, it's late. Nice to run into you, Mrs. Penn."

"I want to tell Mrs. Penn about the movie!"

"You'll see her on Monday," Lena McTavish said with a backward glance at Laura. "You can tell her then."

The McTavishes went into the door of the condo, which was just in front of their car.

Laura looked at Max across the top of the Monte Carlo. "Your condo is the one next door. Right?"

"And that was one of your students, right? The kid who set off the stink bomb?"

They looked at each other, then Laura sighed. "I can't do this, Max." After opening the door, she slid into the car seat. Max got in the driver's side. "You can understand, can't you?"

"Yes," he said finally, reaching for the ignition.

"It wouldn't have worked, anyway. There's my cat, the mail, newspapers . . ."

He drove her home in silence.

"I'll stay here," he said when they were again in her living room. When he saw the indecision on her face, he realized tomorrow was Sunday. Everyone in her neighborhood would be home and would see his car. A reluctant grin deepened the lines framing his mouth. "I have to get an old-fashioned girl."

"The local schoolmarm," Laura said, her smile as filled with regret as his. Stepping up to him, she placed her palm against his cheek. "It will be all right. I think the show is over for tonight. Nothing more is going to happen."

"That's for sure," he said with an exaggerated sigh and they both smiled. He kissed her, his mouth lingering, a promise for the future. "There are extra patrols in this area. I'll increase the frequency of drive-bys."

He sat in his car for a few minutes. The lights went out in her living room, came on a minute later behind her bedroom draperies. He would not have driven away if he had not agreed that nothing more would happen that night.

His hands tightened on the steering wheel. He was going to get the bastard who was doing this to her.

Chapter Eight

Although Dave Penn had been released, he was warned not to leave the Denver area. Because he had no definite alibi for the time of the murders, he was still in the game. But the lack of scratch marks was a telling piece of evidence in his favor.

"Our dentist's attorney is fighting a tissue sample," Max said, leaning over his desk and rubbing a hand across his jaw. "I hate to mention this, but there should be more than one scratch on Smyth's face. St. Marks had tissue under several nails."

"Two good suspects and we can't pin either of them," Eric said in disgust. "Hell, if it wasn't for the impostor thing, Smyth would be back on the street."

"What about the weapon? Let's go over that again."

After tilting backward in his chair, Eric crossed his ankles on top of his desk. "We're looking for a hybrid. A blade that's part serrated, part smooth, about three-and-a-half to four inches long. Same pathology for all three murders. The blade is probably smooth at the tip, serrated near the handle."

"We know it isn't a regular home kitchen knife. Doesn't come from a restaurant or butcher supply, either."

"We've looked at a dozen hybrid types," Eric continued, reviewing it, "but they're all wrong in one way or another. Too long, too curved, too smooth or too serrated." Leaning forward, he stubbed out a cigarette in an overflowing ashtray.

"Okay, we're probably looking for a specialty knife." At this point Max's imagination went blank. What specialty? Where to look next? Eventually they would locate a match for the weapon. In the meantime the problem was another source of frustration.

"All right," Eric said, rubbing his eyes. "Run down the killer."

Although he know the details by rote, Max consulted at his notes. "All the murders occurred on Wednesdays. Either the guy has adjustable time or he has a job with Wednesdays off. This would rule out a white-collar salaried position."

"Dave Penn has adjustable time. So does the dentist."

"It's also true that neither Penn nor Smyth would have to limit themselves to Wednesday. Okay, the killer is right-handed—"

"Both our suspects are right-handed."

"There was type-O blood under Elizabeth St. Marks's fingernails—"

"Penn has type-O blood. According to his sheet, so does Smyth."

"The killer has some scratches on him, probably on his face. Starting to heal by now."

"Dammit. There is where we hit a brick wall again."

"We've looked at every man remotely connected to these cases and none of them has a bunch of scratch marks—just Latka with the one." Max reached for his coffee. "Since the women let him inside, we can assume there is nothing unusual or suspicious about his appearance or manner."

"Since no burglary is involved, we can also assume the attacks are personal, the choice of victim deliberate," Eric said, taking up the recital. "What's the psychological profile say?"

"I've got it two ways. One is based only on hard evidence. The second profile plugs in Laura's items and assumes the intruder and the killer are the same person."

Max and Eric looked at each other. "You and I think he is," Eric said finally. "You know, of course, if we're right, then Smyth isn't our guy. He's not even in the ballpark. He was here when the intruder put the chess pieces in Laura's bed."

Max scowled at the papers in his hand. "If we plug in Laura's items, here's what we've got. The killer is boiling with hate and it's an old hate, dates into the past. As the photo of the car suggests. The bookend, the flowers and the paper crown are meaningful, but the meaning is not yet apparent. The chess pieces are another matter. According to the shrink the chess pieces are the most significant psych clues so far. This guy does not relate well to women. He sees them as far above himself. They reduce him in stature, take something away. He'll get that something back if he kills them. Could be his self-esteem."

"So, when he kills, is he transferring? Or is he killing the specific women who did him wrong?"

"The murders are planned. The items left in the houses suggest it's specific."

"So what set this guy off?"

"The profile suggests it was most likely a series of related things happening in rapid sequence. Several things occurred within a short span, which in themselves probably wouldn't have triggered him. But taken together, they flashed him back and he erupted. Maybe he ran into one of the women accidentally and he remembered her, or she reminded him of someone. Maybe seeing her occurred on a date that was important to him, or he saw something in the newspapers. No way to tell. The only thing we can guess with any certainty is that it connects to his past."

"You saw the bodies of those women," Eric said, frowning. "There was a lot of hate there." The overhead fan squeaked in the silence. Phones rang in the outer room. He gazed at the map of Denver and suburbs tacked to the wall behind Max. Three red pins stood out against a colorless background. "Diane Gates was not an easy hit. Nelson is a busy street with lots of kids home from school at the hour she was killed. The killer took a big risk of being seen and remembered."

Max threw his pencil on his desk. "In the end, it was a safe choice. No one remembers seeing a damned thing."

"Yeah, but the killer couldn't have known it would go that way when he picked Diane Gates. So why take the risk?"

"He had to want her dead. The question is why?"

Eric nodded. "Meanwhile there's our bogus dentist. Let's see if we can get him to agree to a tissue sample."

MONDAY AND TUESDAY were hectic. No one paid attention in class; there was a holiday feel in the air. Wednesday, Laura passed out final report cards, received some gratifying hugs and a few small gifts, then, at noon, the term ended. She and Patty Selwick stood at the window of Laura's classroom and watched the kids streaming across the school lawns.

"I always have mixed feelings when the term ends," Laura commented. "Sad and glad."

"Want to go out for a real lunch with a real martini and celebrate?"

"Thanks, anyway, but there's something I've been putting off for a couple of days that won't wait any longer. Besides, I'm trying to lose a few pounds."

"Maybe you'll win the Sleek Chic drawing," Patty said, shaking her head. "I still can't believe you did that."

"What? Enter the draw?"

"Who knows what happened to those entry slips? For all you know some waiter at the Anchor Bay is running around with the slips in his pocket. He forgot to turn them in for the drawing when he collected them. Or worse, maybe they sell the names later and every salesman in town is going to show up at your door."

"Or maybe I'll win and return in the fall looking thin and fabulous," Laura said with a smile.

They shook hands. "Don't be a stranger," Patty said. "If you need a tennis partner..."

"I'll remember."

The minute she got home, Laura poured a glass of iced tea and settled on the sofa with the yellow pages spread across her lap. She looked up locksmiths and reached for the telephone.

MAX AND ERIC SHOOK HANDS with Tim Gates. "Sorry to trouble you, but we have a few more questions."

"Anything I can do to help, you know I want to." Tim Gates leaned his palms on the registration counter.

The office of the Gates Motel was small but scrupulously clean. A counter placard displayed a list of modest rates.

"When you were packing to move, did you happen to notice a couple of loose chess pieces?" Max asked.

"I threw them away. There didn't seem to be any reason to keep them. Should I have?" Tim Gates looked at them with an anxious expression.

Max and Eric did not glance at each other. "Then you did find some loose pieces. Can you describe them?"

Gates shrugged. "Just a couple of plastic chess pieces. Looked like they came from a cheap set. Why?"

"Do you play chess, Mr. Gates?"

"Tim. Call me Tim. I've played. But the pieces weren't mine, if that's what you're asking."

"Which pieces did you find?"

"A queen and a pawn, I think it was."

Max drew a breath. "The same color or different colors?"

"Let me think a minute. I wasn't paying much attention. I think the queen was black and the pawn was white. Or it could have been the other way around. But I do remember the pieces weren't the same color."

"I know this probably doesn't make a lot of sense, Tim, but bear with us. Did your wife play chess?"

"Diane didn't have the patience for it. Can you tell me what this is all about?"

"Just something we're running down," Eric said. "Where did you find the chess pieces?"

"Well, that was a little strange. I found the pieces in the drawer next to the bed, where Diane kept personal articles."

"I'm sorry to ask this, Tim, but what kind of personal articles?"

"Old letters, her diary, photographs, her nasal spray."

Max's head jerked up. "Your wife kept a diary?"

"She has since she was a kid. You know, the five-year kind. She had two or three of them in the drawer. You guys took them. Or someone did. I don't have them. I'll get them back, won't I?"

Eric swore and patted the pocket where he carried his cigarettes. "Ridley has some explaining to do. He's been holding out on us," he muttered.

Max clenched his jaw. "Tim, where do you think the chess pieces came from?"

"Honestly, I don't have a clue."

When they returned to Max's car, Eric lit a cigarette and slumped down in the seat. "Damn Ridley. He should have told us about the diaries. I am so sick of politics. What difference does it make who solves this as long as it gets solved?"

"If there was anything in them, we would have heard about it," Max said absently. His fingers drummed the top of the steering wheel. He stared in front of him, chewing his lower lip.

"Yeah, well, he should have sent us copies. Let's go, pal."

Two blocks from the Gates Motel, Max cut in front of a 7-Eleven and stopped the car in front of a phone booth. "Listen in," he said to Eric. Nodding, Eric leaned against the phone-booth door as Max dialed.

"You calling Ridley? Good."

"No, Brad Denny." When Denny came on the line, Max straightened. "Brad? Glad I caught you. Did you guys photo the entire St. Marks house? Okay. Do you have the file handy?" He waited. "Take a look at the photo of the son's bedroom."

"The son's bedroom?" Eric repeated, echoing Brad Denny's surprise.

"Now. Tell me if there are two chess pieces on the kid's desk." Max covered his eyes and waited. "Okay. Can you make out which pieces they are? First, let me tell you what I think they are. A black queen and a white pawn."

Even Eric, standing outside the phone booth, could hear Brad Denny's explosion of swearing. He grinned and gave Max a thumb's-up sign.

When Brad had calmed, Max spoke again. "If no one has touched those pieces, have them picked up and dusted. I'll give you five to one the pieces are clean. Another five says the kid doesn't play chess."

After hanging up, he waited for the dial tone, then called the station and asked for the lab. "Walt? What did you get on the chess pieces?" He listened, nodded, then hung up the phone. "Laura's pieces have her prints on the queen. Mine on the pawn. Otherwise, clean."

"This ain't looking good, old son," Eric said, frowning.

Max reached for the phone again, pushing up his sleeve to glance at his watch as he did so. He dialed Laura's number. The phone rang into silence.

"Dammit. No answer."

Eric stared. "It's ten minutes until four. Wednesday."

"The approximate time of the murders." They looked at each other, then ran toward Max's car.

During the ride back to Littleton, Max talked nonstop. It was better than letting himself remember Laura had said she planned to clean house today. She should have been there to answer the telephone.

"Two of the victims have gold lions and odd chess pieces. They both keep diaries," he said.

"Except for Alder. No bookend, no chess pieces, no diary." Eric drew on his cigarette. "Alder is the clinker in this case. She doesn't fit."

Max cut in and out of the afternoon traffic. "If we take out Gates and consider only Elizabeth St. Marks and Ruby Alder, we have no connection to Laura. If we take out the

St. Marks murder and consider only Gates and Alder, we have no connection to Laura."

"I see where you're going. But if we take out Ruby Alder and consider only Diane Gates and Elizabeth St. Marks, then we get a strong connection to Laura and to each other through the mystery items." Eric lit another cigarette. "Can you push this tub any faster?"

"It looks like Diane Gates and Elizabeth St. Marks were visited by Laura's intruder. I think they received the same items—the same messages."

"So how does Ruby Alder tie into this?"

Glancing from the road, Max looked at Eric. "Maybe Alder was the first item. The first message."

"This is starting to make a crazy kind of sense."

"If so, Eric, follow it through. Laura is being set up as victim number four."

"Step on the gas, will you?" Eric stared at his wristwatch.

Horns blared as Max cut sharply to the left, then raced through an amber light. "The question is, which of the mystery items is the last one before the killer shows up at the door?"

Concentration furrowed Eric's brow. "Each of the items is common."

"The last message is still in the St. Marks house. Agreed?"

"Could be. But what the hell is it? We could look right at it and not know what we're seeing."

Max spotted Laura's house ahead, cut toward the curb and skidded to a stop. The house looked deserted.

Pulling their guns, he and Eric ran up the driveway and jumped the steps to the porch. Max tried the door handle and the door opened. He swore under his breath. She hadn't locked it.

"Ready," Eric said, looking at him.

Max kicked the door open and stepped into the foyer. There was no sound. Only silence.

He nodded his head toward the hallway leading to Laura's bedroom and the guest room. Eric acknowledged the nod and stepped quietly into the hallway. The silence ate at Max's nerves. If anything had happened to Laura, he didn't think he could endure it.

Pulse beating in his throat, not sure what he would find, he swung into the kitchen, then came around the counter to the living room. Finally he removed the broom handle and checked the patio and yard. Relief flooded his stomach with acid. He closed his eyes briefly as Eric reappeared, fitting his gun into his holster.

"All clear," Eric said. "Her car is gone."

Lifting his jacket, Max replaced his gun then glanced around the living room. She had left a glass of iced tea on the table beside the sofa. The telephone book was lying across one of the sofa cushions, opened to the yellow pages.

The page showed a list of locksmiths. Max made a sound of exasperation as he ran his finger down the list, following the check marks Laura had placed beside the phone numbers.

"She stopped ticking off names at Markam and Sons."

"We might as well see this through," Eric said. "Let's go."

"I'M LAURA PENN," she said to an older man working behind the counter. "I'm looking for Pete Markam."

"You're talking to him." Pete Markam pushed back a khaki cap that matched his work shirt and pants. "Are you the lady who phoned?"

"Yes. You said you installed a lock at 2022 West Anderson. Is that correct?"

"Right." Extending a pad, he showed her a copy of a receipt. "Put a new lock on the French doors for your husband. He paid in cash."

"Mr. Markam, I have no husband. I'm divorced. I live alone." Anger and excitement mixed in her mind. She couldn't decide if she was furious that a stranger had changed her locks or if she was excited about finally discovering something.

Pete Markam considered the receipt pad. "I don't know what to tell you. The man who ordered this job said his name was Mr. Penn. He said he'd locked himself out and he wanted an extra key made. It happens all the time. I remember he said he was in a hurry, so he told me to install a new lock. It doesn't sound like it, but actually that's quicker when you don't have a key for an impression."

Laura stared at him. "You didn't request any identification?"

"Mrs. Penn, there are damned few people brazen enough to phone a locksmith, wait around for him to arrive, then stand in front of a door that isn't his while the locksmith opens the house."

But someone had done exactly that. With the shrubbery to the east, the vacant house to the west, and the fence in back, there wouldn't have been much risk that he would be seen or challenged.

"What time of day did this happen?"

"It's here on the receipt. Ten-thirty in the morning. Last Wednesday. A week ago today."

The bell over the shop door tinkled and Laura turned to see Max and Eric. "How in the world did you know I was here?" she asked. Before he could answer, she took his arm. "Max, you were right. Someone hired Pete Markam to change the locks on the French doors."

He looked down at her. "You said you were going straight home from school to clean house." He looked upset.

"I wanted to track this down. Is something wrong?"

"I telephoned and there was no answer. You worried the hell out of me. Eric and I rushed to your house not knowing what we were going to find. Your front door was unlocked."

A hand flew to her mouth. "I forgot to lock it? I thought I had. Max, I'm sorry."

"We'll talk about it later. The important thing is, you're all right." He looked at Pete Markam. "So. What have we got here?"

He and Eric showed Pete Markam their badges and Pete Markam gave Laura an uneasy look.

"Okay, I didn't ask the guy for any identification. Maybe I should have insisted on verification. But you have to understand this call was like a thousand others. When I got there, the guy was sitting on the front porch steps waiting for me. He didn't seem nervous or like he was trying to hide anything. I had no reason to think it wasn't his place."

"Why did you change the lock on the back instead of the front door?"

"The guy said—and it made sense—that he and his wife hardly ever used the French doors, and it would be less hassle to replace the lock on the back than to track down and exchange all the keys to the front door. He indicated a neighbor had a key, and a couple of relatives…you know how it is. I didn't think much about it."

Eric requisitioned the receipt and copied the time Pete Markam had arrived at Laura's house.

Max leaned an arm on the counter. "Can you describe the man who identified himself as Mr. Penn?"

Markam pursed his faced into an expression of concentration. "Well, let's see. There wasn't anything unusual. Average height, maybe a little shorter than me—I'm five-ten. Average build. Kinda light brown hair." A shrug accompanied an apologetic look. "I guess I'm not very good at this. I see about twenty customers a day, sometimes more. I can't remember them all."

"Can you remember what he was wearing?"

"Let's see. I think he was the one with black pants and a white shirt."

"You're sure?"

Pete Markam thought about it. "I think so."

"No jacket? No tie?"

"No. I'm sure about that. He looked like a guy who was probably getting ready for work, then stepped outside for a minute and locked himself out. He said he called from a neighbor's house."

"Try to remember. Did he have any unusual marks or moles? A tattoo? Anything at all?"

"The cat had scratched him. You mean something like that?"

Eric looked up from his notepad. "Another bingo," he said softly.

"Tell us about the scratches, Mr. Markam," Max said in an expressionless voice.

"I made some dumb remark about his wife working him over, but he said no, it had been the cat." Pete Markam glanced at Laura's pale face then touched his collar. "Whoever lives there has a big white tomcat. It came outside when I opened the door. The guy said it had scratched him."

"Your first impression was that the scratches had been made by a person?"

"Yeah, the marks were pretty wide apart for a cat. But I didn't say anything. It wasn't any of my business. Hell, what do I know? Maybe the cat did it."

"Mr. Markam," Max said. His smile was thin. "I suggest you cancel any appointments you may have. A lot of people are going to want to talk to you."

Markam blinked at them. "What's this all about?"

Eric had stepped to the telephone behind the counter and was speaking to Brad Denny. When he hung up, he nodded to Max. "Denny will be here in about twenty minutes. He'll call Ridley. Two things, Max. Denny phoned St. Marks's ex-husband in Wyoming, where the kids are staying. None of the family plays chess. The son does not own a chess set. Second thing—Marshall wants to meet with us and Ridley. He also wants to talk to Laura."

Max looked at Laura standing beside the door of the shop. "I think I'll take Laura somewhere for a cup of coffee. It's time to lay this whole thing out."

"Good idea. I'll catch you back at the station."

"Max?" Her eyes were as wide as saucers.

Taking her arm, he led her outside.

LAURA SAT SIDEWAYS on the car seat, studying Max's profile as he drove up I-70 into the mountains west of Denver.

"Are you ever going to say something?" she asked softly.

"I was thinking about when Eric and I drove up to your house. Going inside."

"Something else must have happened. Was there another murder?"

"No," he said, turning to look at her. "But things are coming together." He didn't say anything more for a moment. "We'll stop at El Rancho. Have a cup of coffee."

When he fell silent again, Laura shifted her attention to the pines and aspen rising up from the edge of the highway. In the distance, the far peaks were still capped with winter snow. They didn't speak until they were inside the restaurant.

"I'm sorry I worried you," Laura said. Outside the picture window lay a scenic view of aspens and wild flowers. For a moment it seemed ludicrous to be discussing dark subjects like intruders and murder.

"When I stepped around the foyer in the kitchen..." Max covered his face with his hand and let his voice trail off.

"What did you expect to find?" She was starting to feel uneasy. "Aren't you making a big deal out of nothing? I mean, what's the worst that could have happened? Another mystery item."

"Laura, I think I'm falling in love with you."

Her fingers flew to her mouth and she stared at him. "Tell me when you know for sure," she said softly when her voice returned. It was a silly thing to say, but a blaze of happiness made her feel tongue-tied.

Suddenly he laughed and the tension that had stretched between them during the drive vanished. "I promise you'll be the first to know." His smile held, but his eyes darkened and turned serious. "When I thought something had happened to you..."

"What did you think had happened?" she asked.

"Laura, it's Wednesday."

"Wednesday." Then she made the connection and her eyes rounded. "The murders."

"We've been talking all round this," he said gently. "It's time to face it squarely." Reaching across the table, he took her hands and spoke in a low voice. He reminded her about finding the lion bookends in Diane Gates's and Elizabeth St. Marks's house. He told her about Diane Gates's missing graduation photo and the empty picture hook in the St. Marks house. He told her about the chess pieces. And about how whoever murdered Elizabeth St. Marks had scratch marks on his cheek, like the man Pete Markam had met at her house.

The blood drained from Laura's face as he continued. She closed her eyes and listened in silence until he finished. Her hands felt like ice, though he continued to hold them across the table.

"You and Eric are thinking I may be the next victim. Is that right?" she asked in a whisper.

"Yes. Jim Marshall and Bill Ridley are also considering the possibility. They want to talk to you."

"But . . . why me?" She pulled her hands from his grasp and spread them in confusion.

"That's what we hope to find out."

"Max, as far as I know, I don't have any enemy in the world." A shaking hand lifted to her forehead. "I'm not thinking as clearly as I should be. But I can't think of any reason why anyone might want to hurt me."

"Not hurt, Laura. Murder. I don't want to frighten you unnecessarily, but neither do I want you to minimize the seriousness of what we're discussing."

"Whoever is putting those things in my house is the murderer?" Questions tumbled from her lips as quickly as they came into her mind.

"Eric and I think each of the victims except Ruby Alder received the same items you did. And Laura...they're dead."

Swallowing hard, she pushed aside her cup of coffee. "But that doesn't make sense. If Ruby was murdered by the same man as the others, and if you think...then shouldn't she have received the mystery items, too?" Hope flickered in her eyes.

"I don't know the answer to that. Yes, she should have. But she didn't. Somehow Ruby Alder's murder is slightly different than the others. Everything is the same except she didn't receive the mystery items. The connection to you could be that you knew her."

"But not well."

He nodded. "It's more likely we haven't spotted how Ruby Alder fits into everything. Eric and I are wondering if Ruby Alder's murder was the first item. The first message, if you will."

A shudder constricted Laura's shoulders. "What kind of message?"

"We don't know." Max caught her hand again and rubbed at the chill in her fingers. "We're hoping you can help."

The perimeters of Laura's world had suddenly shrunk to the shape of the table. She was no longer aware of the summer view beyond the window or the other people scattered throughout the restaurant. She clung to Max's strength and didn't look away from his eyes.

"How can I help?"

"Let's try a few questions. Are you up to it?" When she nodded, he squeezed her hand. "What was your first thought when you learned Ruby Alder had been murdered?"

"My first thought." She tried to remember. "Horror. Disbelief. I thought about Dave and how terrible it must be for him."

"Did you think Dave might be involved?"

"No. Not once."

"All right. Try to remember. Did you think anything like, *This reminds me of...?*"

"No. What could Ruby's murder possibly remind me of? I've never known anyone who was murdered. Oh. You mean, like some incident with Dave? Max, do you still think Dave could be involved in any of this?"

"He's looking less and less likely, but we can't rule him out of the Gates and Alder case at this point," he said slowly. "What we've got is flawed and it's circumstantial, but it's there, Laura."

A headache had begun behind her eyes. "I want to help, but I don't know what you're looking for."

"Okay, let's try dates. Does the date of Ruby Alder's murder mean anything special to you? The twenty-fourth of April. Maybe a birthday or an anniversary of some kind. Anything?"

She thought about the twenty-fourth of April. "No," she said finally. The dates of the Gates and St. Marks killings didn't ring any bells, either. To be certain, he asked about Dave Penn's and her wedding anniversary and the date of their divorce. Nothing surfaced there.

"All right, how about Wednesday? Do Wednesdays have any special significance for you?" The murders were erratically spaced, but each had occurred on a Wednesday. "This may sound silly, but do you consider Wednesday a bad-luck day, for instance? And if so, why?"

Laura's cheeks were pale. "No, Wednesdays don't mean anything special to me." She met his eyes. "Max, all the murders occurred on a Wednesday, and this is Wednesday. Did..." She swallowed. "Is it possible that going to the locksmith's saved my life? Do you think the murderer might have...?" She couldn't finish the sentence. It was too unthinkable.

"The truth? I don't know. It doesn't happen every Wednesday. Not even every other Wednesday. The week isn't predictable. All we know for sure is that Wednesday is the day he strikes." When he looked at her, his eyes had softened. "I can tell you this. In retrospect, I'm glad you left the house. You're absolutely positive that none of the dates or the day of the week means anything special?"

Laura spread her hands. "I'm sorry."

Max released a breath and pushed a hand through his hair. "We're getting nowhere. That's okay," he said when Laura apologized. "It's not your fault. We're just getting started. If Eric and I are right and your intruder is our murderer, then you have the solution, Laura."

"Good Lord," she whispered.

"All we have to do is find it." He gave her a reassuring smile.

They paid for the coffee, then walked outside to the car. During the drive back to Denver, Max continued to question her.

"Have you ever had cosmetic surgery?"

She turned in her seat to give him a startled look. "No."

"Have you ever dyed your hair?"

"Not since I was a teenager. I experimented a little then, but not in recent years."

"Do you ever invite any of the neighborhood kids into your house? Maybe some of your students?"

"Occasionally, but not very often. Most of the neighborhood kids play at the other end of the block where the rest of the kids are. And my students see enough of me during the week."

Max kept his eyes on the road. "Have you ever stayed at a motel on West Colfax?"

"The Gates Motel? No."

"Ever attended a party on Braithwaite Street?"

"At the St. Marks house? No. I don't know a soul on Braithwaite."

"Do you keep a diary?"

"Not since high school."

"Ever been to Vancouver in the summer?"

"Vancouver? No." Her eyebrows lifted in surprise. Most of the other questions made sense, but not that one. "What does Vancouver have to do with this?"

"I'd like to take you there. How would you like to go to Vancouver for a week when this is all over?" His smile made Laura's heart turn over in her chest.

"I'd like that a lot," she said softly.

"Getting away for a while might be good for both of us."

She reached a hand to his cheek. "Max...did you mean what you said in the restaurant? About falling in love?"

"Yes." He looked away from the road, his gaze brushing her lips.

"I think I'm falling in love with you, too," she said.

"If Jim Marshall and Bill Ridley weren't waiting at the station for us, I'd pull to the side of the road and show you how happy that makes me." Smiling, he met her eyes. "To hell with them. They can wait a few more minutes."

Guiding the car to the side of the road, he set the brake and the flashers, then turned in his seat and guided her into his arms. His kiss melted the tension from Laura's body and replaced it with tension of another kind. When their lips finally parted, they were both breathless.

"What do you think Sarah Ashbaugh would say about this?" Laura asked when she caught her breath.

Max ginned. "The truth? I think she's already bought a wedding present."

Laughing, Laura moved back on the seat while Max released the brake and eased onto the highway. Right now it was impossible to think of anything other than Max Elliot and the incredible fact that he loved her. And she loved him. There was so much to talk about.

For the next thirty minutes she let herself be happy, let herself talk about Vancouver and loving him. That she might be targeted as the next victim in a series of brutal murders was there, but far in the back of her mind.

But when Max parked in his spot behind the Littleton Police Station and she saw Jim Marshall and Bill Ridley standing at the window waiting for her, she examined their expressions and the smile faded from her lips.

Chapter Nine

"I'm sorry," Laura apologized two hours later. Leaning back against the hard chair, she released a sigh of frustration. "I'd like to help. But I don't know what the items mean. If I knew, believe me, I'd tell you. And I've never met Diane Gates or Elizabeth St. Marks. I'd never heard their names until the murders occurred."

The men studied her a moment longer, then filed out of the small room and left her sitting alone, feeling she had disappointed everyone.

In the hallways outside the door, Bill Ridley pulled his tie loose and took a sip of coffee that had gone cold an hour ago. "Hell, I don't know what to make of it."

Jim Marshall pushed his hands deep into his pockets and stared out the window at the sunset. "Okay, she's tied into it. Laura Penn is targeted as the next victim."

Ridley's face constricted. "Based on a bunch of maybes? That's all we've got. You're going to throw out the dentist based on a lousy bookend and a couple of chess pieces?"

"One scratch, Ridley, that's all he's got. He should look like the guy Pete Markham described, but he doesn't. In fact, Markham looked at a photo of Smyth and said positively Smyth was not the man on Laura's back porch.

When the tissue sample comes back, it's not going to match what Marshall's people found under St. Marks's nails,'' Max said. "You can count on it."

Jim Marshall nodded agreement. "Brad Denny confirmed your dentist was still in California when St. Marks was hit. He's got a solid alibi. Plus we have a positive ID from an airline passenger agent that Smyth was on the Thursday flight he claimed he was on. He may still be an active suspect for Gates and Alder, but he's off our list for St. Marks."

Ridley swore. "Which means he skates on the other two. The same guy made all the hits."

"The same guy placed items in all the victim's houses," Eric pointed out.

"No proof," Ridley said, rejecting a tie-in.

Max felt the heat rise in his face and in his voice. "What's it take, Ridley? Do you want a handwritten note from the killer telling you Laura is the next victim?"

"Maybe you're too involved on a personal level to separate the trees from the forest, Elliot." Ridley lifted an eyebrow.

"You're damn right I'm personally involved. I don't want to see someone I care about end up on the front pages!"

"Let's calm down, gentlemen," Jim Marshall said, making peace. "I see Ridley's point. Alder is the glitch."

"The items scream pattern killer," Ridley interrupted. "If you're right, Max, the killer sends the victim a message via the items. The message is: I'm coming. The items satisfy some quirk in the killer. Maybe he thinks he's giving the women more of a chance than they gave him. Under your theory, the items appear in a certain order, at a certain time. When the message is complete, our boy shows up at the victim's door and the game is over."

"That's exactly what I think. And dammit, Laura is next!"

"A tidy theory except for one giant flaw. Ruby Alder. Pattern killers don't set up the pattern in the middle of a killing spree. You know that as well as anyone, Max. This guy didn't decide to become a pattern killer after the first hit. He either is—in which case Ruby Alder would have gotten the items, too—or he isn't. In which case none of the victims would receive identical items. Face it, you don't have a shred of hard proof that all the items showed up in all the victim's houses."

In a voice thick with frustration Max explained his conviction that Ruby Alder's murder was the first item, a message.

"Thin," Ridley said, shaking his head. "Diane Gates and Elizabeth St. Marks didn't get the message. Neither does Laura. I can't see it."

Both men were becoming heated, and Jim Marshall stepped in again, looking at his watch. "Laura Penn is in your jurisdiction, Max. Can you suggest she leave town until this is over?"

"That could be for a long time. The killer doesn't strike every Wednesday. It could be weeks before whatever drives him kicks in again."

"Listen," Ridley said, still trying to make his point. "A message isn't a message unless someone receives it. The message here is so obscure no one can spot it."

"The killer sees it," Eric said, stepping in before Max exploded. "The threat is so obvious to him that he believes it must be obvious to the victims."

"Too bad it isn't." Jim Marshall moved toward the door. "Meanwhile, we keep pulling in every bastard with a scratched face." He shook his head. "It looks so easy on TV."

"Ridley, why didn't you tell us about the Gates diaries?" Max's voice was sharp.

"Does Macy's tell Gimbels'?" Bill Ridley smiled then shrugged. "Okay, we thought maybe we had something, and we wanted to check it out before everyone else jumped on it. But the diaries didn't amount to anything. As soon as we've finished photocopying, we'll return them to the husband. We followed up what there was. Which was nothing to write home about. The only thing interesting is that Diane Gates turned out to be feistier on paper than in person. Looks like she used the diaries to let off steam."

"For instance?'

"She had a sister-in-law she couldn't stand. She shreds the sister-in-law in the diaries. But when we ran it through, it turns out the sister-in-law had no idea Gates was upset. She thought they had a close relationship."

"Eric and I want copies."

"You guys don't know what you're asking. The first diary begins when Gates was fifteen. She was twenty-eight when she died. And she wrote in her diary every day. We're talking a lot of paper. And I can promise you, there's nothing there."

"We want to see them." Max turned and called to Jim Marshall before Marshall pushed through the door. "And Denver is sending over copies of St. Marks's diaries. Right, Jim?"

"Did we promise that?"

"Damned right you did."

Jim Marshall smiled. "You'll have copies by the end of next week."

Bill Ridley threw out his hands. "I'm telling you, there's nothing in those diaries. It's dull stuff. We've been over all of it at least half a dozen times. *Nada*, guys. Zippo. There's nothing there." When Max said nothing, just continued to look at him, Ridley rolled his eyes in resignation. "Okay. By the end of the week. Try to stay awake. This woman's life will put you to sleep."

After they left, Max returned to the room where Laura waited. Taking the chair in front of her, he sat down and took her hands in his.

"What did they say?" she asked anxiously.

"They suggested you take a vacation, leave town for a while. It's a good idea, Laura."

"I thought about that while I was waiting for you." She drew a breath and met his eyes. "But I decided leaving town wasn't a solution, it was only a delay. If someone wants to kill me, he'll wait until I return." She pressed her lips together and drew another long breath. "I'd rather stay here, face this and get it over with."

"You're absolutely sure?" When she nodded, he pressed her hands. "Will you change your mind about staying at my place?"

Laura thought about Gene McTavish living next door to Max. There was more to teaching than reading, writing and arithmetic. There was also a responsibility to set high standards and a good example. She shook her head. "Max, I just can't. I wouldn't be comfortable running into one of my students under those circumstances. I'd wonder how Gene's mother was explaining my living with you."

"I could tell her—"

She shook her head. "I'm sorry."

"All right," he said after a moment. "Then, how about me staying with you?" He watched a struggle ensue behind her eyes. "I'm going to be assertive and tell you it's one choice or the other. Now that I've found you, I don't want anything happening to you." A smile softened the implication behind his words. "If it will make you feel better, I'll park on the next block and sneak in and out. Not a soul will see me. Your reputation, ma'am, will remain intact."

She returned his smile. "If the choice is my place or yours, it'll be easier if you stay with me. I don't have a student living next door, and no one can see my house anyway."

"Good, that's settled." At least until next Wednesday. But neither of them mentioned that. "We'll swing by my place and I'll pack a few things. Then we'll return to the locksmith's and pick up your car."

"Max . . . I was thinking." She fell into step beside him. "Remember what Pete Markam said about R.C. coming outside when he opened the door? That reminded me. There's cat hair all over my place. I can't keep up with it."

Max stared at her. "Laura, you are brilliant. Sarah is right to start buying wedding presents! Come on, I'll phone Brad Denny."

"What now, Elliot?" Brad said when he came on the line. "Are you going to pull another rabbit out of the hat?"

"Did Elizabeth St. Marks own a cat?"

"I can't believe it. You blew one. No cat, no dog, no animals of any kind. One of the kids was allergic."

"So any animal hair you guys vacuumed had to travel into the house on someone's clothing, right?"

"You're telling me the killer is a pet lover?"

"Stranger things have happened, but no, that's not what I'm driving at. This could be another tie in between Laura Penn's intruder and the murders. You should have found some white cat hairs at the St. Marks house. Carried from Laura Penn's house on the killer's pant cuffs possibly."

"Close, but no cigar. Hepplewhite, St. Mark's boyfriend, has a black-and-white cat. Hepplewhite could have walked the hair in. Just a sec, I'll pull up the lab analysis. Yeah, here it is. We've got a few strands of human hair we haven't matched . . .''

"Light brown? Sandy-colored?"

"Consistent with the locksmith's description of Laura Penn's intruder. Also consistent with Dave Penn and half a million other guys, including me. Okay, here we are—we've got some dog and cat hair. The dog belongs to the second boyfriend. We've got black-and-white cat hairs. About a dozen more whites than blacks."

Max swore. Nothing was conclusive. Hepplewhite couldn't have a black cat; he had to own a black-and-white.

"Our forensic guys are good," Brad Denny was saying, "but not good enough to say for certain if the cat hair came from different cats or the same cat. We think the animal hair dropped off Hepplewhite and the other boyfriend. You're on target there. You heard about the dentist? He's out of it. In case you're interested, he was spending his Wednesday afternoons with a city councilman's wife."

Max took Laura's arm and started toward the door but Eric called him back.

"How much bad news can you take, pal?"

"What have you got?"

Eric handed him a copy of a traffic ticket. "You'll love this. Dave Penn had the best alibi in the world. He just didn't remember."

"I don't believe it." Max stared at the ticket. "He wasn't in Willow Hills—he was in Wallowbrook Hills. About thirty miles from Willow Hills. Hell, he was in Westminster."

"Look at the time," Eric said.

Laura leaned over Max's arm. The ticket had been written at ten minutes to four on the day Ruby Alder was murdered.

"He couldn't possibly have been in Westminster at three-fifty then turn up at Ruby Alder's house ten minutes later," Laura said.

"He couldn't have reached Ruby Alder's house even by four-thirty. It would take at least forty-five minutes if he made all the lights. Plus he would have hit the beginning of rush hour. He'd have to drive like a maniac to make it there by five."

Eric nodded. "There isn't a chance in hell. We can test it, run it ourselves and see how long it would take to reach West School Avenue from Wallowbrook Hills, but it's probably a waste of time." He looked up and scowled. "And there's more. Detective Mifflin located Mr. and Mrs. Charles Whitcomb. Penn was right—they lied about being from out of town. They live in Arvada, and they confirm they were with Dave Penn when Diane Gates was murdered. They lied because Penn had been drinking and they wanted to get rid of him. They didn't want him to call them again." Eric lifted his hands and let them fall. "Dave Penn is out of it."

"Thank God," Laura said softly, sitting down abruptly. When they looked at her, her eyes filled with tears of relief. "I've been worried half out of my mind that he might have . . . and I . . ."

Eric's large hand squeezed her shoulder. "At least something good came out of this. You'll sleep like a baby tonight, honey," he said, smiling. "Penn didn't need your alibi at all. As far as this department is concerned—" he glanced at Max for confirmation "—Dave Penn is free as a bird. There's no way he could be involved."

Max was glad for Laura, but the look he exchanged with Eric was grim. They had lost their prime suspects. The killer was still out there. This Wednesday had technically passed, the killing hour was over. But they still had next Wednesday to contend with. And the next Wednesday and the next, until he tried to strike again.

And they didn't have a clue as to who the hell he was.

LAURA THREW TOGETHER a light supper while Max unpacked his overnight bag. It was nice hearing him whistling in the bedroom. But these were not the circumstances under which she had fantasized sharing house with Max Elliot. He was here because he was concerned for her safety, not because they had taken a deliberate decision toward the next step in their relationship.

While she fixed a salad, she tried to sort out her feelings. It wasn't easy. The relationship with Max was woven into the murders and her intruder. And the shocking revelation that he believed she was the next victim.

Apprehension prickled her skin. And a healthy dose of fear. On the other hand, another part of her rejected any link between herself and something as ugly as murder. It was difficult to reconcile the image of herself as a potential victim with the utter impossibility of such a thing. She had no enemies that she knew of, wished no one ill. Until the last few hours, she would have sworn no one wished her harm, either.

But if Max's instincts were correct, someone wanted to kill her.

Someone was playing games with her, putting items into her home that were supposed to tell her something. She had thought about it until her head ached, and she was no closer to deciphering the message or warning or whatever it was that she was supposed to see.

Discouraged and struggling against depression, she entered the living room where Max was seated on the sofa surrounded by a pile of files. He had changed into jeans and a cream-colored pullover. Lamplight shone across his thick dark hair. "Work?" she asked, indicating the files.

"I keep hoping something will jump out at me."

"Dinner will be ready in about twenty minutes. Nothing fancy." She nodded to the file opened on his lap. "Do you have a photograph of Diane Gates?"

"None I would want you to see," he answered, his expression grim. "Why?"

"No particular reason. Just curiosity. I've seen the newspaper photos of Elizabeth St. Marks, and of course I knew Ruby. I was curious about Diane Gates. Who she was, what she looked like."

"I could get a photograph for you," Max said, watching her. "I'm sure Tim Gates wouldn't mind as long as he was assured the media wouldn't get hold of it. He doesn't want his wife's photograph splashed across the newspapers. Or I could check with Wheatridge. They may have a photo they didn't send us."

"No, don't go to any trouble. Honestly, Max, it's just curiosity. The St. Marks and Ruby Alder murders seem more real, somehow. I think it's because I can picture them. But I can't picture Diane Gates. Does that sound silly?"

"Nothing in a homicide is silly. Diane Gates was small, about your height. A few pounds overweight but nothing serious. She colored her hair, wore it in a reddish shade. She was a pretty woman. Not a knockout like St. Marks, but attractive."

"Is that why you asked if I'd ever dyed my hair?"

"It falls under the category of grasping at straws." Max smiled. "All three victims colored their hair. Alder went blond, Gates red, St. Marks sort of dark gold.'' He shrugged. ''Maybe the killer hates dyed hair. Stranger things have happened.''

Sitting on the ottoman in front of him, Laura clasped her hands in her lap. ''What happens next?''

''We keep looking for the man Peter Markam met when he changed the lock on your doors. We keep searching for a match for the weapon. We dig into each victim's past.'' Leaning forward, he touched her cheek. ''And you and I continue to look for the meaning behind the mystery items. We try to find a link between you and the other three.''

A tiny shudder rippled down Laura's spine. It gave her a spooky feeling to imagine she could be linked to three murdered women. ''I've been thinking about that,'' she said in a low voice, ''going over any way I might have met Diane Gates or Elizabeth St. Marks. The obvious way would be through school, the way I met Ruby Alder. But Diane Gates didn't have any children. And Elizabeth St. Marks's stepchildren went to school in the Cherry Creek system. That can't be it.'' She closed her eyes and tilted her head backward. ''I've thought about every organization I belong to and I've checked the membership lists. No help. While I was in the kitchen I flipped back through the calendar and checked all the appointments I've had since the first of the year. There's no one there who matches the description of Gates or St. Marks. With or without dyed hair.''

''Stay with it. There's a link somewhere.''

She knew he had to be right and the knowledge made her stomach cramp. ''What if we don't find it?'' In time.

''We'll find it, Laura. It's only a matter of asking the right questions, triggering the right memory. Unfortunately, we don't know yet what the right questions are.''

He thought for a moment. "Have you ever tried to find a piece of information in a library?"

She smiled. "Once or twice."

"Of course. Sorry. Well, suppose you wanted to know how colonial women cooked a rabbit. First you try the section on cooking. Maybe you find four shelves of books, but none of them are the right time period. They tell you how to cook rabbit today, but they don't tell you how a colonial woman cooked a rabbit over an open hearth. So you go to the rabbit section."

"The rabbit section?" A grin relaxed her expression.

"Okay, animal husbandry. You learn a lot about raising and breeding rabbits, but nothing about how they were skinned and cooked in the old days. Maybe you try the women's section next. Maybe you find a lot of information about colonial women, but no rabbit recipes. Your problem is you know the information is in the library, but it isn't in the sections where you're looking."

"The obvious approach isn't working—I see where you're going with this."

"Right. The information may be buried inside a volume addressing historical social issues. It might turn up in a biography of someone who lived in that time period. You might find the information in an old journal or a book of etiquette. Or maybe a book about the American Revolution or a book that traces the development of kitchens. See what I mean?"

"I'm beginning to."

"You have the answer to the puzzle, Laura. But right now we don't know which section the answer is filed in. We've eliminated the obvious. Now we need to start probing areas that aren't as obvious."

"How do you suggest we do that?"

"Eric and I will work backward in each of the victim's lives, learning everything we can about their pasts. We'll check everything. At each step, we'll ask you if something in a victim's past matches something in your past or if it holds any sort of association for you."

"That's a big job. If it's all right with you, I'd rather not begin tonight. I've had all the questions I can handle for one day."

He looked disappointed, and she guessed he was thinking they didn't have time to waste. But he nodded. "Fair enough."

When it came time to go to bed, Laura experienced a moment of uneasiness. They took turns in the bathroom and Max chatted and talked to her while he was brushing his teeth, making the situation as comfortable as possible. He hadn't put his things in the guest room; he had assumed she wanted him in her room. And she did. But . . .

"Max?" she said when he came out of the bathroom wearing a blue terry robe. She caught her lip between her teeth and gave him an embarrassed look. "I don't know quite how to say this . . ."

Immediately he understood, and she loved him for it. Gently he placed his arms around her and drew her to him. "Laura, I love you. And I want to make love to you."

She pressed her forehead against his shoulder. Maybe she was wrong. Maybe he didn't understand.

"But not tonight," he said, lifting her chin until she had to look into his eyes.

"You do understand," she whispered.

"It's not every day a person discovers they may be a candidate for murder." He stroked her hair. "I know you have a lot to think about. It's been an emotional day." After kissing her nose, he looked into her eyes. "I want our first time together to be special. I don't want the outside world to intrude. I want it to be just you and me, concentrating on nothing but exploring and learning about each other.''

"That's what I wanted to say," she said, resting her head on his chest. "Do you mind terribly that it doesn't feel that way tonight?"

A laugh rumbled near her ear. "Damned right I mind terribly." She smiled against his chest. "But I'm willing to wait until the time is right. Would you be more comfortable if I moved into the guest room?"

"The truth?" A rush of pink heated her cheeks. "I'd rather you were here with me. But—"

"Good. I promise I'll behave myself." Grinning, he pulled back the bedspread. "Do you know what this feels like? It feels like we're an old married couple."

She smiled. Later, she reached across the sheets and took his hand. "Max?" she asked in a small voice. "Would you just hold me? I'm feeling very alone and a little frightened."

"Come here."

When he opened his arms, she slid across the bed and molded herself into the warm enfolding curve of his body. They fit together like matching pieces of a jigsaw puzzle.

"No one is going to harm you, Laura," he said softly. His warm breath stirred the hair on her neck. His body wrapped protectively around her. She could feel his need for her and recognized his self-control. She felt her own mounting need.

"I love you, Max," she whispered, turning in his arms until she faced him. Her gaze dropped to his firm wide mouth. "Am I allowed to change my mind?" she asked in a throaty voice. Suddenly nothing seemed important but this wonderful man and being with him.

He smiled and touched her cheek with his fingertips. Then he kissed her.

"DO WE REALLY HAVE to do this?" Laura asked, looking up at Max.

It was Friday, and Max had taken Laura to Elizabeth St. Marks's home. "Yes." He pressed her shoulder encouragingly.

"This feels strange," she said uneasily, following Eric into the living room. For a moment she stared with wide eyes at the outline chalked on the oak floor, then hastily averted her gaze.

"No one ever really gets used to it," Brad Denny commented, watching her. He spoke in a normal tone of voice, which startled Laura, who didn't seem able to speak above a whisper. A person had died violently in this room. The impact of that realization closed her throat.

Max placed an arm around her shoulder and gave her a brief hug of reassurance. "Take your time. Look at anything you want to."

Understanding he was trying to make this as easy as possible, she gave him a look of gratitude. Unfortunately nothing was going to help. She felt acutely uncomfortable.

"I feel like an intruder. Like we're trespassing."

Max didn't tell her he was trying to save her life, but she saw the message in his dark eyes.

She swallowed and tried to smile. "I'm okay," she assured him. "It's just that . . ."

"We understand," Eric said.

Max, Eric and Brad Denny moved to stand in front of the sliding doors leading outside to a covered terrace. They talked quietly, casually, watching her while trying to appear they weren't. Laura knew they hoped she would recognize another mystery item. Something she might have overlooked that would provide the key to everything. They were also hoping to spot something like the gold lion bookend that was out of sync with the rest of the house, something that didn't quite belong, something they might have previously overlooked.

What froze her mind was knowing they believed time was running out. The mystery item they were hoping to find was the last item, the one that appeared just before the killer did.

Moving slowly, Laura inspected Elizabeth St. Marks's living room, careful not to touch anything, although Brad Denny had told her she could touch something if she wanted to—the fingerprinting was finished. But she didn't want to touch any of Elizabeth St. Marks's things. To do so seemed like a violation.

After studying the portrait above the fireplace, she turned away with a slight shiver and paused before the bookshelves, then, followed by the others, she walked down the hallway toward the bedrooms. She lingered in the doorways to the children's rooms, then drew a breath and entered Elizabeth St. Marks's bedroom. A bedroom was such an intimate place. She had to force herself to step inside.

Feeling compelled to say something, she noticed aloud that Elizabeth St. Marks had owned several furs. The closet door was open and she could see a row of fur coats in plastic bags, and a stretch of expensive clothing.

"Does that mean anything to you? Trigger something?" Max and Brad stood beside the satin-covered bed, hands in their pockets, watching her.

"No. It was just a comment." She wished they wouldn't watch her so closely. Hands clasped in front of her, Laura inspected the dresser, examined the items scattered across the top, then glanced into the bathroom, admiring the crystal bottles on the countertop.

"If anything doesn't fit, I'm not seeing it," she said finally. "Assuming the last mystery item is here, I can't even guess what it might be." A sigh dropped her shoulders.

She knew what was causing Max's frown. It worried her, too. Although neither had mentioned it, they were both wondering—and worrying—if the chess pieces were the last items. Before the killer showed up at Laura's door.

They walked through the silent house to the front door. Despite Laura's eagerness to depart, she paused in the wide foyer and looked back at the framed portrait of Elizabeth St. Marks hanging over the living-room fireplace.

"She was lovely, wasn't she?"

"Yes, she was," Max said. Eric and Brad murmured agreement.

"I'd say she was also vain," Brad Denny added. "The kitchen is about the only room in the house where she didn't hang a picture of herself."

Laura continued to stare up at Elizabeth St. Marks, at her smile, her shining blond hair, her perfect features.

"What are you thinking?" Max asked, studying her expression.

"Elizabeth St. Marks reminds me of an old friend." When they all turned to stare at her, she indicated the portrait and hastily added, "But that woman isn't Bets."

"You're positive?"

"Positive. The resemblance is strictly superficial. Something about the eyes and expression. That's all."

Max stepped closer for a better view of Elizabeth St. Marks's portrait. "She dyed her hair, Laura. Would that make a difference?"

She tried to imagine it. "I really don't think so."

"And she had cosmetic surgery. Brad? Do we know how extensive her surgery was?"

"Very extensive. Elizabeth St. Marks was a cosmetic-surgery junkie."

"Wait a minute," Laura protested. "Granted, I don't know much about cosmetic surgery, but I can't believe a few nips and tucks could make an ordinary person into a beauty." Turning back, she concentrated on the portrait above the fireplace. Elizabeth St. Marks smiled down at her from the portrait. And suddenly she felt confused. "It couldn't be Bets, could it?"

"Brad?" Eric looked at him. "What was St. Marks's maiden name?"

"Van der Kellen. She grew up back east—Philadelphia, I think. Went to all the tony eastern schools. There was big money in the family." Brad Denny studied Laura. "Does that describe your friend?"

Relief eased the tension in her chest. For an instant a chill had swept her body. "Not even close. My friend was Bets Kosinski. And she definitely did not have a tony background."

"Bets? For Elizabeth?"

"Nothing that fancy," Laura remembered with a smile of affection. "Bets given name was Betty. She grew up in Vincent, Colorado. Her father was an auto mechanic, her mother waitressed at a local coffee shop. Bets used to say the only advantage her parents had given her was that she was an only child. She didn't have to share what little there was. About the only similarity between Bets's life and Elizabeth St. Marks's life is a vague physical resemblance and a love of beautiful things. Except Bets never owned any really nice things."

Rocking back on his heels, Max studied Elizabeth St. Marks's portrait, then looked at Laura with a thoughtful expression. "Brad?" he asked, still looking at Laura. "Do we have any photos of Elizabeth St. Marks before the cosmetic surgery?"

"We haven't located any so far. Frankly I'm beginning to think we're not going to. This lady liked the new look she created, and she had various procedures done at various times. Aside from the nose and chin reconstruction, which were done early on, you can spot slight differences in many of the photographs hanging in the house. She had an eye lift, had her brows reshaped, had her hairline raised, her ears reshaped, and she had a facial peel once a year. Moreover, she had breast augmentation, liposuction—you name it. If there was a procedure to improve her looks, she had it done. Elizabeth St. Marks bought new features like some folks buy new clothes."

"That's sad," Laura commented in a quiet voice. "She must have felt very insecure." Turning away from the portrait and Elizabeth St. Marks's smile, she looked up at Max. "Can we leave now?"

He placed his hand against the small of her back and guided her outside into the bright sunshine. "If you turn up a pre-surgery photo of her, send us a copy, will you?" he said to Brad Denny.

"Don't hold your breath. She even insisted the 'before' shots taken by her surgeon be destroyed. This lady hated the way she looked. She made a new person out of herself and she made sure there were no reminders of how she used to be."

Max helped Laura into the car, then turned in the seat to look at her. "When did you first notice a resemblance between Elizabeth St. Marks and Bets Kosinski?"

She hesitated, answering with reluctance. "The first time I saw Elizabeth St. Marks's photograph in the newspapers, I thought of Bets. To be honest, I'm not sure the photographs in her house remind me of Bets as strongly as the newspaper photo did."

"The newspaper reproductions aren't as sharp and distinct as the actual photographs."

"If I'd seen the photographs and portraits in the house before I saw the newspaper photo, I'm honestly not certain if I would have thought of Bets. Max, why are you pursuing this? Elizabeth St. Marks's background is nothing like Bets's."

"She changed her looks. Maybe she changed her background, too." Frowning, Max tapped his fingers on the steering wheel. "It isn't impossible." He turned the key and pulled the car away from the St. Marks house.

"I don't think Bets could pull off something like that. She would have to have had a certain level of sophistication to pass herself off as someone from tony schools and a wealthy family. Bets was just a plain girl from a modest family who grew up in a small Colorado mountain town."

"Where is Bets Kosinski now?"

"I lost track of her over the years. She married right out of high school. She didn't have the money or the grades for college. I think she married Walt Miller—we called him Ace—more to get out of Vincent than because she loved him. At least that was my impression. Ace joined the navy two weeks later and Bets followed him to San Diego. She was excited about moving to a big city, but she would have preferred Denver to California. We wrote to each other for a while, but the correspondence dwindled and finally stopped."

They drove in silence for several blocks, then Max nodded to himself. "I'll ask Brad Denny to begin a background check on St. Marks."

"He's going to scream," Eric interjected. "Denver isn't sitting on their thumbs like we are, and background checks take time."

"We could do it."

Eric grinned. "Try suggesting that to Brad or Jim Marshall. They'll take your head off. St. Marks is their case. If we start working their territory, we can kiss off any further exchange of information."

Max swore under his breath. "We can ask them to check her out—" he slid a look toward Laura "—and hope they get to it soon. Meanwhile we'll pick up where we left off. We'll drop Laura at home then check out a few cutlery shops. Stay with the knife."

"I really don't think Elizabeth St. Marks could be Bets Kosinski," Laura said firmly. "Honestly I don't."

"Think about the cosmetic surgery."

"I am. Maybe I just lack a vivid imagination, but..." She shrugged, unable to move past the lingering impression of the opulence Elizabeth St. Marks had enjoyed and the sparse shabby existence of Bets Kosinski. The difference was too vast.

When they arrived at her house Max insisted on coming inside, and Eric tagged along.

"Just to check things out," Max explained.

He and Eric walked through the rooms while Laura opened the French doors to let some cool air inside. It was going to be hot today.

"All clear?" she asked, smiling when they reappeared.

"Seems to be." Max touched her cheek. "Look, I don't like the idea of leaving you alone. Come with us."

"To look at knives?" Laura pulled away from him with an incredulous look. Then she burst into choked laughter. "You sure know how to cheer a person, Detective Elliot.

I'm standing here thinking I may be the next murder victim and you want me to go with you to look at *knives*?''

A sheepish smile warmed his expression. "Not a great idea, right?"

"Definitely not a great idea. I'll take a rain check, thank you." The laughter swept the tightness from her shoulders and diminished the depression that had overtaken her in Elizabeth St. Marks's house. "Look, I'll be fine. Stop worrying." When she saw his uncertainty, she kissed Max's cheek and smiled. "There's no reason to be anxious. We know this guy's routine by now." She hated the thought. "Besides, I'll keep the broomstick in the French-door handles. I'll be perfectly safe."

"You're certain?"

"Of course I'm certain." She gave him a little push toward the door. "Go to work."

"I think we need some rules, agreed? You go nowhere, and I mean nowhere without letting me know, okay? Call the station and leave a message or ask them to patch you to my car." She nodded, her expression solemn. "You don't run out for groceries or go over to a neighbor's. Don't go anywhere without checking in."

"Agreed."

"Next Wednesday morning, early, you and I are going to take the day off and drive up to Vail. We'll shop a little, have a leisurely lunch. Ride the gondola up the mountain. Okay?"

Wednesday. The day all the murders had taken place. Laura wet her lips. "Sounds wonderful."

After Max and Eric left, she sat curled in a protective ball on the end of the sofa, drinking iced tea and trying to make herself confront the fact that someone wanted to kill her. She looked at the items on her coffee table and she believed it. Someone wanted her dead.

But why? She rubbed her temples and whispered, "Who are you? What did I do to make you hate me?"

Closing her eyes, she tried to visualize the man Pete Markam, the locksmith, had described. She tried to picture that man standing on her patio as Pete Markam changed her lock. Had he relaxed in one of her patio chairs? Had he picked up R.C. and stroked him? Then she tried to imagine him creeping into her living room, looking at her belongings, maybe touching them. A shudder rippled her skin.

Because thinking about her intruder, the killer, upset her, she turned her thoughts to Elizabeth St. Marks.

Was it conceivable that Elizabeth could be Bets Kosinski? She remembered how much Bets had hated Vincent and how she had always said that one day she would be rich. She would live in the best section of Denver and she would have a life-style a movie star would envy. Elizabeth St. Marks had achieved Bets's dream. The thought made Laura distinctly uneasy.

Suppose, just suppose, Elizabeth and Bets were the same person. Would that make anything clearer? She didn't see how. She hadn't seen Bets for ten years. There was no present connection.

The murders couldn't possibly track back ten years. Two things were wrong with that line of thought. First, she hadn't known Ruby Alder ten years ago. Second, she and Bets and Bumper had been inseparable. Anything involving her and Bets would also involve Bumper. Not Ruby Alder.

The shudder came again, like cold fingers skittering down her spine.

Right now she couldn't bear to think about it—besides there was nothing concrete to go on—but tomorrow, after

dinner with Sarah and Eric, she would remind Max to get
her a picture of Diane Gates. She felt positive Diane Gates
would not remind her of Bumper. Absolutely positive. But
it wouldn't hurt to check.

Chapter Ten

"This is terrific lasagna, Laura." After offering his third compliment, Eric extended his plate for another helping.

Eric and Sarah, and Max and Laura sat around the dining table in her living room. Overhead a Casablanca-type fan turned lazily, stirring the air, which was still hot from an eighty-degree day.

"Do you have any enemies?" Sarah inquired, returning the conversation to Laura. When Laura raised an eyebrow, Sarah shrugged in apology. "I told you I can't stop meddling. Plus, I'm a cop's wife. Plus, I'm worried about a new friend. This is a scary situation. So, do you have any enemies?"

"As far as I know, I don't have any enemies." Earlier today, at Max's suggestion, she had tried to make a list of anyone, anyone at all, who might dislike her. "I came up blank," she explained. She had even thought back to childhood and could think of no one.

"Either you're one of the nicest people I know or one of the dullest," Sarah said, grinning. "There has to be someone who doesn't like you."

"Obviously there is," Laura responded. She was enjoying the evening and the company was marvelous. Discussing the murders didn't distress her as she had expected it would. In fact, the conversation was interesting and stimulating. "But I can't think who he might be."

"Max," Sarah said, "is it absolutely, positively certain that Dave Penn could not be involved?"

"Not a chance," Max answered. "Eric and I drove up to Wallowbrook Hills, then drove to Ruby Alder's house from the point where Penn received the ticket. Thanks," he said when Laura served him more lasagna. "Penn definitely could not have done it."

"Did Max tell you about Diane Gates's diaries?" Eric asked later, when they were having coffee in the living room. "By the way, do you keep a diary?"

Laura smiled. "Not since I was a kid."

"That reminds me. Max, the copies of the Gates and St. Marks diaries arrived yesterday after you left. Susie made copies for both of us. Your set is in the car. Don't let me leave tonight without giving them to you." He sighed. "Maybe we'll find something everyone else missed. Meanwhile at least we have a little good news. Did you tell her, Max?"

"I haven't had a chance," Max said. "Eric and I think we've discovered what the weapon is. We found a possible match today."

Despite herself Laura was interested. "What is it?"

"A clip-lock boot knife. We bought three and sent one to each of the forensic departments. Eric and I believe the boot knife will match the pathology."

"What on earth is a boot knife?" Sarah asked.

"The blade is smooth toward the tip, serrated near the hilt. The handle is flat and has a clip release at the center. You press the clip and the knife comes out of the sheath."

Laura frowned, trying to picture what they were describing. "It's worn inside a pair of boots?"

"Usually on the inside of the leg," Max explained. "That's why the handle is flat, so the knife rests comfortably against the leg. No bulges. The sheath clips over the edge of the boot and the knife is locked to the sheath. A comfortable, secure arrangement."

"If you're into that kind of thing," Laura commented with a grimace.

"This kind of knife can also be worn on a belt or in a shoulder holster," Eric added, "but since it's more commonly worn inside a boot it's called a boot knife."

"Maybe I'm missing something, but what you're describing doesn't sound that unusual." Laura declined more coffee when Max offered it. "Why didn't the killer just leave the weapon behind and buy a new one for the next..." She swallowed hard. "I think I've changed my mind about more coffee," she said, extending her cup toward Max.

After pouring, he took her hand and rubbed it absently. "Aside from the expense—and this particular knife is on the expensive side—the entire assembly is metal. Blade, handle, all of it. Which makes this knife ideal for picking up fingerprints. We're guessing that's the reason the killer takes the knife with him."

"What happens next is we'll start beating the pavement, calling on cutlery shops, trying to find someone who remembers selling this particular knife."

"How likely is it that you'll find a salesman who remembers?" Laura asked.

Eric shrugged. "Someone sold that knife. Maybe we'll strike it lucky and find him sooner rather than later."

"You know," Sarah said in a thoughtful tone, "these aren't clean murders. Whoever committed them would be covered in blood. What about that?"

Max exchanged a look with Eric, then they both looked at Laura. "You're sure you're okay with this conversation?"

"Yes." She swallowed and said, "I've wondered about the blood, too."

"All the departments are struggling with that question. Our best guess is—as the murders are premeditated—the killer brings along a change of clothing."

"Good God." An involuntary gasp of revulsion burst from Laura's lips. "Look guys, that does it for me. I haven't been at this as long as you have. And I have a personal interest in this case. Could we...? I mean, would you mind if—"

"Of course we don't mind," Sarah said quickly. "It took me a while to get used to murder as dinner conversation, too." After dusting her hands together, she gave them a cheerful smile. "Okay, folks. What's it going to be? Bridge, canasta, or Trivial Pursuit?"

Two hours later, Laura and Sarah left the Trivial Pursuit board to slice pie in the kitchen. "Sarah, do you recall the conversation we had the night you and I first met?"

"About living with a policeman?"

For an instant Laura studied the knife in her hand then pushed aside any hint of squeamishness and sliced into the pie. "It's funny how things work out, isn't it? A few short weeks ago, I was concerned about having a relationship with someone in a high-risk job." She looked at Max and Eric through the kitchen pass-through. "Now Max is worrying himself half-crazy that someone is trying to kill *ne.* It's flipped upside down. Max isn't in danger—I am."

he gazed into Sarah's warm understanding eyes and her ace crumpled. "Oh, Sarah."

Sarah enfolded her in an embrace and patted her back. "It's all going to work out," she promised. "The good uys are on our side. They're going to find that bastard, aura, and they're going to put him away for a long, long ime."

Laura tried to smile. "I just hope he doesn't get me irst."

"He won't. Don't even think it."

But she did of course. She couldn't help it.

HE HEARD THE CLOCK chime twice. When she was cerain Max was sleeping beside her, Laura eased out of bed nd stepped to the bedroom window. Peeking outside, she azed at the deep shadows across her lawn, then lifted her yes toward Denver's lights twinkling in the distance.

He was out there somewhere.

Who was he and what was he doing right now? Was he sleep? Was he watching late-night TV? Or was he driving around the city? Maybe past her house. Thinking bout creeping inside.

A shudder convulsed through her, chilling her even hough the night was warm.

"Why are you doing this? Why do you hate us?" she vhispered.

When she realized she had said *us*, that she had grouped erself with Ruby Alder, Diane Gates, and Elizabeth St. Marks, another violent shudder tore down her body.

Spinning away from the window, she hurried back to ed and curled into Max's warmth. He murmured in his leep and his arm moved around her, pulling her into the curve of his body. Laura snuggled close to him, glad they had made love earlier. She didn't know how many nights she had left.

Twenty minutes later, still unable to sleep, she remembered that she had forgotten to remind Max about getting her a photograph of Diane Gates.

THEY SLEPT LATE Sunday morning, then sat in bed eating muffins and drinking coffee and watched *Dr. Who* on PBS, pleased to discover another point in common.

"It's great to find another *Dr. Who* fan," Laura confided, grinning. "Someone who shares my passion for time lords."

"Not only do you make the best lasagna I've ever tasted, but you're a *Dr. Who* fan. What more could a man ask?"

Pulling her pillow beneath her, Laura rolled on it and propped her chin in her hand to look at him. "Remember the episode when Tegan is possessed by the Mara?"

"I like the episodes with Davros." He kissed her nose then swung out of bed. "Up and at 'em, Miz Teacher Lady. We have things to do, murders to solve. Who gets the shower first?"

Dropping back on the bed, Laura sighed toward the ceiling in a gesture of mock resignation. "I suppose I'll get used to talking about murder the last thing at night and the first thing in the morning."

"Actually there's nothing pressing today," Max called from the shower. "I thought we'd work on the dresser in the garage. Or maybe we could go through some of those boxes and organize the shelves."

"You're kidding. That's your idea of a great way to spend Sunday?"

"I thought I saw a box of school mementos..."

Now she understood. When he stepped out of the shower, smelling like Ivory soap, she handed him a towel. "I see through this, Detective Elliot. What you're after is a peek at my high-school photographs. You want to get a look at Bets Kosinski, don't you?"

"Do you have a photograph of her?"

"I'm sure I must have. As a matter of fact, I'd like you to take a look. And I'd like you to have a look at Bumper's photo, too."

He looked at her over his shoulder. "What about Bumper? Would you mind drying my back?"

He had a wonderful back, muscled, a deep tight ridge that ran down his spine. Very sexy, Laura decided. "I want you to tell me if Bumper looks anything like Diane Gates," she said without looking at him.

After dressing, with Max hurrying her along, they went out to the garage, then Max carried the box of mementos inside and placed it on the table in the living room. Laura pulled off the tape and peered inside with a soft expression.

"This is my past, my history," she murmured. A rush of nostalgia overwhelmed her. Removing a packet of letters, she turned them in her fingers. "These are letters from Dave. I don't know why I kept them. It's time to throw them away."

Max winked at her. "You won't hear an argument from me on that one."

There was another slimmer packet of letters from her parents and school friends. And copies of her birth certificate, her divorce papers, diplomas, copies of tax returns—the things people accumulated over the years.

Max removed a photo album, opened a page and whistled around a grin. When she looked to see what had elicited such a response, she laughed. He was ogling a picture of her taken at about age two. She was naked, sunbathing on a towel in front of her parents' house.

"You were cute even then."

"Here's what you're looking for," Laura said, smiling. She removed her school annuals from the box. "Help yourself." After rummaging in the box another minute, she carried a packet of letters to the sofa, intending to read them, but she looked at the items on her coffee table instead, trying once again to figure them out.

"I'm going to throw away the chrysanthemums today," she said out loud. The blooms had turned brown and dried, and bits of dead leaves were crumbling around the base of the pot.

After that neither of them spoke for several minutes. Sunday sounds drifted through the open windows: the click of roller skates against the sidewalk, the sputter of a lawn mower, a radio playing on someone's back patio.

Because she was happy, the kind of silly happiness that comes from being in love, Laura put the paper crown on her head and rearranged the other items on the coffee table, not really believing moving them around would make any difference.

Max looked up and smiled. "Queen of the May. It suits you."

"I always wanted to be a queen. But it never worked out that way. Bets, Bumper and I were always attendants, never the queen. We got to wear crowns, but not the big one."

She straightened abruptly, staring at the items on her coffee table. "Oh my God!" A gasp tore from her throat. "I have it. Max, I know what these items mean!"

At the moment she spoke, Max raised her annual and swore. "Here it is."

The stared at each other across the room then said in unison, "High School."

"You first," Max said in a tight voice. "Run the items down for me."

Stretching a trembling finger, Laura touched the crumbling chrysanthemum. "Blue chrysanthemums, like the corsages worn for homecoming. But it's probably the color that's the message. The blue flowers and the gold ribbon around the pot. Those are Vincent's school colors—blue and gold." Lifting her hands, she removed the paper crown. "I was homecoming attendant my senior year."

"The bookend?"

"If you've been looking at the annuals, you know the answer. All the Vincent teams were the lions."

Max nodded. "How about the car sketch and the chess pieces?"

"I'm not sure about those," Laura said slowly. "Except the car is a 1977 model, which places it during my high-school years. I'm guessing the first items pertain to me. The bookend stands for Vincent. The sketch and the chess pieces probably identify the killer."

Max stared into space. "You graduated in 1980. Diane Gates graduated in 1980. I think we can assume Elizabeth St. Marks did, too." Raising a hand, he covered his eyes. "Dammit. I was right."

Immediately Laura understood. "Oh, no," she whispered. "Poor Ruby."

"It was her address," Max said finally. "1980 West School Avenue."

The realization devastated Laura. Her throat felt hot and tight. Falling back on the sofa, she closed her eyes and tried to grasp the brutality and the callousness behind killing someone because of their address. It was impossible to comprehend.

"Ruby Alder's death was the first message," Max said, sitting at the table. "But I wasn't even close to guessing what the message meant. The murderer used her address to announce the key date and tied it to school." He covered his face. "He must have loved it when he discovered Ruby was engaged to Dave Penn and tracked back to you. It was a double message."

"Oh, my God." Laura dropped her face into her hands. "Poor Ruby," she said again. After a moment, she looked up at Max, her eyes moist. "There's no question, is there? I'm next." Despite everything, she didn't want it to be true.

Instead of answering, Max crossed the room and sat beside her. He set her senior-year high-school annual on her lap and opened it. Vincent High School was small. There had been less than a hundred students in Laura's graduating class. Instantly she saw what caused Max's tight expression and she sucked in a hard breath.

Someone had carefully removed her senior picture. He had cut it out of the page. There was nothing but a neat rectangular hole. The same person had also cut out Di Bumperton's and Bets Kosinski's photos. Her eyes widened as Max silently handed her the annual from her junior year.

"The same thing?" she whispered.

"Yes. The same three photographs are cut from every one."

She felt sick. As if she had received a violent blow to the stomach.

"Max," she said when she could make herself speak. "I'm starting to feel very frightened." The intruder—no, the killer—had obviously been in her home many times. He had been through the boxes in her garage, probably knew every drawer in her house, what her lingerie looked like, what brand of toothpaste she used.

Framing her shoulders between his large hands, Max turned her to face him. Her blue eyes looked very large against her white face. "We're starting to put this together, Laura. We're getting close to the truth."

"I just remembered—about six weeks ago I discovered the latch to the garage door was broken. Since nothing was missing, I didn't think anything about it." She pressed her hand flat against the annuals.

"Cutting out the photos must have been the first thing he did." Rising, Max went to the telephone and dialed Eric at home. When Eric answered, Max spoke in a low tone, explaining what he and Laura had discovered. "Tell Wheatridge and Denver. Tell them to get a look at Gates's and St. Marks's high-school annuals. Get me a photo of Diane Gates so Laura can give us a positive I.D."

"I knew Diane Gates," Laura said in a dull voice. "I must have. She has to be Bumper."

Max looked at her but didn't answer. "Eric, do you have your files handy? What was Diane Gates's maiden name?"

While he waited for Eric to get the files out of his den, Laura forced herself to stand. Moving on rubbery legs, she crossed to the table and removed a photograph album from the box. After leafing through a few pages, she located a photograph of herself standing between Bumper and Bets. Silently, she pulled the photo from the album and handed it to Max.

He studied it for a moment, then nodded, his expression pinched. "Your Di Bumperton is a young Diane

Gates." Eric returned to the phone then and Max pressed the receiver to his ear.

Di Bumperton—her Bumper—was Diane Gates. The sick feeling returned to Laura's stomach and she sat down.

"You're sure?" Max said into the phone. "Okay, Eric. We've got it. High school is the connection. It's a sure thing that Diane Gates came from Vincent. Call Tim Gates and check it, will you? And I'll bet everything I own that Elizabeth St. Marks is Bets Kosinski. We were on the right track about her changing her background just like she changed her appearance. Tell Denver to move the background check to the top of their priority list."

After hanging up, Max knelt beside Laura and ran his hands from her waist up to her shoulders. "You're trembling."

"Bets and Bumper," she whispered. "They're dead."

Max started to tell her they didn't know if Elizabeth St. Marks was Bets Kosinski, not for certain. Not yet. But he stopped himself. He did know. Years ago he had learned to trust his instincts. Denver was going to discover no such person as Elizabeth Van der Kellen existed. Or if they did discover such a person, she wasn't the woman they had found on Braithwaite Street. If a real Van der Kellen existed, then Bets Kosinski had borrowed her name and her history. One thing he knew—the woman who had been murdered on Braithwaite Street had been Bets Kosinski.

He looked over Laura's shoulder at the annuals lying on the sofa. Two of the women whose photographs had been cut out of the pages were dead. He held the third woman in his arms.

At that moment he knew how much he loved her.

"Let's get out of here," he said, lifting her chin so he could see the tears she was trying to blink back. "I told Eric we'd meet him at his house."

"I'm afraid, Max." She stated it simply. No dramatics, no histrionics.

"I'd be worried if you weren't. But no one is going to harm you, Laura. I promise." He kissed her, then replaced the broomstick through the handles of the French doors. "You told me once that you bought a gun after your divorce."

"Yes. A .38."

"Where is it?"

She had to think a minute. "In the kitchen, maybe. In the junk drawer."

"Is it loaded?"

"Yes."

"You know how to fire it?"

"Yes."

They didn't speak much during the drive to Eric's house. After Sarah served iced tea, Max leaned forward and studied her face. "Are you feeling all right?" he asked gently.

"Honestly? I don't know. I feel a little shaky inside. Strange. Sarah, would you mind if I used your guest room for a few minutes? I think I'd like to lie down. I need to think about all this and try to find a little courage."

"Sure, honey." Sarah took her arm. "Could you use a little company?"

"Thanks."

For a brief instant Laura looked at Max, loving him. "Remember when you mentioned there was probably a series of things that triggered the killer? One of them must have been the notice about the ten-year reunion. And I feel like another must have been poor Ruby's address. If the killer ran into Di or Bets or me about the same time..."

Max nodded slowly. "That works."

Laura followed Sarah into the hallway. "Call me if you need anything," she said to the men before leaving.

Eric waited until they heard the door to the guest room close. Then he lifted the file on the floor next to his chair and looked at Max. "She's in big trouble. You know that. It's going to happen soon."

Max stood at the window. He raked a hand through his hair and nodded. "Yes."

"By now the killer knows she's dating a cop, he's known it for a while. He's made you part of the game, Max. Every time he went into Laura's house, he was rubbing our nose in his sense of invulnerability. Maybe knowing Laura is seeing you increased the thrill for him. Bottom line—he knows she'll be a tough hit. He's working on a plan right now."

"He's also a pattern killer. Whatever drives him won't allow him to break the pattern unless he absolutely has to. He'll stick to his own rules if he can."

"Okay, let's walk this through and see what we've got. Alder is the first message—she's killed for her address." Eric shook his head and swore softly. "That she was tied to Dave Penn and thus to Laura was icing on the cake. The killer probably took it as some kind of go-ahead sign. All right. Assuming the other two victims received the same items, then first they received the blue chrysanthemums in a pot tied in gold ribbon."

"The Vincent school colors. Maybe a reference to homecoming."

"Which also ties into the paper crown."

"Laura, Bumperton and Kosinski were attendants to the homecoming queen in their senior year. There's a photograph in the senior annual showing all of them wearing tiaras."

"Brad Denny and Bill Ridley should be calling here soon. They're looking for the other school annuals."

"The bookend is now obvious. It represents the Vincent Lions. It was probably the second item in the chain. First we get 1980 West School Avenue, then the bookend to identify which school."

"Do you think the guy played high-school sports?" Eric scribbled notes down a yellow legal-size pad. "A jock?"

"Maybe. Maybe not. The bookend could be meant only to flag the town and school. The chess pieces and the photograph of the car strikes me as more likely to be associated with the killer. They don't seem to tie in to the victims."

"How about this? Maybe the guy sees himself as a pawn in thrall to three queens. The female chess figure is black—black for evil?—and the pawn is white. Suppose he sees the three women as black and evil and sees himself as white and good. And a pawn is easily sacrificed. Does this circle us back to homecoming? Or is he saying he was sacrificed by or to the queens?"

"The car in the museum photograph must have been his. The dice hanging from the rearview mirror show three dots. Bets, Bumper and Laura."

"This whole puzzle dates into the past. To high school. Suppose this guy is carrying a torch for Laura, Di Bumperton and Bets Kosinski. But they won't give him the time of day. The rejection smolders. Then, ten years later he gets the notice about the reunion. Starts thinking about them being there, laughing at him. Then maybe he runs into one of them—"

The phone rang, and Eric caught it on the second ring. After he hung up, he looked at Max. "Bingo. We've got confirmation regarding Diane Gates's high-school annual. The photos are cut out."

"No surprise. And Brad didn't find any annuals at the St. Marks house, right?"

"St. Marks wouldn't keep a school annual from Vincent lying around if she was trying to maintain the fiction that she'd gone to school back east. Brad has a dozen calls out trying to get a fix on her true background."

"It's only a matter of confirming it. We can guess what he'll discover," Max said. "According to Laura, Bets Kosinski married a boy named Ace Miller—Walter Miller—then followed Miller to San Diego when he enlisted in the navy."

"Wait a minute. That rings a bell." After flipping through his files, Eric found the page he wanted. "Here it is. Elizabeth St. Marks's bio states her first husband was Walter Winthrop Miller, a rear admiral assigned to the Pentagon."

"I think Brad is going to discover Walter Winthrop Miller was a mere swabby who never saw the Pentagon. I'd guess Miller did his time, found himself divorced, then disappeared from Bets Kosinski's life. At some point between divorcing Walter Miller and marrying St. Marks, she became Elizabeth Van der Kellen from Philadelphia."

After a long moment of silence, Eric lit a cigarette and exhaled slowly. "I think you'd better get Laura out of town on Wednesday."

"I thought we'd drive up to Vail. Spend the day there."

"Good. We'll put a team on her street and put some-one inside the house. We'll schedule increased drive-bys for the rest of the week."

"I want this guy, Eric."

"Sounds like every cop movie I've ever seen." His smile faded. "We'll get him."

"LAURA? ARE YOU AWAKE?"

"I can't sleep."

"Me, either."

When Max opened his arms, she moved across the bed and into his warmth, resting her head on his broad shoul-der.

"We've put together a list from the annuals of every-one who was a member of the chess club during the years you were in high school. We'll check out the jocks, too. First thing tomorrow, we'll contact the alumni committee and obtain addresses for the list. Then we'll begin run-ning them down."

"Max?" She hesitated. "I'm having terrible thoughts."

"Want to tell a friend all about it?"

She didn't tell him that she had been dreaming about her own funeral. Terrible dreams that made her wake up in the middle of the night drenched in perspiration.

"Max, where is our relationship heading?"

He chuckled and held her tighter. "Is this a proposal?"

She blushed in the darkness. "I've been think-ing...teaching children isn't enough. I want to have my own."

"That's not a terrible thought." He kissed her neck, then her eyelids. "In fact, that's a nice thought. Maybe I can help."

When his hands slipped under her nightgown, Laura gasped with pleasure and wound her arms around his neck. "Maybe that was a proposal, after all," she said when his lips released hers.

His deep laugh sounded in her ears. "If it was, I accept. And I thought you were an old-fashioned girl...."

Chapter Eleven

The telephone was ringing when Laura came into the house after her tennis lesson. She dropped her racket onto the sofa, tossed back her hair and picked up the receiver, expecting to hear Max's voice.

"Hi, Laura."

"Dave?"

"I called to say goodbye. I'm leaving tomorrow for California. Maybe the real-estate market will be better out west."

"I hope so," she said after a moment. "I hope you find what you're looking for."

A silence opened. "Are you still seeing that detective? Elliot?"

"Yes." She drew a breath. "We're talking about getting married."

"Oh." In the silence, she heard him smoking. "He seemed like a nice-enough guy. Congratulations."

"Thanks." For a moment she considered confiding in him about the situation she was in, then decided against it. Dave was no longer part of her life.

He laughed, the sound short and humorless. "It seems like there should be something more to say. Some kind of last words or something. I mean, I'll probably never see you or talk to you again.''

"Good luck, Dave.''

"Yeah. Good luck. Laura? I did love you.'' The words came in a rush. "I know I treated you badly...but I did love you. I'm sorry it didn't work out. I'm sorry I didn't try harder.''

Briefly she closed her eyes and adjusted the receiver against her ear. "Goodbye, Dave,'' she whispered, then hung up.

For a moment she stood beside the sofa, staring toward the French doors. Finally it was over. Dave Penn would not reappear in her life. And she was glad.

Recently the past had seemed like a living thing, reaching out and wrapping around her. She was surrounded by newspapers speculating about Bets's death, weighted down by her sadness about Bumper and Bets, and items on her coffee table. And Dave had been part of it, too, pulling up memories, making demands. It seemed the present was on hold, unable to go forward until the past was confronted and vanquished.

Transferring her gaze to the coffee table, she studied the symbols of the past. A tremor of revulsion rippled her skin. Suddenly she wanted them gone, out of her house, out of her life. This, at least, was something she could do.

After getting a trash bag from the kitchen, Laura returned to the living room and dropped the items into it. Now that the mystery was solved, there was no reason to keep them anymore. She closed the bag with a twist tie and carried it to the bin in the garage. When she returned she dusted the coffee table. That was better. Much better.

She fixed a sandwich and ate it at the living-room table, sitting where she could see her clean coffee table. The warm afternoon stretched before her, a day that invited gardening or other outdoor activities. The problem was she felt too restless and edgy to commit to any project.

There was something about a death threat that tended to make everything else seem unimportant, she thought grimly.

Yesterday, trying to enjoy the day in Vail with Max, she had found herself distracted, her thoughts continually turning toward home. While murmuring about the scenery and having lunch, her thoughts had strayed to Eric and the team staking out her house. She had imagined the murderer, someone from her past, prowling through her house, searching for her. Had wondered if today was the day that police would catch him. They hadn't.

Who was he?

Most likely he was her age, possibly a year older or a year younger. He had light brown hair, a sandy color. Average height and weight. He wore boots. That thought made her mouth twist. Probably he played chess. Certainly, she thought, he was a game player.

The clock on the wall near the bookcase struck two, and she started, a guilty look on her face. Dave's call had distracted her and she had forgotten to phone Max when she'd returned from her tennis lesson. Jumping up, she went to the telephone and dialed the Littleton station and asked for Max Elliot.

"He's in a meeting now," a woman's voice informed her. "May I have your name and number and he'll return your call when he can."

"Please tell him Laura Penn phoned."

"This is Laura?" A smile sounded in the woman's voice. "He's been waiting for your call. I'll send a message into the meeting."

"Remind him that it's Thursday, will you?" Laura asked, anticipating Max would be angry that she hadn't telephoned immediately upon returning.

The doorbell rang as she was hanging up the telephone, and she jumped. "Not as steady as you pretend," she muttered. Maybe she needed to remind herself that it was Thursday.

Before opening the door, she peeked through the window in the center of the panel. A boy in a messenger's uniform waited on her step. Behind him, she saw a delivery van parked at the curb. McNeese Delivery Service was scrolled across the side in large white letters. Feeling a little foolish, a little paranoid, she opened the door, keeping in place the chain lock that Max had installed.

"Yes?" The messenger boy couldn't have been a day over twenty. He didn't look familiar. This was definitely not a face from her past.

"I have a package for Laura Penn." The boy smiled at her. "You have to sign for it."

"Just a minute." After sliding off the chain lock, she opened the door and looked at the package as she signed a line on the boy's clipboard form. Before she accepted the package and closed her door, she glanced toward the street. The vacant lot was deserted. There wasn't a car in sight. It was a quiet empty summer afternoon. For one crazy instant, she fantasized that she and the McNeese messenger boy were the only people left in the world.

As soon as she had discovered what her package was, she decided, she would call the owner of the rental house next door and insist he trim the shrubbery. If he refused, she would get her hedge clippers and do it herself.

"Thanks," she said, closing the door.

Who on earth would send her a package? A book, from the size and feel of it. She turned the package between her hands and frowned. There was one way to find out. But before she could unwrap the unexpected gift, the phone rang. Pushing back her hair, she went into the kitchen and picked it up.

"May I speak to Laura Penn, please?"

"This is Laura Penn." Cradling the telephone between her ear and her shoulder, she turned the package over, looking for a return address. There was none.

"This is Ron Smith with the Sleek Chic Spa. I'm calling to congratulate you, Laura Penn. You are the lucky winner of a year's free membership at your nearest Sleek Chic Spa!"

"What?" Then she remembered. The drawing. "You're kidding!"

"Nope. Your name was drawn in our grand-prize drawing this morning."

"I've never won anything in my life." Patty Selwick was going to turn green with envy when she heard about this, Laura thought, grinning.

"I'm calling to confirm that you'll be home during the next hour. We're sending over a cameraman and a reporter to interview you for our in-house magazine. We'd like to feature you in the August issue of our magazine."

"The next hour?"

"If that's not convenient, just tell them you can't manage it right now, and reschedule. They should be there in about ten minutes or so."

"Your reporter and cameraman are already on their way here?"

"It's my fault, Mrs. Penn. I should have phoned earlier. But I got busy, and you know how it is. Look, if this is going to cause a problem..."

"No, not really." She tried to think what shape her hair was in and if she had time to freshen her makeup.

"Great. And again, congratulations."

Well, how about that? Something good had happened in the middle of this mess, she thought as she hung up the phone. Suddenly feeling better, she hummed under her breath as she pulled at the tape wrapping the package she had received. When the phone rang again, she looked up and rolled her eyes.

"Laura? I've been worried. You should have checked in a couple of hours ago."

"Hello to you, too. Now calm down, everything is okay. It's Thursday, remember?" Holding the phone between her ear and shoulder, she tried to pull the tape off the package. It was the resistant kind, the kind that would hold together a Boeing 747. "Actually I've been busy." The phone cord was too short to reach the drawer where she kept the knives.

She told him about Dave's call. "Then the McNeese Service brought me a package delivery. A book, I think. I haven't unwrapped it yet." Giving up on the knife drawer, since the cord wouldn't stretch that far, she leaned against the counter. "Then—you aren't going to believe this—I won a year's free membership at the nearest Sleek Chic Spa. They drew my name this morning. Isn't that terrific?" When he didn't respond, she said, "Max? Did you hear?"

"I heard."

"They're sending a reporter and a cameraman to interview me for their August magazine. They should be here any minute." Bending, she looked through the pass-through at the living-room clock. She didn't want to rush Max off the phone, but she did want a minute to check her appearance.

"I don't like this," he said finally.

"It's perfectly on the up and up," she said. "I entered the drawing the day I met you. When I was at the Anchor Bay Restaurant having lunch with Dave." She smiled. "Listen, friend, if I thought there was anything the least bit suspicious about this, I'd be out of here so fast you'd see nothing but dust."

"I don't know—"

"What are you thinking?" She knew what he was thinking. They were all paranoid. Even Sarah called every afternoon, "just to make sure you're all right."

"Laura . . . I love you."

A smile lit her features. Today was turning into a good day. "I love you, too."

He paused then said, "Look, it's a gorgeous day, and nothing is happening here. Why don't you meet me at the station and we'll sneak out for a cup of coffee? There's a café not far from here with outside tables."

"That sounds wonderful. I'll be there as soon as I finish the interview."

"Good. How long will it take?"

Yes, they were all getting paranoid. "I don't know. It shouldn't take long."

MAX HUNG UP and looked absently at Eric across the space separating their desks. He didn't like the business about the Sleek Chic Spa. On the face of it, nothing sounded out of line. People did win drawings. It happened. He supposed it could happen in the middle of a homicide investigation. Still, it wouldn't hurt to check it out.

"Did you finish reading Diane Gates's diary?" Eric asked, snapping Max out of his reverie.

"Not yet. Eric, phone the main office of the Sleek Chic Spa and confirm they had a drawing this morning and that Laura won a year's free membership."

Eric raised his eyebrows as he reached for his phone.

"It's probably nothing," Max said. "All the hits have occurred on a Wednesday. Our boy is a pattern killer." Reaching for the phone book, Max checked a listing, then dialed the McNeese Delivery Service.

Eric started to ask a question, but someone from Sleek Chic Spa answered the phone and he turned away.

Max's call was answered on the third ring. "This is Max Elliot with the Littleton Police," he said, leaning forward in his chair. "May I speak to someone in your records department?" After a lengthy wait, a nasal voice came on the line and Max identified himself again. "Will you check your records and see if you made a delivery to Diane Gates and to Elizabeth St. Marks on or about the following dates..." After a moment he hung up and looked at Eric's expectant face. "McNeese is going to check it out and get back to us."

"Same here. Whoever I talked to at Sleek Chic didn't know from nothing. She said she'd call back when she had the information."

They stared at each other.

"It's just speculation," Max said. "We don't have a thing."

"We're just checking it out."

"There's no reason to be suspicious of anything."

"Nothing to worry about."

They continued to look at each other. Then Max shifted his stare to the telephone on his desk, impatiently tapping his pencil against the desktop as he waited for it to ring.

"OH!" A SMILE of genuine delight curved Laura's lips.

She gazed at the faded cover of the diary she'd kept while she was in high school, then thumbed through a few pages, pausing here and there to read an entry. Almost every page contained a reference to Bets and Bumper. As she read, her smile faded and moisture filmed her eyes.

If only she had known Bets and Bumper lived in the Denver area. They could have met and renewed a friendship that had been important to all of them, a friendship the diary promised would never die.

Now Bets and Bumper were dead; she would never see them again. Never laugh over old times or create new memories. The thought hurt.

She owed a debt of gratitude to whoever had returned her diary, stolen so long ago. This book was a small piece of her personal history, and that of Bets and Bumper. It was an assurance they would never be forgotten. She wished whoever had returned the diary had done so in person. She would have given him a hug.

A sudden icy chill scraped down her spine and the diary jumped in her hand.

Wait a minute, think it through. All the diaries had been stolen. Hers and Bets and Bumpers. Yet Bets's and Bumper's diaries had been found in their homes after they were murdered. How was that possible? The chill deepened across her skin and tiny bumps rose on her arms as she stared at the diary's locking tab. It had been cut long ago.

This was the last item. Whoever had stolen the diaries was the murderer. And his name was probably in the diary.

"Oh, God." Dropping the diary on the living-room table as if it had scorched her fingers, she backed away, then turned toward the kitchen, three names flying through her mind. Frank Blume, Harold Mercer, and Patrick Lightner. It must be one of them. She had to telephone Max. He had to know about the diary and the names.

The doorbell rang as she rounded the counter. From this spot she could see into the foyer, could see a man's face through the small window on the door. And since he could also see her, she couldn't ignore him. Laura looked into the kitchen at the phone and bit her lip in frustration. Hurrying, she stepped forward and, after making certain the chain lock was in place, opened the door and looked at the man standing on her porch.

"Hi. Did someone from Sleek Chic phone and tell you I was coming?"

"Yes." All she could think about was getting to the telephone to call Max and tell him about the diary. "I thought there was supposed to be two of you. A reporter and a cameraman."

"The cameraman is right behind me. He should be here in a couple of minutes." He looked at the chain lock. "Mind if I wait inside?"

"Of course, I'm sorry. I have a lot on my mind." She shut the door and released the chain lock, then opened the door again. "Come on in. Look, something has come up and I'd like to reschedule the interview. You can wait for the cameraman in here," she said, showing him into the living room. "I need to make a telephone call. If you'll excuse me a minute—"

"Sit down, Laura." His eyes glittered above a thin humorless smile.

Her own smile froze and her heart stopped then lurched forward against her ribs.

He was sandy haired. Average in height. He was carrying a briefcase. He wore cowboy boots. His face was marked with healing scratches. And he looked vaguely familiar.

MAX TRIED TO CONCENTRATE on reading Diane Gates's diary, but his mind wouldn't settle to the task. Bill Ridley had been right. It was dull teenage stuff.

After a moment's struggle, he gave in to a growing sense of unease and dialed Laura's number. The phone rang five times. Maybe she was already on her way to the station. Maybe it had been a short interview. After glancing at the wall clock, he turned another page of Diane Gates's diary and continued reading.

"They sure shredded this guy Frank Blume," Eric said with a smile, looking up from his copy of the St. Marks's diary. By now they had confirmed that Elizabeth St. Marks was Bets Kosinski, and could track long-ago events by comparing her diary with Diane Gates's. "Thank heaven I didn't know what girls were saying about me when I was that age."

Max smiled. "Blume isn't the only guy to come under the scathing pens of our teenage heartbreakers. But he does seem to show up the most often."

"Think he could be the guy we're looking for?"

"He's one of the diary mentions I've got Susie running a background check on. Which reminds me—we should have enough to work with by tomorrow to begin some legwork. We'll start talking to a few of these names." He frowned. "Back to Blume. He wasn't a jock, but he's listed as a member of the Vincent chess club. Along with two other guys mentioned in the diaries."

"How are you progressing on the addresses from the alumni committee?"

"Pretty good. We've got twelve possibles in the Denver area. Susie is pulling their motor-vehicle records for an address update, and we're checking for arrest records." He turned a page of the diary and frowned. "Why do I feel like I'm missing something here?"

"Go with it, partner. What are you thinking?"

"I'm not sure. I have the same feeling I had when we cruised past Ruby Alder's town house. Like I'm seeing something without knowing I'm seeing it. Something that's obvious, but not obvious." Frustration tightened his mouth.

"Gotcha. Like not seeing the forest for the trees. That pretty well sums up this whole damned case."

Max glanced at the clock. If Laura didn't show up at the station in five minutes, he'd call her house again.

AS THE NEAREST PHONE was in the kitchen, Laura looked toward the kitchen and started to rise. "I'll just answer that," she said. Her gun was in the junk drawer. She remembered that Max had checked to make sure it was loaded.

"Sit down, Laura. Let it ring."

She swallowed and tried to smile. "I really should—"

"I said sit down."

The menace in his tone chilled her. Slowly she sank back on the chair. They were sitting at the living-room table, facing each other across the diary and his briefcase which he had placed on the tabletop. She kept darting glances at the briefcase, remembering Max saying the killer brought along a change of clothing. Her pulse thundered in her ears. Fresh clothing to replace the clothes splattered with blood. She swallowed hard.

The phone stopped ringing and she felt her stomach tighten. There was no way to be certain, but she felt it had been Max. Now he would think she had left for the station, that she was on her way to him. She looked at the man sitting across from her and drew an unsteady breath.

She was on her own. No troops were going to ride in and rescue her.

"You don't recognize me, do you?"

Her mouth was dry. Her heart thudded painfully against her rib cage. After wetting her lips, she forced a reply. "I'm sorry, but I don't. Should I?"

She had an idea if she could see him in a different setting, she might recognize him. There was nothing remarkable about his appearance. He wasn't good looking, but he wasn't ugly, either. Most likely he had suffered from acne as a teenager, but his features were otherwise regular. Forgettable.

"I am the invisible man." His eyes were pale and unblinking. His stare intensified the chill that lingered on her skin. Although he didn't raise his voice, she heard the unmistakable anger, the fury and resentment boiling under his words. "I am the man you never see, the man your eyes look through. Think about it. You and others like you. You come into the restaurant and you flirt with someone sitting across from you or you watch who comes in the door and who passes your table, but none of you ever see me. I'm just the waiter, the invisible man. No one ever notices the waiter. No one ever flirts with a waiter. Isn't that right, Laura? We are merely the pawns who serve you.

Beneath your notice. That's how it always is with women like you."

"The Anchor Bay Restaurant." She had it now. "You wait tables at the Anchor Bay."

"Very good, Laura." His pale smile raised bumps on her arms and neck.

No cameraman was going to appear at her door. It had been a ruse. No one was coming to help. Telling her that she had won the drawing was just a sham to get in her door. He had probably telephoned from the gas station on the next street over.

Unconsciously she rubbed the bumps on her arms. She couldn't see his cowboy boots under the table, couldn't see the knife clipped inside one of those boots, hidden by his pant leg. But she could see that he had crossed his legs, and his right hand had dropped beneath the edge of the table and was resting on his leg.

A small choking sound emerged from her throat. If only her mind would thaw and start to function. If only she could move past the frozen thought that she was sitting with a man who had killed three women. If she could just make herself think.

"We're old school buddies." His voice was horrifyingly pleasant, a thin crust holding back what lay beneath the stony eyes, which didn't waver from her face.

She could not force her mind to move past the thought of his hand resting on his boot top beneath the table. She visualized his fingertips toying with the clip release on the knife.

"You're Frank Blume," she blurted. Immediately she recognized and regretted her stupidity. She should have recognized him at the door.

The phone rang again, and Laura jumped, then closed her eyes. She would have given ten years of her life to get into the kitchen and get to the phone and her gun. They were still circling each other. Maybe he didn't know that she knew about Bets and Bumper. Maybe... "If you'll excuse me, I'll just answer—"

"Now, Laura. You know I can't allow you to answer the telephone." She heard his fingers drumming against the side of his leather boot. The sharp staccato sounds reminded her of tiny explosions. He smiled, watching her face pale. "I can't let you go into the kitchen. You might take your gun out of the drawer. We don't want that, do we?"

Her eyes flew open wide and her hand clapped to her lips. The phone stopped ringing. "You know about the gun." Of course he knew.

"I know everything about you."

Her stomach cramped and she felt sick.

Now she heard the larger sound of the clip release—a small noise, yet thunderous in the silence. She saw his hand move up from beneath the tabletop. Saw a flash of sunlight race along the metal blade.

MAX READ THE LAST ENTRY in Diane Gates's first diary, thumbed through a series of blank pages at the end before he reached for the next diary and resumed with an entry for the next day.

"Wait a minute." He frowned. "Why start a new diary here?"

"Beg pardon?" Eric asked absently. Lifting a stack of files he searched for his pack of cigarettes.

"This diary breaks off and leaves several weeks of blank pages. Why didn't she finish the pages in this one instead of beginning a new book?"

"St. Marks's first diary does the same thing."

"That's right. Eric, what's the date of the last entry in St. Marks's school diary?"

"November 10, 1979."

"Gates's first diary stops on the same date." Bells went off in his mind. He was starting to see the forest instead of the trees. "Were you with us when Laura mentioned that the diary she kept during high school was stolen? And so were the diaries belonging to Bets and Bumper."

"No." Eric stared, then spoke slowly. "Okay. You're saying someone steals the diaries, reads the putdowns and goes berserk." He studied Max's expression. "You're suggesting that whoever stole the diaries has reappeared. He's our killer."

"Wait. Let me think this through." Max scrubbed a hand across his jaw, staring down at Diane Gates's high-school diary. "All right. Diane Gates and Bets Kosinski had their diaries stolen when they were in high school. So did Laura." He lifted his head. "So how did these diaries turn up at the murder scenes?"

Eric swore. "That's it. The killer's had the diaries all these years. He makes the hit then leaves the diary." He swore again as the phone rang on his desk.

"Either that, or he sent the diaries beforehand. If so, that has to be the last message, the last mystery item before he shows up at the door." He swore, too, as his phone rang.

SHE HAD TO STALL HIM. At least long enough for her mind to thaw so she could think clearly.

The knife was short and ugly, exactly as Max had described it. It was flat handled, made entirely of metal, the blade smooth at the tip, serrated near the hilt. If she let herself think what the serrated teeth would do to flesh, she would start screaming and she would be unable to stop. And no one would hear her.

She wet her dry lips and pressed her hands flat on the tabletop to steady them. "You don't have to kill me, Frank."

"Oh, yes, I'm afraid I do. You have to pay for making me invisible, you can see that. Because I didn't know I was invisible until you and Bets and Bumper told me." He inclined his head toward the diary.

Think, she commanded herself. *Don't just sit here like an idiot waiting to be killed.* There had to be some way to reverse the situation and save herself. Frantically Laura scanned the tabletop looking for something, anything, that she could use as a weapon.

"I loved you. All of you. I loved you like only a teenage boy can love. I worshiped you."

"I didn't know." Could she hit him with the diary? Grab his briefcase and hit him with that? It was hopeless. What on earth was she going to do?

"Don't mess with me, Laura." His knuckles whitened around the handle of the knife. She tried not to look at the blade. "All of you knew. You laughed about me in your diaries. You made fun of me for following after you, begging you for dates. You laughed at me, all of you."

"That was a long time ago, Frank." Stall, it was the only thing she could think to do. Drag it out and hope to God she could come up with some way to save herself.

A cunning look dropped across his pale eyes and he laughed, the sound ugly and abrasive. "You always thought you were so clever, all three of you. Right now you're thinking if you keep talking, your cop boyfriend is going to burst in here and save you."

She stared at him, watched him shrug.

"You can stall all you like. We have all day. Your boyfriend thinks you're safe because it's Thursday." When her face paled even more, he smiled. "Do you see how stupid all of you are? Did you really believe I'd set a trap for myself, then walk into it by insisting you have to die on a Wednesday? The day of the week was never part of it. Wednesdays don't mean anything except that's usually my day off. I've been a step ahead of the police all the way. And none of you were clever enough to figure out the messages. I warned you. I gave you more of a chance than you ever gave me."

She had to find a way to get into the kitchen. The gun was her only chance. And getting to it was impossible. Frank Blume had maneuvered her into the corner seat. She couldn't get anywhere without passing by him first.

"Oh, Frank," she whispered. "We were all so young. We didn't know what we—"

He stood then and her heart stopped. Then it resumed pounding so hard she thought it would burst from her chest. Slowly she pushed to her feet, trembling, and she faced him across the table.

"It's time," he said, watching her, speaking in a voice that was quiet, almost dreamy. "I'm not invisible now, am I, Laura?"

MAX SLAMMED DOWN the receiver. "McNeese Delivery confirms they made a package delivery to Diane Gates and to Elizabeth St. Marks on the days they were murdered."

Eric reached for his jacket. "Bad news, Max. The Sleek Chic drawings ended two weeks ago. If Laura got a call saying she won in a drawing held this morning, it's bogus."

They ran for the door.

"Laura's delivery has to be the diary. She said she hadn't unwrapped it yet. Said it felt like a book." The car didn't start immediately, and Max struck the steering wheel with the heel of his hand.

"Easy, old son. Don't flood it."

"The killer is with her now. She thinks he's from the spa."

Eric glanced at his watch. "Not now, she doesn't. By now she knows who he is."

"So do I." Max shot out of the parking spot, leaving tire marks on the pavement as he squealed into the street. "Get on the box. Get some black-and-whites over there right now."

"Who's the guy?" Eric reached for the radio unit.

"Frank Blume. It has to be." Max cut around a car, raced through a red light and took the next corner on two wheels. Eric leaned out the window and clamped a flasher onto the car roof. "The chrysanthemums. Blooms. Blume."

"He's the guy the diaries shred the worst."

"Stall him, Laura," Max muttered between his teeth. "Stay cool, darling, and stall him." Too late to make an avoidance turn, he skidded into the midst of a horrific traffic jam piled behind what looked like a fender bender. Before Max could slam the car into reverse, a truck and a station wagon slid in behind him. The Monte Carlo was pinned.

A message squawked over the radio. "No black-and-whites available at this time. Will respond when possible."

"YOU SAID WE HAD all day, Frank. There's no rush, is there?" Laura spoke through dry lips. She swallowed and tried to clear the panic from her thoughts. "You killed Ruby Alder because of her address, right? But how did you get into her house?"

"You're stalling."

"Don't you want to tell someone how you worked it all out?"

He hesitated and one sandy eyebrow twisted as he considered.

"It was the same with all of you," he said finally, giving in to the urge to boast as she had prayed he would. "The Sleek Chic promotion gave me the idea. I was the one who removed the entries from the ladies' room after the restaurant closed every night. Ruby Alder entered the drawing. I saw her address, and everything came together." He smiled.

There had to be a way out of this. Please God, there had to be a way. Laura dropped her gaze to the knife clenched in his right hand. The serrated teeth took her breath away and she hastily looked aside.

Her stupidity was going to cost her her life. She had to think of another question. "How did you know Elizabeth St. Marks was Bets?"

"The alumni committee had her address."

"You found us through the alumni committee?" He wasn't listening to her. "Tell me about your car," she said desperately.

"No good, Laura. You're ten years too late." Leaning forward, he applied his weight against the edge of the table. The table slid and Laura involuntarily stepped backward. Which was a mistake. Now she understood that he intended to pin her in the corner. Lifting the knife, he ran his thumb lightly over the edge of the blade, watching her expression as she realized she had about two minutes left to live.

THEY LEAPT OUT of the Monte Carlo and raced toward the front of the traffic jam, jackets flying behind them. Max jerked open the door of the first car in the jam. The fender was crushed and the bumper crumpled, but it looked drivable.

"Out. Get out of the car!" He flashed his badge in the face of a wide-eyed woman clutching the steering wheel. "Move!" Eric was already sliding into the passenger seat.

When the woman continued to sit behind the wheel, her mouth open in astonishment, Max reached inside and dragged her out.

"You can't do this!" she shouted, realizing they were going to take her car.

"Call LPD and leave your name," he called over his shoulder. He twisted the key savagely, the wheels spun, then the car shot forward.

"FRANK, WAIT!"

The pressure of the table's edge steadily increased against the top of her legs. Stumbling, the table forcing her, Laura took another step backward into the corner.

"Frank, please. Just please listen for one minute. Okay?" Laura had no idea what she would say until the next words fell out of her mouth. Her voice was thin and shaky. "You're going to kill me, and there is nothing I can do to prevent it. I accept that." The words were so terrifying that a wave of dizziness passed over her. But the pressure against her legs eased somewhat. She glanced at the knife in his hand and swallowed hard, then drew a gasping breath. "I am about to die."

"Yes," he agreed.

"I have a last request. Just one thing."

"No."

"Every condemned person gets one last request." Her eyes pleaded with him. "Please, Frank."

"No." Stepping forward, he leaned his weight against the table and Laura stumbled again as the edge pushed her backward. She could feel the corner walls behind her, trapping her.

"I want you to hug me!"

The words tumbled over each other, surprising her as much as they surprised him. But the appeal in her eyes was genuine.

"Please, Frank. I'm very frightened. I've never been this frightened. I need someone to hold me. Just for a moment. Just give me one moment of warmth and comfort before I die. Please. Please, Frank? Just hold me. Only for a minute."

Her request was not what he had expected. She saw the indecision flickering in his pale eyes and hope blazed in her chest. If it was true that once he had loved her, that once he had fantasized about her, then maybe, just maybe he would agree. Laura didn't know what advantage an embrace might provide or even if she could bear to have his arms around her, touching her. But if he agreed—*please, God, let him agree*—it would get her out of the corner.

"You'll try to knee me in the groin," he said, watching her. But the indecision in his eyes had deepened; she heard it in his voice. He wanted to touch her, wanted to embrace her. She could see it in the way he looked at her, could feel it at a primitive level.

"No. I promise I won't. If you hold me tightly enough, I won't be able to."

The thought had certainly crossed her mind. But she knew she was only going to have one chance at escape and she could not risk blowing it. A knee to the groin was not a sure thing. She might miss. The blow might not be incapacitating.

For one endlessly fearful moment, she watched him waver and she thought he would not agree. Then, he slowly stepped backward from the table and gestured with the knife, beckoning her forward, watching her carefully.

Summoning her courage, Laura clenched her teeth and straightened her shoulders, and made herself walk toward him, toward the knife, until the tip of the blade pressed against her blouse. She felt a sharp prick against her skin through the thin material. If she looked at the knife she knew she would scream, so she kept her eyes fixed on Frank Blume's face. Trembling, she slowly raised her arms, feeling hideously vulnerable, more frightened than ever in her life.

"Please, Frank," she whispered, her voice nearly inaudible. "Move the knife out of the way and hold me."

A sighing sound resembling a sob or a groan issued from his lips. His eyelids drooped and he blinked heavily. Then his hand moved and the knife disappeared behind her as his arms tightened around her waist and he pulled her closely against him.

"Oh, God," he said in a whisper.

Cautiously, slowly, heart crashing in her chest, Laura laid her head on his shoulder, felt him turn his face into her dark curls and inhale the scent of her hair. One chance. She was only going to have one chance.

Easing back slightly from him, she lifted a shaking hand, moving slowly so as not to startle him, and she placed her palm against his cheek. His body was rigid against hers; a tic jerked beneath his eyelid. She sensed he was struggling for control.

One chance. She had to make it count.

Now.

She drew a breath and felt the adrenaline rush through her body.

With one swift fluid movement, she brought her hand down from his cheek then swung it up hard. She hit him at the base of the nose with the heel of her hand. His nose crushed with a splintering sound and blood gushed over her hand and wrist.

At the same moment she heard his scream, she felt a sharp hot pain slice across her side. The knife blade had slashed her waist as he jerked his hands up to his face. Somewhere she had read that a blow to the base of the nose could kill, but Frank Blume was not dead. His nose was broken and his eyes streamed tears, but he was still on his feet, still alive, the knife still in his hand.

Her only thought was to get to the gun. Pushing backward, she spun away from him, but he caught her wrist and gripped it as they fell to the floor, hitting the table, knocking the diary and briefcase down on top of them. The briefcase landed on Blume's arm, the impact knocking the knife out of his fingers.

If his eyes had not been tearing so profusely, Laura would not have had a chance. But she saw where the knife had spun before he did. Clawing forward, she got her fingers around the slippery handle and managed to hang on as he jerked at her legs, at her ankles.

Frantically, he wiped at his eyes and nose, both streaming, and he tightened his grip on her ankles, dragging her toward him.

Panting, gasping for breath, Laura shoved herself into a sitting position and struck at his hands with the knife. He screamed again and his grip on her ankles loosened enough that she could jerk free. Crawling, a sob in her throat, she got away from him, then scrambled to her feet and ran into the kitchen. Frantic fingers pulled at the drawers where she kept her gun. She spun the chamber in shaking hands and her heart hit her toes. The gun was not loaded. Oh God. At some point, he must have unloaded it.

What should she do? Try for the phone or for more bullets? The bullets were closer and faster. Jerking off the lid to her tea canister and praying he hadn't found and removed the bullets, she thrust her hand into the canister and pulled out the box of ammunition, which she spilled over the counter top. *Thank you, thank you.* She was shaking so badly she could hardly curve her fingers around a shell.

Snatching a bullet, she ran back into the foyer. Blinking against the tears clouding his vision, Blume had crawled forward and was almost at the kitchen door. Blood continued to pour from his nose and had soaked his shirt front. His eyes gushed tears. But he had not given up; he was coming for her. Hands shaking violently, not looking away from him, Laura loaded her one bullet into the gun and pointed it at him.

Now what should she do? If she tried to reach the living-room telephone, she would have to step over him. He would grab her. If she tried for the kitchen phone, she wouldn't be able to keep him in her line of vision. And she knew he wasn't going to just sit there and allow her to telephone for help. She bit back a sob of indecision.

Frank Blume pushed up on his hands and knees and looked at her through his streaming eyes. Incredibly he smiled at the gun, an ugly malignant smile she would never forget.

"It's not loaded," he said, his voice raw and nasal.

"I loaded it." She held the knife in one hand, the gun in her other. She was shaking so badly, she didn't know if she could aim steadily enough to hit him unless he was on top of her.

"Even if you did, you won't fire it. You're not a killer. You don't have the guts." His teary smile burned into her brain. An evil thing.

Sweat trickled into her eyes. She could feel her blouse sticking to the blood seeping from the slash across her waist.

Was he right? She bit her lip. If he came at her, could she pull the trigger? Raising the hand that held the knife, she wiped at the sweat on her forehead. She saw his body gather and tense.

"Don't," she whispered, begging him. "Please, Frank, don't make me do something that—"

He lunged forward, his hands clawing for her, his mouth twisted in hatred.

The front door crashed open behind her, and two shots were fired.

Chapter Twelve

"I didn't think I could do it," Laura admitted. It was a week later, but talking about the experience, remembering, still sent an icy tremor down her spine. "I didn't think I could pull the trigger." Her fingertips strayed to the bandage under her blouse. The cut at her waist was long but not deep. Additionally, there were scratches on her ankles from the cuts she had made when striking at Frank Blume's hands.

"Of course you fired," Sarah commented in a dry voice. "You were motivated."

They were seated at the picnic table in Sarah's and Eric's back yard, having demolished Sarah's famous barbecued steaks.

Max slipped an arm around her waist—carefully—and kissed the tip of her head. "You were terrific."

"Damned right," Eric agreed, smiling. "I never saw anything like it," he explained to Sarah, repeating a story that would be retold a hundred times during the next years. "Max goes flying in the door expecting God knows what and I'm right behind him. And there stands Laura like an avenging angel. She's got this bastard down on the floor, bleeding like you wouldn't believe, *and* she's got his knife *and* she has a gun.'' He shook his head in exaggerated amazement and grinned at Laura. ''I'll say one thing. I I'm ever in a fight with you, I hope to hell you're on my side.''

She laughed. ''You might want to reconsider, Eric, in view of where my shot went. It was Max's shot that hi Blume, not mine. I shot my old diary.''

''Killed it dead,'' Sarah said with a satisfied smile. ''And if that isn't a nice piece of symbolism, I don't know wha is.''

''The past is dead. Long live the future.''

''Hear, hear.'' Raising his snifter of Amaretto, Max sa luted her with a toast.

''What will happen to Frank Blume, Max?''

''He should get out of the hospital some time next week Eventually he'll stand trial and spend the rest of his life in jail.''

Eric nodded. ''We found the painting of your cat in Blume's apartment, and the pictures he replaced in the Gates and St. Marks houses. He also kept the cutouts from the school annuals. By the time this goes to trial, we'll have Blume nailed down tight on all the murders, as well as at tempted murder.''

''It's sad, isn't it?'' Laura turned her gaze toward the sunset. ''Those stupid hurtful things we wrote in the dia ries...''

''You didn't know anyone would ever read them.''

''I wish no one had.''

''You can't blame yourself. The guy is a nut case,'' Sarah pronounced.

''It's over now,'' Max said gently. ''That's the impor tant thing.''

Laura returned their smiles, but she couldn't stop thinking about Bets and Bumper. Her heart wept for the young women they had been, and the older women they would never be. For foolish words and for dreams of the future that had died in the past.

Max touched her cheek. "Let's go home."

AT HER DOOR, Laura paused with her key in the lock and gave Max a tremulous smile. "How long do you think it will take before I can step inside without wondering if someone has been in my house? Without wondering if something else will show up on my coffee table?"

"It may take some time," Max conceded. "But remember that you won, Laura. And...not all mystery gifts are unpleasant."

She looked at him a moment, then pushed the door open and stepped into the foyer. Instantly she froze. Her heart accelerated and her pulse pounded at the base of her throat.

The lamp was on beside the sofa.

"Max! I know I turned off all the lights before we left the house!"

"We'd better investigate," he said, smiling down at her.

His smile was as confusing as his apparent unconcern. Frowning, she turned her head to follow his gaze.

A small box sat in the middle of her coffee table.

"Hmm. What have we here?" Max's dark eyes twinkled. "I believe you have another message."

Slowly Laura entered the living room and approached the coffee table. A tiny smile eased the anxiety from her expression as she recognized a jeweler's box.

"I think you'd better open it," Max suggested. "Maybe there's a clue inside."

"How did you manage this?" Laura asked softly.

"A detective can't reveal everything," he said. "But did I mention that Sarah's and Eric's daughter is home from college for the summer?"

Bending, Laura lifted the jeweler's box and held it in her palm. After gazing up at him, reading the blend of eagerness and anxiety in his eyes, she opened the lid and gasped. "Max! It's beautiful!"

An exquisite diamond surrounded by emeralds sparkled up at her from a bed of green velvet. Taking the ring from the box, she slid it on her finger. Then, eyes dancing, she wound her arms around his neck. From the corner of her eye, she noticed Eric's and Sarah's daughter had also left a bottle of champagne nestled in an ice bucket.

"I think I can guess what this item means," she murmured in a throaty voice, smiling up into his warm dark eyes.

"Really?" His hands circled her waist and he held her close. "Tell me."

"I could be wrong, but I think it means you love me almost as much as I love you."

"You're getting very good at police work. Now the question becomes, what are we going to do about you loving me and me loving you?"

"I'll send you a message," she said, laughing.

Then she kissed him, again and again until he swept her into his arms and carried her toward the bedroom, carrying her toward the future.

Harlequin Intrigue ®

COMING NEXT MONTH

#135 SWITCHBACK by Catherine Anderson
When kidnappers stole Mallory Christiani's little
daughter Emily, she was warned not to tell anyone.
Mallory desperately wanted to meet the kidnappers'
demands and make the switch but, despite her
efforts, she couldn't keep private investigator Bud
Mac Phearson out of her life. Mac and Mallory were
strangers, with no one to turn to but each
other... and their future and happiness depended on
holding nothing back.

#136 UNDER THE KNIFE by Tess Gerritsen
When a patient perished on the operating table
during routine surgery, Dr. Kate Chesne was accused
of malpractice. Had she misread an EKG... or was
something, someone else the cause of death?
Prosecutor David Ransom certainly didn't believe in
her innocence despite his admiration for her. He only
hoped she was wrong. For if murder had been
committed in OR 7, Kate was the next target of a
fiendishly clever psychopath.

**In April, Harlequin brings you the
world's most popular romance author**

JANET DAILEY

No Quarter Asked

Out of print since 1974!

After the tragic death of her father, Stacy's world is shattered. She needs to get away by herself to sort things out. She leaves behind her boyfriend, Carter Price, who wants to marry her. However, as soon as she arrives at her rented cabin in Texas, Cord Harris, owner of a large ranch, seems determined to get her to leave. When Stacy has a fall and is injured, Cord reluctantly takes her to his own ranch. Unknown to Stacy, Carter's father has written to Cord and asked him to keep an eye on Stacy and try to convince her to return home. After a few weeks there, in spite of Cord's hateful treatment that involves her working as a ranch hand and the return of Lydia, his ex-fiancée, by the time Carter comes to escort her back, Stacy knows that she is in love with Cord and doesn't want to go.

**Watch for *Fiesta San Antonio* in July and
For Bitter or Worse in September.**

JDA

You'll flip . . . your pages won't!
Read paperbacks *hands-free* with

Book Mate · I

The perfect "mate" for all your romance paperbacks
Traveling • Vacationing • At Work • In Bed • Studying
• Cooking • Eating

Perfect size for all standard paperbacks, this wonderful invention makes reading a pure pleasure! Ingenious design holds paperback books OPEN and FLAT so even wind can't ruffle pages — leaves your hands free to do other things. Reinforced, wipe-clean vinyl-covered holder flexes to let you turn pages without undoing the strap . . . supports paperbacks so well, they have the strength of hardcovers!

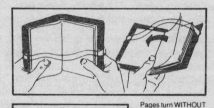

Pages turn WITHOUT opening the strap

SEE-THROUGH STRAP

Reinforced back stays flat

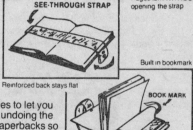

Built in bookmark

BOOK MARK

BACK COVER HOLDING STRIP

10" x 7¼", opened.
Snaps closed for easy carrying, too

Available now. Send your name, address, and zip code, along with a check or money order for just $5.95 + .75¢ for postage & handling (for a total of $6.70) payable to Reader Service to:

Reader Service
Bookmate Offer
901 Fuhrmann Blvd.
P.O. Box 1396
Buffalo, N.Y. 14269-1396

Offer not available in Canada
*New York and Iowa residents add appropriate sales tax.

BM-G

Harlequin
Superromance®

LET THE GOOD TIMES ROLL...

Add some Cajun spice to liven up your New Year's celebrations and join Superromance for a romantic tour of the rich Acadian marshlands and the legendary Louisiana bayous.

CAJUN MELODIES, starting in January 1990, is a three-book tribute to the fun-loving people who've enriched America by introducing us to crawfish étouffé and gumbo, zydeco music and the Saturday night party, the *fais-dodo*. And learn about loving, Cajun-style, as you meet the tall, dark, handsome men who win their ladies' hearts with a beautiful, haunting melody....

Book One: *Julianne's Song*, January 1990
Book Two: *Catherine's Song*, February 1990
Book Three: *Jessica's Song*, March 1990

If you missed Superromance #386 • *Julianne's Song*, #391 • *Catherine's Song* or #397 • *Jessica's Song*, and would like to order it, send your name, address, and zip or postal code, along with a check or money order for $2.95, plus 75¢ postage and handling, payable to Harlequin Reader Service to:

In the U.S.
901 Fuhrmann Blvd.
P.O. Box 1325
Buffalo, N.Y. 14269

In Canada
P.O. Box 609
Fort Erie, Ontario
L2A 5X3

Please specify book title with your order.

SRCJ-1A

This April, don't miss Harlequin's new Award of Excellence title from

CAROLE MORTIMER

Award of Excellence

elusive as the unicorn

When Eve Eden discovered that Adam Gardener, successful art entrepreneur, was searching for the legendary English artist, The Unicorn, she nervously shied away. The Unicorn's true identity hit too close to home....

Besides, Eve was rattled by Adam's mesmerizing presence, especially in the light of the ridiculous coincidence of their names— and his determination to take advantage of it! But Eve was already engaged to marry her longtime friend, Paul.

Yet Eve found herself troubled by the different choices Adam and Paul presented. If only the answer to her dilemma didn't keep eluding her....

HP1258-1

"Nothing is more satisfying than a mystery concocted
by one of the pros."

—*Los Angeles Times*

THE
FOURTEEN
DILEMMA
HUGH PENTECOST

George, Helen and 12-year-old Marilyn—the Watson family—are
the super all-American, super-lucky winners of the Carlton's Creek
lottery. The grand prize: $250,000 and one luxurious week at the
New York's legendary Hotel Beaumont.

But the dream vacation that begins in a gorgeous suite on the VIP,
celebrity-occupied fourteenth floor turns into a ghastly nightmare
when beautiful Marilyn is found murdered. What had this innocent
deaf-mute girl seen that caused someone to kill her? As manager
Pierre Chambrun digs beneath the lacquered surface of the pow-
erful and elite occupants of the floor, another murder takes place.
Time is running out for Chambrun as he uncovers the hidden
secrets of a dozen hearts ... and the unimaginable brutality of a
killer.

Available in April at your favorite retail outlet, or reserve your copy for March shipping by sending your name, address, zip or postal code along with a check or money order for $4.25 (includes
75¢ for postage and handling) payable to Worldwide Library Mysteries:

In the U.S.	In Canada
Worldwide Library Mysteries	Worldwide Library Mysteries
901 Fuhrmann Blvd.	P.O. Box 609
Box 1325	Fort Erie, Ontario
Buffalo, NY 14269-1325	L2A 5X3

Please specify book title with your order.

 WØRLDWIDE LIBRARY